Copyright Notice

Prologue

"Hello? No, he's not in right now. Sure, I can take a message for him. Okay, and what's your name? Julie Wilson? Okay, I'll tell him!"

As Miracle hung up the phone, she walked upstairs to her room. She turned on her radio and flopped down on her bed. She picked up her cell phone and looked through her call log. She called her best friend, Melanie.

"Hello?" Melanie answered.

"Melanie, what's up?" Miracle spoke.

"Not much, girl. You know how things normally are. Super quiet and super boring, since no one's home," Melanie replied.

"I know how that life is. I'm just here home alone, chilling in my room and listening to music."

"That's cool. What's going on?" Melanie asked Miracle.

"I just got a call; some lady calling for my papi. She said her name was Julie Wilson. I've heard that name quite a few times before, but I've yet to ask about her."

"Don't you think you should be calling the cop about that? I mean, the call *was* for him, not me." Melanie asked her with a laugh.

"Well damn," Miracle started to chuckle, "I just felt I could talk to my best friend about some things. Guess I was wrong," Miracle joked with Melanie.

"Who's spoken of Julie Wilson?"

"My *mami*, my *papi*, my best guy friend and your boo-thang, Jacob, my *tío* Jared, my *tía* Madison; pretty much everyone!" Miracle thought for a second as she played with her curly, brown hair. "Girl, let me call my father and let him know of this call." Miracle mentioned.

"Alright Miracle, well you know I'm here for you," Melanie replied. "Call me back."

"I will. Love you," Miracle mentioned.

"Love you, too," Melanie added before she hung up.

Miracle thought for a second. She picked up her phone and dialed her father's number.

"Hello?" Richard answered.

"Papi!" Miracle replied.

"Hey baby, how are things going at home?"

"They're quiet, Papi. You just got a call."

"A call? From who and what'd they want?"

"The woman said that her name was Julie Wilson and that it was urgent to speak to you," Miracle answered.

Richard stopped and looked at his phone.

"Repeat the name, Miracle."

"Julie Wilson."

* * *

Author's Page

Since the release of "Flirting With Death", I have continued with my schooling; it is honestly a top priority for me, at the moment. I've managed to remain on the Dean's List throughout my semesters, and have managed to earn a 3.74 GPA. I've also gotten my Associates' Degree in General Studies, now it's time for the Bachelor's Degree.

This work was honestly not going to happen, until I got a great concept for a sequel, a few months after the release of "Flirting With Death". This is a more advanced and complex work, and switches between the viewpoints of the two main characters: Richard Young and Miracle Young, with a slight touch of the Spanish language. The story takes place in both Puerto Rico and the Dominican Republic, and it's been about 16 years since the birth of Miracle.

With this work, I've tried to not only capture your thoughts but to also touch your emotions with different situations occurring through the piece. Although this work is completely fiction, many events that happen with some of the characters may be relatable to you, the reader.

Although the work is fiction, I have made use of street, location, and structure names within the piece, to capture the experience and to give you a general concept of the situation(s).

So, sit back, sip some wine, or apple cider, (it's your choice), and enjoy my latest piece. As always, I value all feedback; https://facebook.com/officialbmgage or by leaving your reviews. Thank you!

Remember; don't let anyone tell you what you can't do! Do you, because only you can do you the way that you do, you...

1

Miracle

***

"Did she leave a number?" My father seemed to be in shock when he asked.

"Yeah, it's on the caller ID."

"Miracle, don't erase the number; I'll call it once I get home."

"Who is Julie Wilson, Papi?" I asked him.

"We'll talk about it later, baby. I have to get back to work," he mentioned. "I love you."

I sighed out of irritation.

"I love you, too."

I ended the call with my father and called Melanie back.

"What'd he say?" she asked.

"He didn't say anything. He said that we'd talk about it later. Same thing he always says," I mentioned to her as I grabbed my sunglasses and towel, and laid them both on my bed.

"Well, just be patient. He'll come around and tell you eventually, Miracle." Melanie assured me. "What are you up to?"

"About to go lay out on the beach. It's a beautiful day and I don't want to let it go to waste by staying indoors," I stated.

"I heard that. Why don't you get the car, swing by here, and pick me up?"

I thought for a second and then answered Melanie's request.

"Yeah, I guess I could use my car and ride over there. You got gas money?"

"On second thought, I'll walk," she laughed.

"Girl, you're right around the corner anyway," I stated. "Better put those legs to good use."

"I was just messing with you, girl. I'm already getting my stuff together. I'll see you in ten," Melanie stated as she hung up.

I put my phone in my purse and put my purse on my bed. I took off my clothes and changed into my two-piece swimsuit. I put my purse on my arm, grabbed the towel and sunscreen, put on some *Michael Kors* sunglasses, and I walked out of the house, locking the door behind me.

I walked over to the beach and put the towel on the sand, and lied down on my back.

I grabbed my iPod out of my purse, put in my earbuds, and closed my eyes.

"Damn girl, you got your mama's body," a guy stated; causing me to open my eyes.

I recognized the voice and instantly became irritated.

"*¿Que quieres*, Quincy?" I stated and sat up.

"I want that body of yours," Quincy replied as he sat on the sand next to me and he put his left hand on my right thigh.

"Watch your hands," I stated as I slapped his hand away.

"Alright, I'll move my hands, but it won't stop me from looking," Quincy stated while removing his hand from my thigh.

"Q, what do you want?"

"I told you," he added with a chuckle.

"Oh, hell no," Melanie mentioned. "*¿Tu sabes qué,* I know you aren't over here feeling up my girl."

"Oh, this is your girl? I thought I recognized her," Quincy laughed.

"You know it," Melanie added as she flipped her hair and sat down next to me.

She kissed me on the cheek.

"Well maybe later, you can bring your girl back to my bedroom, and we can have a *ménage a trois.*"

"A what?" I asked.

"You know, so I can fuck two bad bitches at the same damn time," Quincy mentioned.

"Yeah and if you attempt to get any closer to these ladies than you already are, I can and will whoop your ass," a gruff voice spoke as it approached us.

"Jacob!" Melanie exclaimed.

"So, Q, how about you leave these two women alone?" Jacob added.

Quincy approached Jacob and looked him in the eye. Jacob didn't back down.

"What will you do if I don't?" Quincy questioned.

"Lay another finger on Miracle or Melanie, and trust me, you'll find out," Jacob mentioned.

Quincy looked back at Melanie and me and turned back to Jacob.

"Y'all keep looking sexy, ok?" Quincy mentioned, staring Jacob down. "Miracle, that ass will be mine." Quincy brushed past Jacob and left with his group.

Jacob shook his head and walked over to Melanie and me. He kissed Melanie and then he hugged me.

"What is wrong with these football stars thinking that they can get any girl that they want?" I asked.

"See, Mami, that's why you need to get you someone like Jacob," Melanie added before kissing Jacob.

"I don't think so. I'll stay single until I find someone actually worth having," I stated. "Jacob, I want to ask you a question."

"What's up, Miracle?" he asked me.

"This woman called for my father today. Her name was Julie Wilson."

"Julie Wilson?" Jacob questioned.

"Yeah. Who is she?"

"I honestly don't know much about her. The story goes that she put our fathers through hell before we were born. Well, I know for sure they were saying it was before you were born. I heard she died before your birth. I don't know what relation she was to him or your mother. I know the little I know from hearing my moms and pops talk about her," Jacob answered.

"Damn, still doesn't answer much. *Pero,* I thank you; it's more than I know. Every time I ask my father, he never tells me and my mama just tears up when I mention her."

"I wish I knew more," Jacob stated.

"It's fine," I added.

I looked at the sun and put back on my sunglasses.

"Miracle, how does it feel to be able to step outside and be on the beach?" Melanie asked with a chuckle as she and Jacob held hands.

"It's beautiful! I love it! Too bad we don't always live here."

"Yeah, that must suck. Why are you all here right now?" Melanie asked.

"We're only here now because my father was called here for work, but it is our house. We're going back to Chicago in a little bit."

"Damn, girl, y'all banking like that to be able to travel back and forth at will?" Melanie asked with a laugh.

"We're pretty well off. Plus, my father oversees the helicopter issued by the police force. And with some money from the various investments and work, he's purchased us a private jet. The chopper can only be used during work, and my father uses the private jet for vacations and personal use."

"So, wait; you all have a helicopter, a private jet, four cars, and two large homes, what's missing?"

"A ship to send my car back and forth. My mami and papi already have cars in both locations." I added while rolling my eyes.

"You are one spoiled little bitch," Melanie joked. "Why don't you just ask your rich daddy to buy you a new car?"

"Let's keep that on the hush-hush," I stated in a lower tone.

"What's wrong?" Melanie added.

"I don't want for people to know that my family is, 'rich', as you put it," I whispered.

"Understandable. If they knew you were rich, you'd have friends for all the wrong reasons. You're a smart and beautiful young lady, and if people only want to befriend you for money or your body, they're some *pendejos.*" Melanie remarked.

I twirled my hair and wrapped it around my finger.

"Yeah, I guess you're right."

"Speaking of your car, Miracle," Jacob spoke, "when are you going to bring it by my house and let me work on that body and engine?"

"Which home?" I asked. "Do you mean your home here or in Chicago?"

"Either one. You know I'm pretty good with cars. I know you've seen mine." Jacob added.

"You want me to bring it by later on tonight?" I asked.

"Yeah, that'll be cool. My pops is letting me keep the place to myself. I'm sure he wouldn't mind if you and Melanie came over. I'll ask him later."

Melanie wrapped her arms around Jacob's bicep and kissed him on the cheek.

"You know, I love how you and Melanie keep a relationship. Even though you're back and forth, you all stay happy and loving." I remarked in admiration.

"Nothing's perfect, Mami," Melanie stated, "but communication is important in a relationship like ours."

"I love how you all work through your issues, you know?" I added.

"All we can say is that it's hard, but you have to work hard and really have the commitment and devotion," Jacob added.

"Yeah. But I'm not looking for a relationship of my own right now. I just admire yours," I chuckled.

A man selling drinks passed by with his cart.

"Would you all like something to drink?" he asked.

"Yeah, can we have three wine coolers? Cherry?" Melanie asked.

"Now you kids know that you all are too young for any wine. What I can do is give you all these sprites that I have, or mockups that I create; all the flavor, but without the alcohol."

"We'll try that," Jacob mentioned as he held Melanie's hand.

The man prepared the drinks and passed them to us.

"That'll be $24," the man spoke.

Melanie and Jacob both went into their pockets to pull out the money.

"*No te preocupes,* I have your back this time," I laughed as I pulled a wad of bills out of my purse.

"Damn girl, is that your allowance?" Melanie asked.

"Shush," I spoke.

I unrolled the money and pulled out a fifty-dollar bill.

The man started to give me my change.

"*Mantenlo,*" I spoke.

"*Gracias,*" he replied and continued to walk along the beach.

Jacob, Melanie, and I continued to talk. Quincy and his crew walked back up to us.

"Ay, Miracle!" Quincy shouted.

"¡*Pinche cabron*! Would you leave me alone?" I asked.

Quincy walked in front of me and kneeled.

"You seem stressed, baby. Do you need to be relieved of the stress you may be feeling?" He put his hand on my calf and started to rub it.

"Get the fuck away from me," I spoke and kicked at him.

Jacob rose to his feet and pushed Quincy back so hard, that Quincy fell into the sand.

"I need for you to back away from Miracle," he spoke as Quincy started to get up.

Quincy's crew walked forward and formed a circle around Jacob.

"Or what?" Quincy spoke as he attempted to intimidate Jacob, for he was alone and the crew had Jacob surrounded.

A bullet whizzed past Quincy into the sand.

"Well, for one, if you ever touch my daughter again, the bullet won't miss," my father mentioned as he stood behind us while removing the silencer and putting the gun away.

"Oh shit, it's the cop!" Quincy stated.

He brushed past Jacob again. He walked away and his crew followed.

"Papi!" I shouted as I sat up.

"How are you all?" my father asked.

"Well, we were just enjoying this sun until you came out here shooting bullets," Melanie stated, jokingly, but appeared to have a slight attitude.

"It's nice to see you too, Melanie," he replied.

She gave a slight wave and smile to my father, and I walked over to him. I embraced him and I kissed him on the cheek.

"Papi, I have a question for you," I asked in my childish voice.

"What do you want?" he asked with a chuckle.

He could tell I was about to ask for something.

"Can I go over to Jacob's house tonight with Melanie? He wants to work on my car."

"Did you ask Madison or Jared?" my father asked with a concerned look.

"With all due respect, Unc, they won't be there. I think that you should know that we'll be the only ones there."

He studied Jacob carefully.

"Jacob, have you spoken with your parents about having these two young ladies over?" my father asked.

"I haven't spoken to them about this night in particular. However, I have had Melanie over before, and, besides, my father said it was okay to have a few friends over when I would like."

"Miracle, now you know how I feel about you hanging out at unsupervised functions, but seeing as though I know Jacob is a good kid and I know his parents, I'm going to permit it," he told me.

I jumped for joy as I kissed him on the cheek and hugged him again.

"All this sand has got to go!" he joked as sand started to transfer from my body to his suit. "I'm about to head inside, just come and let me know when you're about to leave, Miracle."

"I will, Papi," I replied.

My father disappeared into the house.

"Like I said, you're such a spoiled little bitch," Melanie laughed.

"I could have sworn he was about to say no," I stated.

"Nope! He said yeah; you know we are definitely about to do it big tonight!"

***

I informed my father that I was about to leave with Jacob and Melanie, and I got into my pink 2014 Ford Mustang. I started the car and lowered the top. Jacob climbed into the back seat and Melanie climbed into the passenger side.

I revved the engine once, as I usually did, and pulled off.

"It rides nicely," Jacob stated, "once I work on this engine for you, I think you should definitely consider putting it to the test, and taking it out to the streets."

"What do you mean? Racing?" I questioned.

"That's a good idea, girl! Think about it; you could win hella money from it, and, if you're good enough, possibly cars." Melanie added.

"Yeah, but not to mention that if my father finds out that I'm racing, my ass will be grounded for life," I mentioned. "Besides, it's no guarantee that I will win."

"I have a guy, Miracle. Maybe he can work out a few things and find out how you can start small and simple. Challenge the easier cars first, win the races, and improve your car, to race better cars." Jacob mentioned. "Put this baby to the test, now, let's see how fast you can go in a three-second time frame. Pull over for a second."

I slowly pulled the car over.

"I can use my phone to time you," Melanie offered. "You ready, Miracle? Nothing but open road."

"Don't stop at three seconds; drive and see how fast you can get," Jacob spoke.

"Honestly, I don't feel comfortable driving so fast. Jacob, why don't you come and do it?" I asked him.

"Alright, let's switch seats."

Jacob and I both got out of the car and we changed positions; now, I sat in the backseat and Jacob was in the driver's chair.

"Damn, she is a beauty," Jacob mentioned as he studied the car.

I put on my seatbelt.

"Let's do this," he mentioned.

"Hold on!" Melanie stated as she started the stopwatch. "Okay, go!"

Jacob stepped on the clutch, switched gears, and stepped on the gas; the car climbed in speed.

"3 seconds are up," Melanie stated.

Jacob continued to accelerate but spoke.

"0 to 60 in three seconds," he mentioned as the car approached a hundred miles per hour.

He passed 100 and sped even more; climbing to the maximum speed of 180.

"Can we slow it down a bit?" I asked while I clutched onto my seatbelt.

Jacob heard me and pulled up the handbrake as he came to a turn and drifted. He released the handbrake and started to decrease speed until he came to a gentle stop.

"You have a beauty, Miracle. Put her to the test," he spoke. "I really think you should go for at least one drag race and see how it goes," he mentioned.

"I don't know… maybe," I answered.

"If Jacob suggests it to you, you should try it, girl," Melanie assured me.

"I don't know. I'd have to think about it. It would be a big risk to try it." I responded.

Jacob drove the car, at regular speed, towards his house.

As Jacob pulled into the parking lot, Melanie hopped out of the car.

"Let me take it out for a race. I know of a good one going down tonight, Miracle," Jacob stated.

"If you get a single scratch on my baby, I will kill you, Jacob," I joked.

"I won't," he stated with a chuckle, "let me work on your engine a bit."

He drove the car into the garage and onto a platform.

He and I exited the car, and he walked towards the button to lift the platform the car rested on.

He walked back over to the car and opened the hood; I walked over to Melanie.

"Yeah, girl, when are you going to get a man?" Melanie asked as her arms were folded across her chest.

"Please… I'm more focused on my art and my schooling. I don't need a man," I immediately retaliated.

"Yeah, I hear you. I don't know how much longer me and Jacob are going to last," she admitted shyly.

"Why do you say that?"

"There are so many issues between us right now. I mean we're trying to work through them, but it's hard. We show that we love each other very much and our emotions show it, but, I mean, we haven't even had sex yet," Melanie spoke.

"Nothing wrong with that; I'm a virgin myself."

"Yeah, but I'm not, girl. Jacob says he is, and I don't have an issue with that, but shit — I need some," she joked.

I laughed as I observed Jacob work on my Mustang.

Melanie and I walked over to the Mustang and watched Jacob work on the vehicle, as he walked back and forth to get parts for improvement.

About two hours later, Jacob finished working on the car.

"Damn, girl, you got the hookup," Melanie spoke and she ran her hand on the body of the car.

"Jacob, what did you do?" I asked in admiration.

"I upgraded and improved your engine and rotated your tires. I took the liberty of giving you a paint job, changing your oil, and, although I haven't put any in, your car is now compatible for nitrous," Jacob spoke. "Are you going to try to race it?"

"I don't even know to be honest," I spoke as I looked at the new rims.

My cell phone rang and I answered it. I was surprised to hear my father's voice on the opposite end of the phone.

"Miracle, I need to talk to you about something," my father told me over the phone.

"Hey, Papi, what is it?"

"I was just sitting here speaking with your mother; do you have the number to the lady who called earlier?"

"*¿Sabes qué?,* her name should be on the phone," I answered.

"You said her name was Julie Wilson?"

"*Sí,*" I spoke.

"Thanks, Miracle. How are things over there?" he asked me.

"Great! Jacob just fixed up my car: changed the oil, rotated the tires, you know, the works," I stated joyfully.

"That's great; you kids have fun and if you need anything, you know I'm only a call away. I love you, Miracle," he mentioned

"*Te amo, tambien, Papa,*" I spoke and hung up the phone.

Jacob unlocked the car doors.

"Hop in," he spoke.

"Where are we going?" Melanie asked.

"I told you all already; we're going to put this baby to the test. I know of this spot where they have quarter-mile drag races. It's definitely worth checking out."

"Jacob, if a scratch ends up on my baby, it's over," I mentioned as I got in the car. "I hope you know that I'm not racing. I can't."

"Don't worry, I won't scratch her. We're not racing for cars, just $200 in cash. I'm putting it up, since I'm only trying to see if this car can handle it," Jacob mentioned.

He drove for about five minutes until he reached the location of the race.

"I know this pink and black Mustang isn't coming to race," the opponent criticized and laughed.

"Yeah, *puta*, we'll see who's really laughing after that ass loses," Melanie spoke.

The spectators let out noises of surprise.

"Well, uh, why don't you say we up the stakes a bit; my beautiful Charger for your Mustang?" he spoke.

"No, we're here to race for money. We aren't racing for cars," Jacob spoke.

"Oh, so we have a little *puta* here," the opponent laughed.

I looked around. This was a new environment for me and I had never seen anything like it before.

"Let's do it," I spoke.

"Miracle, are you crazy?" Jacob whispered.

"Yeah, girl. ¿*Sabes qué?* Your father will kill you if you lose this car!" Melanie exclaimed.

"Let me worry about my father," I responded. "He's always taught me to stand my ground, and that's what I'm going to do. Jacob, do you have those canisters of nitrous?"

"It's in the trunk," he spoke. "I'll throw those in before I do this race," he added.

"Hey, hey, hey; no additional customizations. All cars must be raced as they were brought!" the opponent shouted.

"Fine… Let's do it," Jacob mentioned as he closed the hood.

He drove to the starting line, and both cars got positioned to drive off.

"I want a clean race. The rules are simple: down to the barrels and back. At the time that both cars return, loser hands over the cash as well as the keys and slip to their vehicle. Do you all understand?" the coordinator asked.

"*No te preocupes, para mí,* I'm going to win," the opponent stated.

"I gotcha," Jacob stated as he revved the engine.

"Alright then," the coordinator began, "let's do this!" he stated and everyone cheered loudly.

"Ready, go!" the coordinator shouted.

Jacob and the opponent both raced off.

2

-*Richard*

While Miracle was with Jacob and Melanie, Jamie and I were at home going over a few things, including the mysterious phone call that Miracle received earlier.

"Miracle got a call today, baby," I told Jamie.
Jamie twirled her hair. "A call from who?" she asked.
"The person said their name was Julie Wilson," I mentioned.
Jamie let her hair go as she looked at me.
"Julie Wilson? My aunt?" Jamie was confused.
"I don't know who it could have been, but I know, as well as you do, that your aunt is dead."
"Unless someone is playing a terrible trick," Jamie stated.

"They'd have to be pretty damn good to pull this off, Jamie," I assured her.

"*Todo la razón*," she spoke. "I wonder who could be messing with us."

"Maybe your aunt is calling from the grave," I joked as I leaned in and kissed Jamie on her neck and put my hand on her thigh.

She put her hands on my head and laughed and she flipped her hair back.

"*¿Sabes qué? Tu juegas demasiado*," she laughed as I lifted my head.

I looked at Jamie admiringly and kept my hand on her thigh.

"Just when we think that we've caught a break, it starts again," I told her.

"I need a drink," she stated as she stood up.

She walked over to the cabinet of wine and poured herself a glass.

"I need some Jamie," I stated as I stood behind her and placed my hands on her waist. I kissed her on the back of her neck.

"Oh really?" she asked as she put the glass down and turned around. "Well, I need some Ricky," she stated as she put her arms around my neck.

I kissed her on the lips, picked her up, and put her on the counter.

Jamie wrapped her legs around my waist as she took off my shirt. I lifted her shirt above her head as she rubbed on my body. As she let out moans of pleasure, she swiped her hand back and knocked silverware and spices from the counter.

Just as I started to kiss down her body, the phone rang. I continued to kiss Jamie.

"Papi, we should answer the phone," Jamie spoke.

"Let it go to voicemail," I spoke as I continued to kiss her.

"Baby..." she spoke.

I already knew what she meant, as she had a stern expression on her face.

I stopped kissing her, walked over to the phone, and answered it. She got off the counter and picked up her shirt.

"Hello?" I answered in a frustrated tone.

"Hello? Can I speak to Detective Young?" the voice answered.

"This is he. May I ask who is calling?"

"Detective Young; so nice to finally hear your voice," the woman spoke.

"Who is this and how'd you get my number?" I asked.

"You know about a decade-and-a-half ago, some shit went down and I lost one of my family members."

"I'm giving you three seconds to…"

"Julie Wilson, you know her?"

My heart sank a little as I heard this.

"You killed her. Little did you know that you were killing someone's guardian, their best friend, their mother. Did you stop to think about anyone besides yourself?"

"Julie Wilson had no children," I spoke as Jamie came closer.

"*Au contraire,* because you're speaking to her daughter, Julie Wilson Jr.," she stated. "She was such a loving and caring mother. I guess that means that you weren't fully doing your job; otherwise, you would have known of any children."

I sat down with the phone in my hand.

"And if you think I will let my mother's death go unavenged, you thought wrong, buddy."

"Look, I'm sorry about what happened to your mother, but at the same time, I'm not. Your mother has put many people through living hell and…"

"I'm not here for any explanation," she interrupted. "Now, I'm going to set a few terms and you will agree."

"And if I don't?" I asked, curious to see what she would say.

She chuckled. "That's funny. I didn't think I gave you that fuckin' choice," her tone intensified.

"Forgive me, what do I have to do?" I asked her.

"You're going to fix all of this. Or else I'll be visiting baby Miracle, and your lovely wife, Jamie."

"Go to hell," I stated and hung up the phone.

"Was that…" Jamie started.

"Yeah, Julie Wilson," I mentioned.

"How?" Jamie questioned.

"Apparently, your aunt had a daughter, Babe. She wants me to give in to demands, or else she's threatening to do something to you and Miracle."

"My Miracle? She threatened our child?" Jamie asked.

"Baby, don't even get worked up over this. When things like this happen, they're normally bullshitting and call back if they're hung up on."

"So, I have a cousin named Julie Wilson? Wow; now I really need a drink," Jamie spoke as she rose to her feet and walked back over to the counter.

"Or, we could finish what we started," I stated as I stood back up and took Jamie's hand.

"I don't think we should until we figure out who's calling on the phone," Jamie added, followed by a kiss on my cheek.

The phone rang again.

"Go on and get it, cop," Jamie spoke as she walked towards the back.

"Young, speaking."

"Ah, you're back. Have you blown off the steam?"

"Listen, I can't undo the past, but right now, you're making a really foolish decision to call and threaten a police officer," I spoke.

"Oh really?" she spoke. "Well, my bad. But if you think I don't have access to you, you're dead wrong."

"Don't let this turn ugly today, Ms. Wilson," I told her.

"Doesn't have to," she spoke. "Just follow my orders. I'd like for you and your crew to come to the Dominican Republic. No cops and you need to quit your job," she cleared her throat. "You're going to come and work for me. You will be racing, performing missions, and many other activities that will be very dangerous and risky. You're going to come and get my cars back and take back my property. If I find out that any cops are behind you, I will get you and your family!" she threatened.

"You should know better than to threaten a man's family, let alone a cop's" I spoke.

"Poor Richard, trying to act tough. You humor me." She chuckled. "As long as you follow orders, everything will be fine." "When does this start?" I asked.

"We'll be in touch," she spoke before hanging up.

I hung up the phone and Jamie was walking back to the kitchen.

"What'd she say?" Jamie asked.

"Basically, the same crap. I'm not too positive that we will do her demands, but, just in case, brush up on your driving, Jamie," I replied.

"What did you do?" she asked me; concern filled her voice.

"Something we may regret."

3

Miracle

We arrived back at Jacob's home and I parked the Mustang; he parked the Charger.

"Two canisters of nitrous, but he couldn't beat hard work and a 420-horse powered engine," Jacob spoke.

"You still don't think you can race, Miracle?" Melanie asked.

"I'm telling you, my papi would kill me... but I guess that if I can win easy money and cars, ¿porque no?" I answered.

"I'm not going to lie to you, Miracle, it's not as easy as it looks. It's more-so about timing than speed. It's not about the speed of the car, it's about the person driving," Jacob answered.

"So, train me," I replied. "Right now; we have three cars here. I'm in the Mustang, you take my new Charger. Melanie, you take Jacob's Camaro."

"It's not going to be easy," he spoke as he walked towards the Charger.

"Try me," I spoke as I got in the Mustang.

"Neither of y'all are ready for what I'm bringing," Melanie spoke as she got in the Camaro.

We each started the engines and drove off.

"Follow me," Jacob spoke over his phone.

"I'm feeling this app," I spoke.

"Makes it hella easy to talk while we drive, huh?" Melanie asked.

"Just keep up," Jacob spoke as he shifted gears and sped up.

"Fuckin' show-off," Melanie shouted as she shifted gears and passed Jacob.

I didn't know how to do what they were doing, so I switched to the third gear and stepped on the gas harder, but I wasn't keeping up with their vehicles.

"Miracle, where are you at?" Jacob spoke. "Your Mustang just beat this Charger and you're in last place."

"*Callate pinche cabrón*," I retorted. "This is new to me," I stated as I approached 120 miles per hour.

"Gotta want it, Mami," Melanie spoke as she drove even faster.

"Oh yeah?" Jacob spoke as he changed gears again and drove in front of Melanie before lifting his handbrake and performing a drift that turned his car 180 degrees. He continued to drive in reverse as he looked at Melanie.

"Ah, *besa mi culo*," Melanie spoke.

Jacob laughed.

"Don't crash my Charger, Jacob," I shouted.

He did another 180-degree drift and changed gears again. He performed one more drift, but this time, he stopped the car.

Melanie performed the same drift and I pulled up nearby and came to a regular stop.

"Come on now, you gotta do better than that," Jacob spoke.

"Now you both know that I am new to this," I retaliated.

"Come on girl," Melanie started. "We're gonna teach you a few things."

She walked back to the Camaro.

"Miracle, don't be scared. Nothing but open road out here, and no buildings in sight. Just do as we tell you; become the car," Jacob spoke as he lifted my chin.

He walked to the Charger and I got into the Mustang.

"Miracle, do you see your gear selector?"

"Yeah, I was switching gears as I was racing," I answered.

Jacob got out of the Charger and walked over to the Mustang. He opened the door and got in the passenger's seat.

"Why are you in this car?" I asked him.

"I gotta show you how to do it," he spoke. "Racing is all about timing," he spoke and put on his seatbelt.

"I heard you when you said that the first time," I stated.

"So, when I say go, I want you to switch gears and accelerate."

"Okay, I guess," I spoke.

"Ready… go!" he spoke.

I switched gears and the gear went from 'N' to '1'. I stepped on the gas and the car accelerated.

"You're doing great, Miracle. Now, you hear how the engine is holding the same tune; it isn't progressing?"

"Yes," I spoke as I kept both hands on the steering wheel.

"Switch gears."

I stepped on the clutch, switched gears, and the car sped a little more.

"Now, you have to work on timing," he spoke. "You have to be able to count in your mind how many seconds it will take before you have to switch gears. It should become an automatic instinct," Jacob told me.

As the car continued to climb in speed, it steadied out at 50 miles-per-hour. I switched gears and the car climbed some more.

"Okay, you have your switching in order," Jacob mentioned as we sped at 85 miles-per-hour. "How about your turns? At the next intersection, make a left."

"Are you sure?" I asked him.

"Let me see you do it," he reiterated.

As I approached the intersection, I stepped on the brakes and proceeded to turn left.

"Too slow," Jacob stated. "As you stepped on the brakes and started to turn, the car lost all of the speed it has gained. Let's work on a drift to turn."

"¿Sabes qué? I've seen drifting and it takes a lot of practice… Honestly, I don't think I can do it." I responded.

"Melanie, speed up and hit this left turn," Jacob spoke.

I saw the Camaro speed up and quickly turn left with a drift.

"Alright Melanie, now make a right at the next intersection," Jacob stated.

As she approached the intersection, she got close to the curb and immediately turned right.

"Let's work on yours," he directed his attention back to me.

As time progressed, we worked on more basics; we practiced drifting with U-turns, left and right drifts, gaining and maintaining speed while having complete control of the car.

Thirty minutes passed, and we slowly started to hear sirens in the far distance, but it was apparent that they were coming in our direction.

"Oh shit, time to go! Melanie, where are you?" he spoke over the phone.

"Coming back to the start," she responded.

"Don't!" he exclaimed. "Just head back to the house. We have company headed our way."

"Damn it, this is exactly what I've feared!" I exclaimed.

"Miracle, turn the car around and take me back to the Charger."

I obeyed his command as I drove back to the Charger.

He hopped out of the Mustang and got into the Charger and started the engine.

"Let's bounce, Miracle," he spoke as he sped off in front of me.

I sped behind him and made sure there was little distance between us. I pulled up to the side of him and we sped side-by-side.

A police car started to drive in our direction and turned on his siren.

"Shit, shit, shit," I spoke out of fear.

"Miracle, don't worry; just follow me."

Jacob made an immediate right and I followed right behind him down an alley.

The police turned on his bright lights and turned down the alley.

"Come on, Miracle, we're going to lose them in a second," Jacob spoke.

We sped faster and noticed that the officer was getting further and further behind us.

I slowed down as we exited the alley and didn't see any police officers.

"Don't slow down, Miracle. We need to make sure that we've lost them."

"I don't hear any sirens nearby," I responded.

"True, but let's give it another few minutes. Come on," Jacob spoke as he turned in an empty lot and turned off his engine as well as his lights.

I followed behind him and turned the car off. We both stepped out of the vehicles and stood side-by-side.

"Now that's how you're supposed to drive, Miracle," he spoke as he embraced me.

My body shook as I accepted his embrace.

"Calm down," he spoke, "everything's okay now."

"I can't believe I just did that," I spoke. "All this time, I've been taught to respect the law…"

"And you still are. Look, Miracle, everything will be alright. It was this one incident that occurred and I'm glad that we're okay, but we can't hold this against our conscience."

As Jacob finished his statement, an officer drove past us, but reversed his car and drove into the lot. He stepped out of the vehicle.

"Seems like you kids are out pretty late," he spoke.

"We're just out for a drive," Jacob spoke as he held my hand.

"Kinda late, isn't it?" he mentioned. "Let me see some identification."

Jacob reached into his back pocket and pulled out his wallet. I opened my car door and grabbed my purse.

I got my license out of my purse and handed it to the officer. Jacob passed his license over to the officer as well.

"Miracle Young? You're Richard Young's daughter," he spoke.

"That's me," I responded while twirling my hair.

"Does he know that you're out this late?"

"I believe that he does," I mentioned although I knew I was lying.

"And you're Jacob Hubbard; Jared Hubbard's son."

"Yes sir," Jacob spoke.

"I guess we'll just have a law enforcement party," the officer joked. "Listen, have you all seen any street racers out here?" he asked.

"No, we've been out here for the past two hours," Jacob lied.

The officer looked at our vehicles and it felt as though my heart was about to stop.

"Nice rides you all have here," he spoke as he approached the cars.

"Thanks," I spoke.

I felt like my heart was going to beat out of my chest.

"Well, you know how we teens are," Jacob spoke.

"Yes, I know. My niece and nephew are teenagers and are a handful. Miracle, ¿*como está tu padre?*"

"*Esta bien. Estamos preocupados por una llamada que recibimos más temprano.*"

"Who was it from?" he returned our licenses to us.

"Julie Wilson."

The officer was silent for a moment and finally spoke.

"Do you know who Julie Wilson is?" he asked me.

"I'm trying to figure that out myself… Maybe you can help me." I mentioned as I loosened up.

"I don't feel it's in my position to say. I will tell you that she was notoriously famous all over. The things she's done and accomplished have made her one of the most famous criminals from all over the world."

"Nobody will tell me anything, but it's more information than what I've previously known," I spoke as I was surprised to hear this.

"Yeah, but I'm about to go back on patrol and look for these racers. You all stay safe out here. Think about heading home before it gets too late," he spoke as he handed us back our licenses.

We retrieved them and he walked back to his car.

"You too, Officer," Jacob spoke.

The officer got in his vehicle and drove away. I let out a sigh.

"*Ay Dios mio*, that was close."

"A little too close. But look at it this way, we live to race another day," Jacob mentioned as he got into his car.

"*Estás loco*," I responded with a chuckle as I climbed inside of my vehicle.

We both drove off and shortly after arrived at Jacob's home.
***

"Damn, what took you all so long?" Melanie asked as we pulled into the driveway.

"Police pursuit. You know me though, I had to find a way to get out the jam," Jacob joked as he touched his goatee.

"*Eres loco*," I spoke. "We almost got caught, girl," I told her.

"Jacob, you can't be getting my girl caught, now. You know her daddy's a cop and will have that ass if she's caught doing anything illegal."

"I doubt it," I interrupted, "I can't remember ever getting a whooping from either of my parents."

"Truly a spoiled bitch," Melanie joked. "So, if you've never gotten a whooping, why in the hell aren't you wildin' out or in the streets?"

"I have a mind of my own. I don't let other people influence me or make decisions for me. I know what's right and what's wrong, and that won't ever change."

"You let us influence you and persuade you into racing," Jacob joked.

"Well, that's because you're my best friends. If one of us goes down, all of us go down." I added.

"Mmhmm, well just don't get too caught up with what Jacob says. This nigga can get you in all kinds of trouble," Melanie joked as she put her arm around him.

"That's what you say now," he mentioned.

I looked at my Mustang and nodded my head.

"I have a question for you all," I spoke. "How did I do?"

They both looked at each other and then back at me.

"After you learned the basics, you did well. I can see that it won't be a thing to you and you'll be an excellent driver and racer," Jacob spoke.

"Yeah, girl, now let's see if you can beat someone for a bit of cash," Melanie mentioned.

"Well, I'm not doing anything tonight. I'm going in this house and taking my ass to bed," I laughed.

"Such an early bird," Melanie joked.

"Well, you know where the blankets are and where you can sleep," Jacob spoke.

"I suppose, since you can't be a gentleman and lay everything out for me," I retorted.

"Ugh!" Jacob stated out of disgust. "Melanie, let's go inside. Apparently, someone's arms don't work," he let out a slight chuckle.

"Thank you," I stated.

We all walked inside and retired for the night.

4

Miracle

When I awoke the next morning, I walked to the washroom and freshened up. I finished brushing my hair and I heard Melanie and Jacob in the kitchen arguing.

"*Pendejo*, how are you going to tell me about my parents and that they keep me under lock and key? Your daddy's the cop and is one of the highest officers in his unit!" Melanie raised her hand and was about to strike Jacob. As she hit him, Jacob grabbed her.

"Woah, woah, woah!" I shouted as I ran into the kitchen and grabbed Melanie. "What are you all fighting about?"

"Miracle, you need to get this boy before I kill him," Melanie stated as she tried to reach over me and attack Jacob.

"She's mad because we were late returning here last night," Jacob spoke.

"No, I'm mad at the fact that you can't keep it real with me."

"Melanie, calm down," I told her.

She ripped her arms away from me. "I'm calm, I'm calm."

"Why do we always get into it?" Jacob asked her.

"*No me hales,*" Melanie retorted.

"So, you're mad at me?" he questioned.

Melanie ignored the question and walked out of the house.

"¿Jacob, *que pasó?*" I asked him.

"I want to say it was just an argument, but I don't know. Seems like Melanie is pretty angry with me. I can't be sure as to why she is."

I took his hand.

"Maybe she just needs to calm down," I stated.

"You know what's funny?" he asked me. "It's not about us coming in late or any of that."

"¿*Como?*"

"It's actually about you," he suggested. I've known you since you were born; I saw you when you came out of the womb," he laughed.

"Ew, so you so my mama's diamond? Wait; even worse, you saw *my* diamond." I started to blush.

"Eh, don't worry, I didn't see… Plus, I was three; I didn't know what it was."

"Mmhmm, ¿*Sabes qué?* You better not be having dreams about me, Jacob." I told him.

"I guess I should keep my mouth shut before I get in trouble, then," he mentioned with a chuckle.

"¿*Que dice?*" I asked.

"Nothing, Miracle," he spoke as he walked out of the kitchen and out of the door to find Melanie.

"Melanie!" he shouted.

Melanie screamed as she stood by the beach.

Jacob and I jogged over to where she stood.

"What's wrong, Melanie?" I asked.

She pointed towards the water, and I looked down. I saw a person's body lying in the water; their eyes were closed but there were lacerations on the body.

"Come on," Jacob started, "grab an arm, and let's pull it out."

We pulled the body out of the water and into the sand. I pulled out my phone and called my father.

"Papi," I spoke.

"What's going on, Miracle?" he could tell that something was wrong based on the tone of my voice.

"Papi, I need you to come out here, now! We've found a body in the water."

"Baby, leave it alone. Mommy and I will be there in a few minutes with a few units." My father hung up the phone and I noticed Jacob as he kneeled to the body.

"Do you all know who this is?" he spoke.

I looked very carefully but the water caused discoloration of the skin and hair. The lacerations on the face made it very difficult to identify the face of the person; the arms and legs of the individual were severely bruised that they were unidentifiable.

"I can't tell," I spoke.

"Doesn't look familiar," Melanie answered.

"Jessie Parker," Jacob spoke. "She goes to our school in Chicago, Miracle."

I looked closer at the body and I covered my mouth.

"She sits in the back of Mrs. Johnson's class," I mentioned.

"Question: what is she doing out here in P.R.?" Melanie asked.

Jacob and I shook our heads in disbelief as we heard sirens quickly approaching.

As we turned around, multiple police cars turned down the beach. My father drove in front of the other vehicles and Uncle Jared's car appeared next.

"Papi," I shouted as all the officers rushed out of their vehicles with their guns raised.

"Stand back!" they shouted.

My mother and father got out of the vehicle and my mother ran over and hugged me.

"Miracle!" My mother shouted as she embraced me.

Her long dark hair touched my face and I'd never felt safer and protected.

"I want for you all to run anything you all can find on this person! I want a complete biography of who this is and I want you all to find out how they died. You can't find out minor details, that's what the coroners are for, but find out the basic information," my father spoke to the other officers. Uncle Jared walked over to us, as well as Aunt Madison.

"Ma!" Jacob spoke as he hugged Melanie.

As Madison reached Jacob, she was frightened at the sight of the woman's body.

"Let's go inside," she spoke.

As my mother, Jacob, Melanie, Madison, and I all walked inside, I glanced at the body and couldn't help but think Jessie was speaking to me.

***

As nighttime fell upon us, emergency personnel and police officers were still outside of the home regarding the body we found.

They locked down the house, so we couldn't leave, and nobody was able to arrive. Also, they shut down the beach to prevent any tampering with any evidence they may have collected.

My father walked into the house and stood against the wall.

"Baby, come sit down next to me," my mother stated. My father walked over to us and sat down. His phone rang and he quickly answered it.

"Young, speaking."

"I hope you realize things are becoming very serious, very quickly."

"You're behind this?"

"I refuse to comment on that. But, things are escalating for you and you will need to back down before you get too involved in this. Remember, you need to come to the Dominican Republic and come get my cars. Time is winding down, Mr. Young. I will need your decision within the next 48 hours. Are you coming or going?"

"Don't worry about me; but I do want to know, what is my benefit from this?" my father spoke as he rose to his feet and paced the floor.

"Your wife and kid continue to live!"

"Again, you're threatening an officer. What do you possibly think will happen once I identify who you are?"

"No, what do you think will happen if you don't follow my orders? I will call you back tomorrow with your flight number. Your tickets will already be registered; I just need to know how many I need to book."

"I'm not coming," my father retorted firmly, although I could tell he was nervous.

"Really? Okay, cool."

The call disconnected and my father placed his phone on the table. My mother rose to her feet.

"Richard, what did you do?" she asked.

"I will not be intimidated by a wanna-be criminal, Jamie. It's not going to work on me. I've been through too much in my life to be worried over someone so simple-minded. I can't even get mixed up with it."

"Are you forgetting how we met?" my mother asked.

"Richard, don't do anything crazy," Uncle Jared interrupted.

"Yes, but you were an accomplice to your aunt, and—," my father abruptly stopped in his sentence.

"*¿Como,* Papi?" I asked as I rose to my feet. "My aunt?"
"Let's not do this in front of Miracle," my mother added.
"No, Mami, let me hear about my aunt."
"Do you want to hear the truth? Or are you just looking for an argument?" my father asked.
"*¿Que coño?* I just wish to know the truth!" I shouted.

In an instant, my mother grabbed my arm and walked me into the living room; squeezing my arm tightly. She released my arm as she pushed me to the other end of the room.

"Where in the hell do you come off talking to your father that way? That man in there has been through hell for both of us; even when you were born was a wild moment!" my mother exclaimed. "No, I've never told you, but you were a month-and-a-half early, Miracle. That's the reason we named you 'Miracle.' So many things occurred during our relationship and during the pregnancy, we felt it was a miracle to have you."

"*Perdoneme,* Mami. But I'm sick of not knowing answers to things I think I have a right to know."

"Miracle, there's a time and place for everything. Right now, isn't a good time with everything that's going on…We have a deceased individual, and someone is threatening your father on the phone."

"Mami, this is extremely hurtful that I can't find out something as simple as this," I walked out of the room.

"Miracle!" my mother shouted.

I grabbed my car keys off the table and walked out of the house. Melanie ran out of the door behind me.

"Miracle, nena, what happened?" she asked.

"Miracle!" my father stated as he walked out of the house behind me.

"I need to take a drive to clear my head," I retaliated.

I unlocked my door and got in the car. I started the vehicle and drove off.

As I drove onto the road, I noticed all the traffic, and I felt it was weird that so many people were out at 9:30 in the evening.

I passed the first light at my intersection, and a police vehicle pulled up behind me and flashed its lights.

"*Ay dios mio,*" I spoke as I pulled over.

"License and registration, Miss?"

I pulled out my license and looked at her uniform and noticed the last name read 'Wilson'.

"Miracle? As in Detective Young's Miracle?"

"Yes, that's me," I spoke.

"Excellent," she replied as she dropped the license, pulled out her gun, and aimed it at me. "Step out of the vehicle."

I revved my car's engine and she prepared to shoot.

"Move this vehicle and I'll blow your brains out," she spoke.

I opened the car door and put my hands up.

"Who are you? You can't possibly be a cop doing this."

"Shut the fuck up," she retorted as she put the gun to the back of my head.

I let out a tear as she continued to speak.

"Now, your father needs to come to the Dominican Republic. I need to get these tickets for him to come on down, but I need verification that…"

"Look, why don't you call him about that?" I asked.

She hit me with the gun in the back of my head and I fell, but I didn't lose consciousness.

"You talk too damn much," she spoke

She tossed her gun to the side and turned me over on my back.

She scratched at my face as I fought back to get her off me. I punched her in the nose and she started bleeding.

"Assaulting an officer, baby girl…. That's going to cost you a bit of time in prison," she stated as she started to pick me up by the arm.

I slapped the woman and scratched her face as I ran towards my car.

I picked up my license, climbed inside, and I quickly drove off. The lady got in her car and drove behind me with her siren on, to insinuate a police pursuit.

"Pull the fucking vehicle over!" She shouted over her loudspeaker.

I drove faster, desperately trying to lose the woman that assaulted me.

As I performed a left drift, I almost hit a few pedestrians so I blew my horn.

"¡*Muévete*! Get out of the way!" I shouted.

As the woman came to the same turn, she drove against the building and damaged her vehicle.

She drove to the side of me and pulled out her gun. She aimed it at me and prepared to shoot, when someone crashed into the back of her car, pushing her forward.

I looked back and noticed Jacob as he pulled forward and drove side-by-side with me. As the lady pressed on her brakes, Melanie appeared out of the intersection and drove ahead of all three of us.

Melanie applied her handbrake and the lady crashed into the back of her as Jacob pulled up to the side of the woman and rammed her over into the building.

Her car collided with the building and immediately burst into flames. Melanie, Jacob, and I continued to drive at top speed until we reached his home.

We all got out of our vehicles and closed the doors. I leaned against my car door and slumped down until I was sitting on the ground and I covered my face as I cried.

"Melanie, go get my mother and father, as well as Uncle Richard and Aunt Jamie," Jacob stated as he walked over to me.

She ran into the house and he crouched down next to me.

"Miracle," he stated as he put his hands on my shoulder.

I turned my head and cried on Jacob's shoulder.

"Jacob, *dios mio*. I don't know who she was or what she wanted, but I can tell that she wished to kill me. If you all hadn't shown up, I would not be alive," I cried so much that Jacob's shirt quickly became soaked.

"Miracle, don't cry. I'm here for you and I am not going to leave your side."

At this moment, Jacob felt like he was more than a friend to me.

He wiped my eyes and lifted my chin: this is when our parents came running outside; my father and Uncle Jared had their guns aimed and their hands rested on the holsters.

"Miracle!" My father shouted as he ran over to me.

My mother pulled me close kissed me on the cheek and hugged me tightly.

As my father reached me, his cell phone rang. He answered it.

"I hope you now realize how serious I am," the voice stated.

"You!" he scolded as he looked around. "I will fucking kill you," my father threatened.

The lady ignored his threat.

"Be at the airport tomorrow at 5 pm; your flight leaves at 7:01… If you miss it, the deal is off and you see your daughter right now?" The voice asked and my father looked at me, "next time, you'll be picking her up in a fucking box. There will be no weapons, no wires, no tricks. If I so much suspect you as to even mumble a code under your breath, I will shut everything down and it will be the last time you see your family alive."

My father sighed.

"How many tickets?" he reluctantly gave in.

"Shit, that's up to you. You tell me how many tickets you need, and I'll provide them. I'm holding up to what I said I would do; now you must do the same for me."

My father had a dazed look on his face as he stared at me.

"Give me six," he spoke.

"Now you're talking. I need details on who's coming with you. Date of birth, age, names; the basics."

"Richard Young is the first ticket; I'm sure you have the details on me. I'm 46; birthday is December 2nd, 1984," he mentioned.

I could tell at this moment he was doing something he honestly didn't want to do.

"Richard Young, reminds me of a funny story..."

"Please, save it. The next ticket goes to -..."

"Woah, now don't think you're in a position to try to control this situation. This is still my party and we celebrate how I want to celebrate."

"I just figured you would need to book the tickets; considering the flight leaves tomorrow."

"Ah, *Señor* Smart-ass is trying to play mind games with me, huh?" the woman asked. "It doesn't matter; I'm still one step ahead of you, whether you want to believe it or not. Second ticket?"

"The next ticket will be for Jamie Young. She's 45 and her birthday is February 14th, 1986."

"Ah, so we have a Valentine's day baby. No wonder you all are compatible; Sagittarius and Aquarius... beautiful couple. Ticket three?"

"Miracle Young." I quivered at the way he said my name.

I had never seen my father look so spooked before.

Jacob held my hand as Melanie held the other; my mother was now pacing the floor. "She's 16 and her birthday is July 11th, 2017."

"I hope I didn't cause too much damage to her face and body; my car was damaged by two jackasses in a black Charger and a blue Challenger. They fuckin' ran me off the road."

My father looked up and noticed Jacob and Melanie's cars were damaged. He knew she was referring to them.

"For the final three tickets, you need to tell me the information quickly. This battery is about to die."

"Jared Hubbard, 47, August 7th, 1983; Madison Hubbard, 45, October 12th, 1985; Jacob Hubbard, 19, March 12th, 2014." My father hurried.

"*Gracias, mi hermano*, I look forward to seeing you *mañana*."

"I'm not your brother." My father hung up the phone.

He shook his head and opened his eyes before speaking again.

"You two," he stated as he pointed to Melanie and Jacob. "Come here."

Melanie grabbed Jacob's hand as they both walked toward my father.

"With all due respect, Unc, Miracle was in danger, and as her best friends, we promised her we'd always have her back," Jacob started.

"We didn't mean for it to cause damage to the city. But whatever happened was to save Miracle."

"Don't worry, calling you all over here isn't bad. You all saved my baby girl's life. She's blessed to have friends like you all in her life. Family first," he held his head high.

I could tell he was truly proud of Melanie and Jacob.

"How did you all know what was going down?" he continued.

"After she drove off, we had to trail her to make sure she was okay. After we saw the fight with the cop, Miracle ran to her car and drove off. We knew something had to be done," Jacob spoke.

"Wait, the woman was a cop?" he asked them.

"Well, she was dressed in uniform and drove a police vehicle."

My father was in awe as he shook his head.

"Thank you both," he spoke to them.

He took a few steps and called my uncle. As Uncle Jared came outside, he and my father stepped to the side as Melanie and Jacob both walked over to me.

"You really handled that shit," Melanie spoke to me as she touched my shoulder.

My mother brought out a warm towel for my cuts and bruises.

"Yeah, well I would be dead if you all hadn't shown up. I could have sworn I saw a gun being aimed at me before Jacob hit her car from behind," I spoke as I used the towel and wiped my cuts.

My mother walked over to my father and Jacob replied.

"I guess you are glad we did that small training session on driving, huh?" Jacob chuckled as he touched the hair on his chin.

"Yeah, I guess it was worthwhile," I stated as I felt a chill run down my body. "*Dios mio*, does anyone else feel cold?"

"Miracle, it's 90 degrees. How can you possibly feel cold?" Melanie asked me with a chuckle. "You're tripping," she laughed as Jacob jogged over to his car and retrieve his jacket for me.

"I don't know; it's just like…" I started and I heard a voice in the distance.

I tried to focus in on the voice and the more I listened, the more I could piece out who it was.

"Jessie!" I spoke as I quickly got up and ran over to the beach where the body still lay.

"You all need to stay back," the medical examiner and the officers told us.

I ignored them and ran under the tape and kneeled to her body.

"Miracle!" my father shouted as he jogged over to the beach.

Jacob put his hand on my arm and tried to hold me back.

"No, let me go. I know it sounds weird, but I can hear her speaking to me." I spoke.

"Maybe that gun to the back of your head has knocked you loopy, Miracle," Melanie spoke as she helped Jacob pick me up.

"No, like, I can legit hear her voice. I can hear her talk about how she died," I tried to explain.

"Miracle, so now I guess you hear dead people?" Jacob joked. "Some people claim to see them, not hear them."

"I'm not joking," I mentioned.

My father overheard our conversation and interfered.

"Hold on," he interrupted. "Miracle, tell me what's going on."

"Papi, I can hear her. She's telling me how she died and everything. It's like she's haunting me."

"What's she saying?" he asked, sounding a bit more concerned.

"She's quieting down now, but she was telling me that she was suffocated. While she was unconscious, her killer must have gotten scared so she tried to dispose of her body. After the killer thought for a while, they decided to throw her body in the ocean and tie weights to hold it down. She told me that she's been floating in the water for over 3 months," I explained every detail.

"Come on," he whispered as he helped me up and walked the three of us, Melanie, Jacob, and myself, away from the crime scene.

"Do you believe me, Papi?" I asked him.

"You have no reason to lie, right?" he asked in a stern tone.

"Lie about hearing dead people?" I slightly rolled my eyes. "I don't want to hear this, but I do. No, Papi, I have no reason to lie."

"I believe you," he replied and quickly changed topics. "Miracle and Jacob, I need for you all to learn how to drive. I'm not talking about NASCAR, I'm talking about drag-racing and extreme driving."

For a moment, my heart seemed to drop.

"¿*Que quieres,* Papi?" I asked.

"I need for you all to race. Some stuff has gone down and tomorrow we're going to fly out to the Dominican Republic. We have to drive and help this woman get her property back. At this point, it's no longer an option," my father didn't look either of us in the eyes.

He looked down and finally turned away after speaking.

"Street racing, huh?" Jacob suggested with a laugh.

"Let's do it," I mentioned.

5

-*Richard*

Jared and I were in the kitchen discussing what was about to happen, as nighttime fell.

"So, Julie Wilson called you and just demanded that you come to the Dominican Republic, and that you race for her?" he asked.

"That's not all. I have to quit my job and can't inform any police of this."

"Well, you told me. You've already broken her rules," he slightly laughed.

"Yeah, but you're a part of my crew, and she instructed me to bring my crew," I responded. "So, I told her you were coming along."

"You told her what?" Jared asked.

"Calm down, bro," I laughed. "We're not going to quit. We're gonna let Roberts know what's going on and we're gonna bust this girl; at least for assault against Miracle."

"Rick, now you know I got your back through thick and thin, but I wanna know why you're submitting to her," Jared asked. "Why don't you just let her come to you?"

"If she's anything like her mother, she's smarter than that," I mentioned. "Remember, Julie had a response for *everything* we threw at her," I scratched the stubble under my neck. "Shit, she probably won't even show us who she is until the last minute," I told him.

Jared walked to the cabinet and retrieved a cup before filling it with water from the refrigerator.

"What makes you so certain that this thing is legit? If she won't show you who she is, who's to say she'll leave your life once this is done?"

"I got a plan," I mentioned with a devious smirk.

"B, don't get us killed," Jared laughed as he placed the cup down.

"I got you," I assured him.

I picked up my cell phone and dialed Abel to inform him of the situation.

"Julie Wilson, huh?" Abel asked. "Young, we can't send units to the Dominican Republic. We can interact with Puerto Rico because it's a U.S. territory, but not the D.R."

"Damn," I spoke with disappointment. "Well, I'm requesting that you send me over a resignation document, per Julie's orders."

"I'll draw up the paperwork and see what I can do to assist you."

"No, Roberts!" I retaliated. "Jared and I are going to handle this on our own. My wife and child are in jeopardy. But I'm gonna keep you in the loop, and if needed, I'll reach out to you," I told him.

"I'll send you a proofed form in a few minutes. Things have been crazy," he mentioned. "You two stay safe, and you know you have the team behind you if needed."

"Trust me, I know. Thanks, Roberts." I stated before hanging up the phone.

Jared and I continued to speak of the situation and soon walked away to pack our things.

When we awoke the next morning, Jared and I swiftly moved our items to the front to be able to easily transport them to the vehicles. Jamie and Madison were in the living room finishing their packing and

Miracle was talking to Jacob and Melanie; I'm guessing they were discussing our flight this evening and what would happen.

Miracle walked into the kitchen. As I viewed my daughter, it was no secret that she resembled her mother in every way: her smooth, tan skin tone; her curly brown hair; her eyes; her smile; her walk; the way she spoke; the little things that she did, reminded me of Jamie.

The only resemblance I could see of myself in Miracle was her personality. She wasn't a weak-minded individual and she always fought for herself.

People that knew Miracle could easily tell that she was my daughter.

She twirled her hair in her finger, similar to the way Jamie did, and I knew she was about to ask me for something.

"Papi, can Melanie come with us to the Dominican Republic?" she put on a pair of sad eyes to influence my decision.

"Baby, I can't say that she can," I stated. "You know the woman that assaulted you?" I asked.

"*Sí*," Miracle replied as she continued to twirl her hair.

"She left specific instructions." I thought for a moment. "I would need to call her back. If she says yes, Melanie can go," I finished.

Miracle squealed with excitement as she jumped up and left out of the room.

I picked up my phone and called Julie back.

"Ah, Richard. What's going on? Are you ready for tonight?" She answered the phone and asked me.

"That's actually what I wanted to talk to you about. Is it possible for me to get one more ticket?"

"Ramón," she stated, which allowed me to know she knew about my radio station, "you aren't plotting against me, are you?"

"No, not at all Julie, it's just that Miracle wants her best friend to come along. It will work out in your favor, as you'll have another person to help," I tried my hardest to identify any background noises to figure out who this woman was.

"I'm warning you, Richard, if you're trying to pull a trick…" I could tell Julie was serious by the tone of her voice.

"No tricks," I assured her.

"Uh-huh," I could tell she was skeptical. "I'm sure we can make that happen. Give me the details," she spoke.

"Melanie Cartel, 17, June 15th, 2016."

"I will call you in a bit with all of the specifics," Julie spoke.

"I have one more question: what about the cars? Are you going to have them shipped over?" I asked.

"Great question. It would be helpful, huh?" Julie chuckled.

I forced a chuckle from my system.

"Yeah, I can do that. How many cars?"

"5," I spoke as I mentally counted the number of cars. I'd paired the adults together and put the children in separate vehicles

I heard Julie typing information on a computer.

"Everything's set," she spoke a few seconds later. "I will see you tonight."

I hung up the phone.

"*Milagro*," I called to Miracle in Spanish.

"*¿Si*, Papi?" she stated as she and Melanie came into the room.

"Melanie, pack your bags. You're going to the Dominican Republic," I announced.

"*Gracias*, Papi," Miracle thanked me with a hug.

"You all better be ready by four," I stated as they ran into the other room.

"We'll be ready by 3:45," Miracle shouted back.

Jamie came into the kitchen and stood behind me. She put her arms around my neck and leaned down.

"No matter what happens, you'll always be my hero, daddy," She kissed me on the lips and hugged me tightly.

"*Te amo*," I stated to Jamie.

"*Te amo, tambien*," she mentioned.

As we exchanged emotional gestures, Miracle and Melanie went to Melanie's home to get a few of her things.

***

At five, we were pulling up to the airport and my phone rang.

"Don't speak, just do as instructed. Drive your vehicles to the airport's dock. Put the cars in neutral and leave the keys in the ignition," the male voice hung up the phone and I informed Jamie to step out of the car.

As she got out, we unpacked the suitcases and Jamie waited while Jacob, Miracle, Melanie, and Jared drove their cars over to the dock.

Once we drove the vehicles into position, we each stepped out of the cars and walked back over to where Jamie stood.

"You all ready?" I spoke.

"Let's do this," Madison spoke as we walked to the service desk to check in our luggage.

"Tickets for Richard Young to the Dominican Republic," I spoke.

The desk operator typed in the last name into the computer.

"Okay, I have the tickets in the system. I'll need to see some identification."

We all pulled out our licenses and put them on the counter.

"Okay," the lady spoke as she looked at each ID and matched it with the corresponding boarding pass. "You'll be flying first class and everything's already been paid for, including your luggage. Just place them over here and we'll send them over for you. You'll be at gate B21 and your flight leaves in two hours," the lady spoke.

"Thanks," I spoke as we all walked into the building.

Time was passing us by as we headed to the gate.

"Hold on one second, guys," I spoke.

I pulled out my phone and answered it, putting it on speaker.

"Glad to see that you can follow instructions so far," Julie stated.

"Yeah, what's up?" I asked.

"Your journey has just begun," she started. "You have a short flight but once you land, you must quickly leave the plane and get to the hotel. They are expecting you. Remember, Young, I am on top of you," she threatened before hanging up.

We still had a bit of time before we needed to board the plane, so we walked over to a restaurant and grabbed a bite to eat.

As time progressed, we all took our seats on the plane after boarding.

Madison and Jared were paired together; Jamie and I were sitting directly behind them. Melanie and Jacob were behind us, and Miracle was set to sit in the middle row of the plane.

"If you need anything, Miracle, I'm right here," I spoke over the chatter of the plane.

"Okay, papi," Miracle spoke.

She put her earphones in her ears and a guy sat down next to her.

6

Miracle

I turned on my iPod and listened to my music when a guy sat down beside me. He had on sunglasses and a leather vest.

He took off his sunglasses and I noticed it was Quincy.

"*Ay dios mio*," I rolled my eyes.

"Miracle Young," he stated as he got comfortable in the seat. "What brings you to this flight for the D.R.?"

My father looked back to check on me and noticed Quincy.

"If you so much as to lay a finger on my daughter, I will kill you; I swear," he spoke.

"Calm your hype ass down," Quincy replied. "I wouldn't hurt this beautiful body."

"That's my father!" I asserted. "Watch who you're talking to like that."

Quincy chuckled as he touched his goatee.

"You guys are so funny. We all know that you won't do a thing to me," he spoke with a smirk.

My father and mother both rose out of their chairs and approached us.

"You wanna take us up on that offer?" My mother asked.

Quincy eyed my mother up and down.

"Another body that I'm loving. You can do whatever you want to me," he spoke and I slapped him.

"Mami, Papi, you can sit down," I started. "I'll handle this," I glared at Quincy.

He rubbed the side of his face and smirked at me.

"Handle it then, baby," he replied.

When my mother and father sat down, Quincy put his hand on my thigh.

I decided to play along and put my hand on his thigh.

He ran his hand up my thigh and I did the same, but I grabbed his testicles and tightened my grip and he quickly let my thigh go but I held on to his testicles.

"*Pinche cabron,* listen up. I will break them. I will keep squeezing harder until you black out."

He gritted his teeth and made a face of pain as I squeezed tighter.

"I do not want to sit next to you on this flight, but I have to. Leave me alone and I won't break you."

Melanie looked in my direction and stifled her laughter as Jacob chuckled.

"Nod your head if you understand, and I'll release you," I continued to hold Quincy and he finally nodded in agreement.

I released my grip and put my hands on my lap. He put his hands on his groin and a tear fell.

"Keep trying me, Miracle," he spoke after a few minutes.

"Whatever," I replied.

The pilot spoke over the intercom and greeted us.

"Welcome aboard flight 258; nonstop service to Santo Domingo, Dominican Republic. It's currently about 89 degrees in the D.R. and it appears we might hit a bit of turbulence, so please keep those seatbelts fastened. We will be together for the next hour, so buddy up and let's make friends. There is absolutely no smoking on this plane.

If you must take a smoke, please step outside to do so; we'll wait for you," the pilot joked as a few people laughed.

"I sure hope you need to smoke, Quincy," I spoke.

He glared at me as the pilot continued.

"We hope you enjoy the flight and thank you for flying with us."

Ten minutes later, the plane started to take off and I could barely hear anything over the roar of the engine.

Quincy put his hand on my leg again and when I grabbed for him again, he grabbed my hand mid-way.

"Not twice in a row, baby" he spoke as he slowly put a hand on my vaginal region.

"Quincy, let me go," I spoke and squirmed.

"Why? You know you're wet. I can feel it," he whispered as he put his whole hand on my leggings.

Jacob looked over and saw that I was uncomfortable and knew something was going on. He pressed the button for the flight attendant and called for my father, but my father couldn't hear him. He nudged Melanie to notify her of what was going on and to get my parents.

Quincy put his lips to my neck as he turned in his chair to face me. He started to kiss my neck and feel on me.

Jacob emerged from his seat and walked towards the back.

"Quincy, *detente*," I stated as he put one of his hands inside of my leggings and inside of my panties.

"Feels so damn good," he spoke as he continued.

He was so discreet with touching my body, even the people sitting beside us didn't notice anything. I tried my hardest to fight back but he held me still.

Jacob crept behind us and grabbed Quincy's head. He pulled Quincy's head back to stop the kiss, punched Quincy in the face, and slammed his head on the back of the chair ahead of us.

The woman sitting in the chair ahead of us jumped out of her seat.

Passengers on the plane turned around and some passengers screamed.

Security could be seen coming in our direction and my father and uncle jogged our way.

Jacob slammed Quincy's head a second and third time on the chair and Quincy began to bleed.

"Didn't I tell you to leave her alone?" Jacob asked as he held the back of Quincy's head and slammed it against the chair once more.

My father and uncle quickly grabbed Jacob's arms to prevent him from fighting. Quincy held his face and as he took his hands away, he noticed blood; however, it wasn't until he saw the bloody table ahead of us that he realized how badly he was bleeding.

Security grabbed at Jacob but my father intervened.

"We'll handle it from here," my father spoke.

I sat in my chair and wiped my lips as I stood up; tears filled my eyes and I hugged Jacob tightly.

"He will be prosecuted, right?" Quincy asked as he glared at Jacob and me.

"Airport policy. When we land, there will be officers on the ground waiting for this young man," the security guard stated.

"That won't be necessary," my father started. "I'm a..."

"Concerned parent who will take disciplinary actions for my son's actions," Uncle Jared interrupted.

"Correct," my father stated as he realized he almost confessed to being a police officer.

"If we're calling the police, call them on him," I pointed to Quincy. "I was just molested," I spoke.

Jacob glared at Quincy as Quincy still looked at me.

"What?" My father asked as he heard me say this.

He grabbed Quincy and held his collar.

"Didn't I tell you not to touch my daughter?!"

"Her body was calling me," he whispered with a chuckle.

"You son of a..."

"Hell nah, I didn't touch that girl," Quincy lied out loud.

"Why don't we all forget about this?" Uncle Jared asked since he knew that Julie must have been around or watching in some way.

I thought as the men argued around me.

Melanie, my mother, and Aunt Madison walked in my direction as one of the flight attendants walked to the front to get the pilot.

"I'm not going to jail," Jacob stated. "As far as I see it, I haven't done anything wrong but defend my friend. If Quincy won't get prosecuted for touching my best friend, don't say a thing to me," he argued.

The pilot arrived at our row and asked what was going on; I figured the co-pilot must have been flying the plane.

My mother took my hand and led me to the washroom, along with Melanie and Aunt Madison.

I broke down in tears when she closed the door.

"Miracle," she stated as she hugged me. Melanie reached over and grabbed some tissue for me.

"Mami, I hate him," I stated as I wiped my eyes, but I was still crying.

"*Milagro,*" my mother stated as she put her hands in my hair. "Has he hurt you?"

"No. He only kissed and rubbed on me. But I've never been so humiliated in my life." I cried more, and the tears continued to flow heavily.

"Jamie, what do you suggest we do about this?" Aunt Madison spoke as she held my hand tightly.

"We can't do anything right now, Madison," my mother whispered. "Richard and Jared are not supposed to be cops. I think that's why Jared just wants to drop the situation. He doesn't want Jacob to go to jail and he doesn't want to risk our lives."

"May I make a suggestion?" Melanie spoke.

My mother and Madison looked at her and nodded in approval.

"When Jacob and I saved Miracle's life, the woman seemed as though she wasn't about playing any games. Quincy needs to regret what he's done, but let's wait until we fulfill her requests, and then take them both," Melanie shrugged her shoulders as she finished speaking.

"I agree with Melanie," I spoke as I wiped my eyes, "although if it were up to me, I would kill him right now."

"Well, murder's definitely out of the question," my mother stated.

I combed my fingers through my hair as we all exited the restroom.

As I walked back towards my seat, I could see the men were still arguing.

"Mr. Young, we are going to need for you to calm down," the pilot stated as my father shouted at Quincy and held his collar.

"Can a cop really do this?" Quincy asked.

"I'm not a cop anymore," my father spoke.

Uncle Jared held my father and Jacob separated my father and Quincy.

It was interesting to see how it had shifted; at first, my father and Uncle Jared were holding Jacob, and now, Uncle Jared and Jacob were holding my father back.

"How about this? Mr. Wright, do you mind if we move you to another seat to avoid further confrontation and to safely land in the Dominican Republic?" the pilot asked.

"That would be perfect," Quincy spoke as he glared at me.

"Captain, there's a problem with moving him. There are no more seats here in first class; only in coach," the flight attendant spoke.

"Let's get this young man to coach, then. Walk him to the washroom as well to get cleaned up."

As Quincy grabbed his coat, he adjusted his clothes and walked with the flight attendant to the washroom.

"Now, Mr. Young, I know you're upset, but this is battery and I don't know how the D.R. will take care of it, but there will be officers on the ground waiting for Mr. Hubbard," the pilot spoke. "I apologize, but rules are rules."

He walked towards the front and a flight attendant arrived at the seat with a towel to clean Quincy's blood.

Once she finished wiping the chair free of Quincy's blood, I sat back down, by myself, and turned on my iPod. I let out tears as I put on my sunglasses. I isolated myself from the rest of the plane for the rest of the flight, although I could still make out that people were whispering about what just happened.

     ***

When the plane landed in the Dominican Republic and we exited the aircraft, police officers were waiting outside for Jacob. My father and Jared walked in front of him as we exited the airport with the luggage in hand.

"Jacob Hubbard?" one of the officers spoke.

"What's up?" Jacob spoke without fear as he kept one arm around me, held Melanie's hand, and had his bag strapped around his shoulder.

"You have the right to remain…" the officer started as we approached him.

"We won't allow you to arrest him," Uncle Jared spoke.

"Your first mistake was thinking that you had a damn choice. You're not in America anymore," the police officer spoke with an accent.

My father looked sternly at the police officer. As the officers reached for Jacob, a woman came to the front and started to speak to the men. She was dressed in all black, wore sunglasses, as well as a shawl. She spoke softly so that no one could hear. My father and uncle turned and faced my mother and Aunt Madison.

The only word I could make out that the woman said was 'Julie Wilson'.

As she walked off, the officers spoke.

"We're leaving you with a warning. Battery is a serious offense here in the D.R. and will not be tolerated," the officer spoke.

He nodded to his partner and they walked back to their vehicle. Once they drove off, my father's phone rang.

"Hello?" he answered on speaker so that everyone could hear.

"Close call on the plane, huh? I could have sworn you were setting me up," the woman spoke.

"Nah, I'm not a snake. I'm living up to my end of the deal; I hope you're doing the same," my father replied.

"Time will reveal," she spoke. "I see everyone is off the plane. Get the next taxi and take it to the Renaissance Santo Domingo Jaragua Hotel & Casino. I will talk to you once you get there."

The woman hung up abruptly without giving my father a chance to reply. He turned to look at us.

"Come on y'all, we have to go," my father spoke as he whistled for a taxi.

The taxi drove up and we loaded all our suitcases into the back.

"That's a lot of baggage," the driver spoke as he adjusted his hat.

"Literally and figuratively," my father spoke. "You wouldn't believe the flight here. Please take us to the Renaissance Santo Domingo Jaragua Hotel & Casino."

The drive was silent: Jacob cuddled with Melanie, my father held my mother's hand tightly, Jared fell asleep on Madison's lap, and I sat there holding my iPod and still wearing my sunglasses.

As we arrived at the hotel, a bellman helped us with our suitcases as we walked into the hotel. He put them on a luggage cart.

"You must be here for Julie Wilson. Please, come on in. We've been expecting you," a man with an Italian accent spoke to my father as he and Uncle Jared finished getting the room keys.

"Baby, you all take the children upstairs. Jared, come with me," my father spoke.

As Melanie, Jacob, my mother, Aunt Madison, and I got on the elevator, I couldn't help but sense that our lives would be changing from that point forward.

7

-Richard

"Ms. Wilson has been expecting you," the man stated as the three of us entered the casino.

Neon lights filled the room as people gambled and chattered among us. He walked to a table where several other men sat surrounded by scantily dressed women.

"So, you're the famous Richard Young? Investor in Double X-L?" another man asked.

"That's just a side gig," I started. "But we're not here to discuss my personal life, am I correct?"

The man puffed his cigar and lowered it into an ashtray. He flicked ashes and raised it again.

Jared adjusted his tie. The man pointed towards me with the cigar.

"Funny guy, I like that."

"Where's Julie?" Jared asked.

"Ms. Wilson will make her appearance later. Right now, you must deal with me; Joey Carrelli. Take a seat."

Jared and I looked at each other before sitting.

"Does Julie normally associate with Italian mobsters?" Jared asked with a chuckle as we sat.

I knew right away which angle he was taking to feel out Joey.

"Watch your mouth, you fuckin' mooly," he stated as he pointed his finger at Jared.

"Strike one," Jared spoke as adjusted himself in his seat.

I could see a sense of suspicion arise amongst Joey as he had a slight smile. He looked at Jared and me.

"Stand up," Joey stated as he rose to his feet.

Jared and I looked at each other.

"The two of you, stand up, now," Joey directed.

Jared and I stood, and Joey walked over to us.

Looking at Joey, I could tell he was about 6'1 and weighed about 250 pounds. "Search 'em," he stated as two larger men approached us.

"Feet shoulder-width apart and place your arms straight out," the men mentioned in unison.

Jared and I stood in the position to be frisked and the men patted us down.

"Check these two well for any weapons or wires; Ms. Wilson wouldn't be proud if she's being set-up."

The man patting me down stopped as he patted my chest and felt something that felt like a wire. I chuckled at him stopping, because he was feeling a chain, and not a wire as he assumed.

"What the fuck is this?" the man asked.

"What's this?" I asked, mimicking him.

"See, you're always getting us into some shit," Jared intervened.

"Hey, man, why don't you shut the hell up and focus on your man over there?" I argued with Jared.

"I asked you a fuckin' question," the man spoke.

"He asked you a fuckin' question," Jared mimicked the guy.

"Hold the fuck up," I shouted to the man. "Jared, if you got something to say, bring your ass over here and say that shit to my face," I asserted.

"Aye, you two; stop all the bickering," Joey spoke.

I held a finger up to Joey.

"You stay out of it," I responded.

"Don't get your head popped," Jared suggested to Joey.

"Bring it then," I shouted.

Jared turned and hit the man frisking him in the face and I kicked the guy frisking me in the testicles.

Two more large men came out and we all stood there shouting.

"Enough," a woman stated in a gentle tone as she approached the front.

The arguing seemed to stop in an instant.

"Richard, Jared, please have a seat. Joey, fall back," she stated.

We all adjusted ourselves and Jared and I sat down. The woman sat and reached her hand over the table.

"Julie Wilson; so nice to meet the both of you," she spoke.

"So, you're the one who's been threatening me and assaulted my daughter," I stated as I shook her hand.

Part of me wanted to pull her over the table and rough her up, but I considered many factors before deciding not to.

"You don't look like a criminal," Jared spoke.

She chuckled as she shook Jared's hand.

She drew her hand back and ran her fingers through her shoulder-length hair.

"I never said I was a criminal, Jared," Julie spoke. "Just trying to settle some things." She directed her attention to me. "Nah, I didn't touch her. That was one of my people. Just like you haven't been talking to me on the phone. The very first time, yes that was me, but not the other times."

"So, what's the deal?" Jared spoke as a woman came by and poured each of us some whiskey into a glass with ice.

"To keep everything simple," Julie sipped her drink, "you all are going to race for me and do the jobs I need. See, I've been fucked over and have lost so many cars and hella property, but thanks to you all, I don't need to worry about getting fucked over anymore. Richard," another woman brought out a cigar and lit it, "I don't have to worry about you fucking me over." Julie blew smoke and continued. "We share a relative: Jamie Perez. I don't have to worry about you wearing a wire or having any weapons on you. I trust that you love your wife and my cousin more than that," she finished.

"So, what is it that you want from us?" Jared spoke.

She put her cigar down, sternly looked at us, and spoke with a chuckle.

"I want my shit."

"And what do we get in return?" I asked.

"Money and peace. I'm a woman of my word. I want you to be comfortable while doing this," Julie cleared her throat. "Yes, you did kill my mother, and I realize that can't be changed, but I can get my shit back and I can ensure that you assist me with this."

She reached down and pulled out some papers. Joey walked over to us.

"These are some of my guys," he spoke as Julie laid the papers in front of us. "Paulie Rivera; great guy, excellent driver. If you're going to face him, you're going to need speed on your side," Joey pointed to a description under Paulie's image. "Paulie has possession of a '69 Mustang. He's going to be the very first person you race."

There was a moment of silence before another word was spoken.

"Do I have your help?" Julie asked as she sipped her drink again.

Jared and I looked at each other.

"Where are the cars that were being shipped over?"

"They're on their way. Trust me, they'll be here before the race," Julie looked up and noticed people walking into the casino.

"Get those children out of my casino," she spoke as Joey walked over to them.

"Papi," I heard Miracle's voice.

"Julie, let her in," I spoke. "That's Miracle and her friends. They will be helping me help you."

"Bring them in, they're with Richard."

Joey brought Miracle, Jacob, and Melanie to the back of the casino.

"Julie, meet Miracle, Jacob, and Melanie," I introduced. Miracle stared at Julie.

Julie put down her drink and reached out her hand.

"Julie Wilson; it's so nice to finally meet my second cousin."

"Nice to meet you, too," Miracle stated as she rolled her eyes.

"Your father tells me that you and your friends will be doing missions for me and help me get my property."

"I guess." I could tell Miracle was irritated at Julie's presence.

"Well, let's start small and see what happens," Julie responded. It was clear that she felt Miracle's negative energy.

"As I said, let's begin with Paulie Rivera," she looked at me. "Richard, I'm assigning you to this first race. Since your personal vehicles are being imported, I don't need to supply you with any. I will provide any maintenance you may need, but that's it. Once we see how this race goes, we'll proceed with further missions. Remember, losing is *not* an option."

"Who said anything about losing?" Jacob asked.

"Are you the one who messed up my client's car?" Julie inhaled on her cigar and puffed out a perfect circle of smoke. "You can drive, kid."

Jacob didn't show any emotion.

"All three of you can drive very well." Julie rose to her feet and raised her glass to her lips. "You all reminded me a lot about some of the street racers I know."

Miracle, Jacob, and Melanie were all silent as Julie put her glass down.

"Yeah, I know this won't be any trouble at all," Julie spoke again as she eyed the three teens up and down.

"We received word from Paulie that he will be wagering two thousand dollars for the race. No cars, just money. Can you put up the money to race?" Joey asked as the lady refilled Julie's glass.

"I'll do it," Jacob spoke.

"You can put up the money, but Richard is doing the first race."

"No cars?" I asked.

"Just cash," Julie spoke. "Consider this to be a trial run."

I lifted my glass and took a sip.

Jared adjusted his tie. He decided to speak after letting me take the lead.

"Well, we didn't come down here to go fishing. Coulda stayed home for that shit," he chuckled. "I'm in."

"Well, ladies and gents," Julie took one final inhalation on her cigar, "we're in business. Let's raise our glasses."

"Can we get some of that?" Melanie joked.

"I'm your cousin Julie," Julie responded with a chuckle, "you can do whatever as far as I'm concerned. "3 more glasses of Henny!"

The waitress brought three glasses over and filled them with Hennessey.

"I was only joking, but hey, I think we should be involved with this toast since we'll also be racing."

"*Nena*, you are so messed up." Miracle chuckled and smiled for the first time since the plane. "Can I have a lemonade?"

"3 lemonades would be good," Jacob shook his head and chuckled. "You are something else, babe," he kissed Melanie on the cheek.

"May as well mix it," Melanie joked as the waitress brought three glasses of lemonade over.

"What are we toasting to?" I asked as we all raised our glasses.

Julie puffed another cloud of smoke; by now, it was very cloudy in the area.

People continued to play games in the casino as Julie thought.

"A toast: to new beginnings." Julie finally spoke.

"To new beginnings," we spoke in unison as we all tapped our glasses together.

I didn't dare take my eyes off Joey as we toasted.

***

We returned to our rooms and we explained to Jamie and Madison what was happening. Once we explained, we decided to go to bed; Julie instructed us to be downstairs at 9:00 the next morning.

As we slept, I heard Miracle talking in her sleep; she seemed agitated so I got up and walked to her room.

Upon entering, I could see her tossing and turning while mumbling something under her breath.

"Miracle," I stated as I got alongside her bed and shook her gently.

She slowly opened her eyes.

"Papi?" she stated as she woke up.

"You were moaning in your sleep. Are you okay?"

"No," she confessed. "I just dreamt I was in a room with Quincy and Jessie. He killed her, Papi," Miracle stated.

I adjusted myself on her bed as she sat up.

"How are you so certain?" I asked her.

"I don't know how to explain it, but Jessie is speaking to me. Like, I can hear her voice; her spirit is kind of haunting me."

I looked at Miracle.

"Miracle, I have something to tell you," I told her as I adjusted myself. "It's a lot so I need for you to pay attention."

She rubbed her eyes and sat up.

I told her about my sixth sense and explained that I think the gene may have been mutated but passed down at birth.

"So, that's why I can hear Jessie?" she asked.

"I believe so. It only makes sense to me." I explained to her. "Now, for the larger question: why are we here?" I switched subjects. "Do you know?"

"Because of Julie, correct?"

"Yes, but you wish to know who she is, right?"

Miracle nodded her head.

"Julie Wilson is your great aunt. Not the Julie Wilson downstairs, but her mother. Before you were born, your great-aunt has tried repeatedly to get me fired or to kill me. Once your mother and I started to date, Julie wasn't our biggest fan," I remembered and shook my head. "Anger and hatred filled her body and she repeatedly tried to break us up or kill us. It even came to a point where she held your mother hostage and another time she almost killed us."

Miracle was in disbelief. "What happened to her?"

I let out a big sigh and proceeded to tell Miracle the story.

"Honestly, I had to shoot her. I had to kill her before she killed your mother and me."

Miracle started to cry a little and I hugged her.

"I just felt that you needed to know the truth about who Julie was and what she was about."

Miracle didn't reply. Instead, she lied back down and pulled the covers over herself.

"No matter what may happen Miracle, just know that your mother and I truly love you." I kissed her on the cheek and exited her section of the suite.

     ***

Morning came and we all got dressed and went downstairs. Julie was sitting at a table of the breakfast lounge coffee shop watching the news.

"This just in. Detective Young has reportedly resigned from the Chicago Police Department. The reason for his resignation is unknown and when we reached out to him, he respectfully declined our interview invitation. *Detective Young ha resignado de su puesto de oficial en el departamento de Policías de Chicago. La razón no se sabe, lo hemos contactado, pero declinó nuestra invitación para una entrevista.*"

Julie tapped her cigar on the ashtray. "Don't you just love the news," she spoke as she saw us standing there. "Glad to see you all," she spoke.

I saw Joey as well as the guards we fought the day earlier.

I shook hands with Julie, as did Jared, Madison, and Jamie.

"This must be my beautiful cousin, Jamie." Julie stood up and passed Joey her cigar.

She hugged Jamie. "I'm your cousin, Julie."

"Nice to meet you, Julie," Jamie was nervous as she remembered her aunt.

"I hope you can race, cousin," Julie spoke as Joey answered his phone.

"Julie, when is the race?" I asked her.

"Joey's finalizing the deets as we speak. You guys can catch a cab over to the pier and get your cars. They've just arrived."

"Alright, make it quick. The race is at 7:30 tonight," Joey spoke as he hung up the phone.

Jamie and the others followed me out of the building after shaking hands with Julie.

We told the taxi driver to take us to the pier and when we arrived, we got our vehicles.

Jacob winked at Miracle and Melanie as they got inside of their cars.

"Papi, where are we going?" Miracle asked through the window.

"To the hotel," I replied while still trying to figure out what the children were up to.

Jacob revved his engine, as did Melanie and Miracle. In an instant, they each sped off.

Melanie, Miracle, and Jacob all drove side-by-side as they came to a turn; they each made a drift to the right as Jared, Jamie, Madison, and I were approximately 10 seconds behind them. Minutes later we were arriving at the hotel and we parked on the street. We each walked to the hotel and saw the children sitting down.

"You all have some explaining to do," I spoke as I pulled out Jamie's chair.

"Explaining about?" Jacob asked.

"Where did you all learn to drive like that?" Jared asked.

"You told us to learn to race," Jacob replied.

I looked at them. There was no way they learned what they just did in a matter of hours.

The two bodyguards walked up to us and frisked us, once again.

"Gotta make sure your punk ass isn't trying to set us up," the man stated as he frisked me.

"I'm not worried about Richard setting me up," Julie spoke as she smoked her cigar.

I looked at her sternly as she had a smirk on her face.

"Lemme guess, you're checking me for weapons," I told her as the man finished frisking me.

"It's standard procedure," she added as placed her cigar in the ashtray. "Any time you leave the hotel, you'll be checked upon return."

"So, how many of those things do you smoke a day? Like seven?" Jared asked her as the man patted him down. Julie chuckled.

"I like you," she stated as she pointed at him. "You're a comical one, huh?"

"I'm just being honest. But you know that's not good for you."

"So stressed. You don't know my story."

The man finished clearing Jared and the two of them walked over to Jamie and Madison.

"Um, they're clean," I spoke before the men touched them.

"Customary, Rick," Julie stated as the men proceeded to pat Jamie and Madison down.

"Arms and legs shoulder-width apart," they stated in unison.

I couldn't even begin to watch as he patted down Jamie; I knew I would lose control if I saw him doing anything the wrong way.

They frisked them down and Jamie walked over and grabbed my hand.

"Here. Take your cars over to this garage," Julie handed me a card. "It's a lot closer to the race and you can get your cars tuned up."

"All I need is a private place to work. We don't need a garage," Jacob spoke.

"Nope." Julie put down her drink and stood up. "We use my garage. Now, if you need to work there, that's fine."

"I don't think that will work," Jacob argued.

"But, we'll definitely make it work," Jared spoke.

Jamie and Madison stood back with Melanie and Miracle as they started to head out towards the vehicles.

"7:30 is when the races start. Don't be late," Julie finished her drink and walked off.

"Jacob, don't start with this woman. Right now, we're all in jeopardy and we can't afford to get on her bad side." Jared reminded his son.

"Hopefully we end all of this soon so that we can get this woman," I added.

Anxiety filled my body as time sprung closer to the race.

We all walked back to our vehicles and drove to the address that was on the card that Julie gave to me.

"Papi, have you ever raced before?" Miracle asked me as we arrived at the garage.

"Baby, when you're a cop, it's all the same. You have to speed and pursue people anyway, so in a way, yes." I shook my head as the mechanic walked out.

"You must be Richard," he stated as he wiped his hands on a towel. "Julie told me you would be by," he reached out for a handshake.

"And you are?" I asked as I shook his hand.

"Terrance Gringer: I'm the guy people come to if they need anything done to tune up their vehicles."

"Oh, is that right?" Jacob asked.

Terrance looked at Jacob inquisitively. "Yes, really. And you are...?"

"Jacob. "I'm the one who works on the vehicles back at home. And, to be honest, I think I could do a slightly better job than you."

"Oh, is that right?" Terrance asked.

"That's right," Jacob stared at Terrance.

"Well, where do we get started?" Jared asked as he cleared his throat.

"What are you all trying to get done?"

"Tune-ups, I presume," I spoke.

"Leave it to me," Jacob spoke before Terrance had a chance to. "Julie stated that I could do some work on the cars in the garage."

"Well, it seems we are at a bit of a debacle," Terrance spoke.

"I guess so," Jacob didn't seem as though he was going to back down.

"Nobody's touching my car, but Jacob," Melanie spoke as she stepped closer.

"Well fuck it then," Terrance spoke. "You all just go on and race these top fighters with amateur vehicles."

"Just watch me work," Jacob spoke before directing me to drive my car into the garage. A few hours later, Jacob was finishing the work on the cars and we all drove our vehicles to the race; Julie was the first person I saw.

"My star racer," she spoke as we exited our cars. People and cars were all around as loud music played from each car.

"How are you doing tonight, Julie?" I asked her as I tugged on the ends of my vest to pull it down.

"I'm about to make money, right? Shit, I'm doing fine," she replied as she walked over to me without any bodyguards or Joey.

"So, this is the chump that I'm racing, Julie? You'll never get your cars back with this kind of bullshit," the guy laughed.

"I'm sorry, I didn't know Victoria's Secrets made menswear," I insulted.

"We'll settle this on the street," he mentioned. "Do you have the money?"

"Always ready," Jacob spoke as he pulled out the money. "But there's no need to worry about our money; just kiss your two-grand goodbye."

"Let's do this," the guy spoke as he returned to his car and we both pulled to the starting line.

"Listen up! Out here, we like to do things either the fast way or no way at all. This the Dominican Republic, baby!" the crowd cheered as the announcer paused. "But one thing is for sure: get yours, by any means necessary. Get ready." the lady continued.

Paulie and I both revved our engines.

"Go!" she shouted.

We both sped off as she dropped her arms and remained side by side for the first five seconds. I switched gears and pulled ahead of the guy but I could tell he was serious. He switched gears and pulled ahead of me while driving 25 miles per hour faster than I drove.

We arrived at our first turn and we started to approach traffic, so we needed to swerve in and out to avoid hitting anyone.

"Gotta want this shit," I could hear him shout as he stuck his middle finger out of the window.

I switched gears again and sped forward but he pulled ahead of me once again. We approached the finish line and I could see the crowd cheering us on.

I flipped the switch for the nitrous boost and immediately sped up, and slightly passed Paulie. We both continued to drive at top speed as we got closer to the finish line, but in the end, my car crossed the finish line by a few milliseconds before his.

People ran to the car; Jamie was the first to arrive over. I stepped out and hugged her.

"I believe the wager was two grand," I mentioned as I held Jamie in one arm and Julie walked over to us.

"We're one step closer to our goal," she spoke.

She handed me a total of $4,000 in cash and patted me on the back. "You all go on back and get a good night's sleep. Tomorrow is when your driving will be put to the test."

Julie vanished like a thief in the night and Paulie stepped to me.

"Don't think it will be easy. Julie Wilson, eh, not so trustworthy. Since she told you that tomorrow won't be easy, I would advise you to prepare for the worst."

"Tell me about her. You seem to know quite a bit about her," I spoke.

"I don't know much, but she isn't a pushover. Just when you think it's over, it's only beginning," he shook my hand and walked off.

Jared, Jacob, Madison, Miracle, and Melanie all walked up to me. I passed Jacob the $4000 and Jared spoke.

"So…. Who's playing whom?"

"Guess we'll find out soon enough," I spoke as we each got in our vehicles and drove off.

8

Miracle

Once we were all awake and dressed the next morning, I heard sirens going off; not police sirens, but a loud, piercing siren that was emitting from the television.

"Guess that's for us," my father spoke as we all exited the hotel suite.

I expected to see Julie sitting downstairs, but where she sat the previous morning, I saw Quincy.

"Miracle, Miracle, Miracle," he spoke as he rose.

I let out a sigh and spoke. "*Dejame solo*," I retaliated as Jacob walked in front of me with Melanie.

"Calm down guys, I'm just here to present what's on the agenda for the day," he answered as he adjusted his belt. "Today, Julie told me that Miracle can't participate. She's to stay behind while you all do whatever's needed."

I felt a chill go down my spine. "I'm not staying behind while everyone else is out in the D.R."

"Well, maybe I should call Julie and tell her how you all aren't following the rules of the game."

"Excuse us for a moment," my father spoke as he pulled me to the side. "Miracle, you have to do this. Everything's at stake right now, but trust me, everything will be alright. Take this $500 and go on a spree in the D.R. We all have our cell phones on us, so just call us in case something goes wrong."

"Don't worry; everything will be alright," Quincy spoke as he eyed me down. "Plus, I'm riding with you all to the mission."

"I love you, Papi," I told my father as he hugged me. My mother walked over to me and kissed me on the cheek before Jacob and Melanie walked over to me.

"Give me a call at the first sight of danger," Jacob spoke.

"Yeah, girl. You know we'll be there quick and fast," Melanie answered.

"Well, you all go on. I'll manage this. I'll stay out of sight and keep a low profile."

Jacob and Melanie each walked off with my parents, and everyone drove off.

I walked back up to the hotel room and turned on the television.

"This just in, Richard Young, formerly of the Chicago Police Department, was spotted here in the Dominican Republic, but this time, he's not serving for good. We have video footage from last night where he was at a street race. Whether or not he was racing is unknown, but he sure isn't on the good team anymore. *Richard Young, ex – policía de Chicago ha sido visto aquí, en la Republica Dominicana, pero esta vez él no está sirviendo al bien. Tenemos imágenes de vídeo de anoche donde él se encontraba en una carrera callejera. Si era él o no quien estaba corriendo es desconocido, pero sin duda el ya no está en el buen equipo.*"

I turned off the television and walked to the window. I saw people standing outside and the clouds were dark and gray. I decided to go outside and go for a ride around the Dominican Republic to clear my mind. Considering I didn't know my way around the city, I decided to catch a taxi.

I walked out of the room and waved a taxi driver down and got inside.

"*¿A donde te gustaría ir?*" the driver asked.

"*Llévame a algún lugar popular entre los turistas. Tal vez cerca de los lugares donde pueda comprar y pasar un buen rato.*" I replied.

He drove for 30 minutes before arriving at the strip. As I got out, he stated 'good luck,' in English before driving away.

The wind blew and my hair covered my face. As I moved my hair, there was a man waving in my direction.

"Oh my God, you're Miracle Young," he stated.

So much for keeping a low profile, I thought.

"That's me," I stated as I fixed my hair.

"I've heard so much about you," he mentioned as he motioned for me to come to him.

"And what have you heard?" I asked as I walked towards him.

"Your great-aunt: notorious on this island, and around the world," he paid homage to her. "In all honesty, she has helped us to stay alive because of the revenue she'd bring in."

"I've heard a little something about that," I added as I reached inside of my purse for my phone.

"Now you, you were a miracle baby, or so I was told."

I was confused at the fact that he knew this.

"How do you know?"

"Your name says it all," he laughed. "Nah, but word on the island and around the way is that she was kicking your daddy's ass up and down Chicago until you were born," the guy chuckled.

"That couldn't be further from the truth," I added.

The guy eyed me up and down.

"That ain't what I've heard," he added as he put his hand on my shoulder.

I touched his hand to move it; he stepped closer to me.

"Be careful and watch your back while here in the D.R. Everything isn't peachy like it is in Chicago or Puerto Rico." He walked off.

"*¿Que dices?*" I asked and he turned around.

"You'll learn," he stated.

Time passed and I couldn't help but think of several things: the stunt Quincy pulled on the plane, the things my father told me the night before, and Jessie. It seemed as though with every step I took, I could hear Jessie's voice.

"*Don't be naïve. Quincy was involved. Look at how he operates and you'll see his involvement in my death. But please, please, please be careful and watch your back.*"

She didn't speak in full sentences all the time, but this was one of the first times I heard her speak so clearly.

As I focused on reality, a car pulled up beside me and two men jumped out and grabbed me. I didn't have time to scream, because as I started, they quickly covered my mouth.

"*Pinche cabrones*," I shouted as they finally got me in the van. The driver turned on the light in the back of the van and revealed who sat inside.

"Miracle Young," the woman spoke as they closed the doors.

"Depends on who's asking," I responded.

The woman chuckled.

"You have your father's attitude," she smiled. "Veronica Edwards. I'm one of Julie's accomplices and she said you were my assignment, so I need for you to listen to what I tell you, Miracle, if you want to stay safe."

I was worried about this.

"Sorry, but I don't need a watch-person," I stated as I opened the door.

She pressed a button and the door closed shut.

"Look, Miracle, I don't want for anyone to get hurt, so you should let me help you."

Veronica tapped the driver on the shoulder and he got out of the van.

"What do you want?" I asked her.

"I want to keep your family safe. If I didn't care, I would be following Julie's exact rules."

"Oh yeah, and what's that?"

"I will not get into details about her plans here, but, it's not pretty." Veronica's voice started to crack but she quickly reformed herself.

"How do you know who I am?" I asked her.

"I know all about who you all are. And one of the things I know, but I promise to keep between me and you is that your father is still a cop."

My heart slightly dropped, but I didn't show weakness. I quickly put up my defense.

"*¿Sabes qué?* You don't know what you're talking about," I shouted in retaliation.

"Shhh," she whispered. "I'm on your side, Miracle. The guys outside of this van, aren't. Work with me, Miracle. Soon enough, it'll be over."

"You're fucking crazy," I stated as I opened the van door and got out.

"Miracle, I will be there when you need me. Right now, you're confused. But don't worry," Veronica continued to speak as I walked away.

Her voice got quieter and quieter, and I could finally hear my thoughts. I decided to visit shops on the strip to pass the time and clear my mind.

***

The sky darkened as I finished shopping and strolling around.

I looked at my phone and noticed the time was 8:00 pm. I put in my earphones and was waiting on the corner for the taxi to arrive.

A car pulled up beside me; it was Quincy.

"What are you doing out here at this time, Miracle?" he asked me.

"Just waiting on my taxi to come and pick me up," I replied.

"Well, I don't understand why you would pay for a taxi when I can just take you back to the hotel for free."

"Nah, *estoy bien*. It should be here any minute," I stated as I nervously looked around for the taxi.

"I'm serious. A free ride back, no strings attached. I promise," he stated.

I looked at him in the eyes. He looked sincere, but it was probably just the hazel color of his eyes speaking.

"After what you did on the plane, why should I get in the car with you?"

"I apologize for that. But I find you extremely attractive and I just couldn't help myself."

I thought to myself for a few seconds.

"Look, you can either wait here for another 30-40 minutes for a taxi, as the weather continues to drop, or you can just let me take you back to the hotel.

"No tricks?" I asked him out of curiosity.

"I swear. I'll keep my hands to myself and behave. You don't even have to say a word to me for the whole ride."

He pushed open the passenger door.

"No tricks, Quincy," I stated as I got into the car.

He quickly moved his sweater and threw it into the backseat. He turned on some music and drove off.

"You like Sean?" he asked a few minutes into the drive.

"I thought you said we didn't have to speak," I responded.

"We don't," he stated, "but it'd be kind of boring to ignore each other when we have to work together," he spoke.

"¿*Que dices?* Work together?"

He glanced at me while he drove.

"Yeah, we gotta work together. Tomorrow's mission hasn't been announced yet, but some people have fucked over Julie and we're gonna get them back for the bullshit they've done."

"I have a quick question. How do you know Julie?" I asked him. He chuckled.

"She's my aunt," he looked at the open road.

"That explains it," I mumbled.

"Huh?" he asked.

"Nothing," I stated. "So, what will this job be about?" I asked.

"Well, hopefully, it'll be simple. You and I will go visit this group of Jamaicans. Julie is going to issue us both guns. You have shot a gun before, right?"

"Yeah," I lied.

"Good," Quincy adjusted the steering wheel as he drove. "Well, hopefully, we won't have to use them, but they're holding her cars and have had them for a while. We're going over there to get the cars back. There'll be a truck that'll be there that we'll use to retrieve them." Quincy stated as he continued the drive.

"Who else will be doing this?" I asked as I became more involved in the conversation.

Quincy chuckled and looked at me. "You ask a lot of questions."

"Well, that's how you learn. I know that I'm not expected to just go do something I'm not sure of how to do," I slightly shrugged my shoulders.

"*Touché*," he replied. "Julie will have a few people around the corner to make sure everything goes as planned, but ultimately, it's just me and you."

"Shit," I stated as I sat back in the chair.

"Yeah; just relax your mind," he stated as he turned the music up.

He started rapping along with Big Sean.

"*All I care about's my crew, my family, and women. 'Cept these women that's hoein', and these hoes that be stealin'. Tryna give 'em a cut, that's how you end up with stitches. I tell her, 'bitch quit playing, and play ya position'.*"

"You jammin', huh?" I asked him as he rapped.

"Sean's my nigga. I fucks with him," Quincy eagerly stated.

"That's why you know every word to his raps," I mentioned as I rolled my eyes.

Quincy looked at me and changed songs. I melted when I heard Miguel start singing, but I didn't show Quincy my satisfaction. We listened to 'Ashley' in silence as he approached the hotel.

"Look, I know you think I'm responsible for what happened to Jessie. I had absolutely no parts of that, honestly," he finally spoke.

He must have overheard my conversation with Jacob or my father.

"All I know is that she is dead. I can't speak on who did it or why they did it. But soon enough, the truth will come out. Everything that's done in the dark eventually comes to the light."

Quincy parked the car in front of the hotel.

"Well, we're here," he stated as a bellman opened the car door.

"I'll see you tomorrow, Quincy," I stated as I got out.

"Dress light… just in case there's a lot of movement," he stated as the bellman closed the door.

I walked inside the hotel and rode the elevator to the top floor and walked to my room. No one was inside, so I decided to lay on the bed and think about tomorrow.

When I awoke the next morning, my father and the team were awake and dressed.

"*Vamos, Milagro,*" my mother stated in Spanish. I got dressed and we all walked downstairs for breakfast.

"So, how was your day by yourself?" Jacob asked as we ate.

"It was interesting, *pero,* Papi, I have to tell you something," I spoke as I remembered the interaction with Veronica and the news that Quincy told me about Julie. "Yesterday, I was stopped by a woman named Veronica Edwards, and she knew everything!" I whispered.

"Everything?" my father asked.

"Yes. She knows you're still a cop, she knows about our family, *todo lo que.*"

"I want you to let me know immediately if you come in contact with her," my father spoke.

As he finished, Veronica was walking towards the table.

"There she is," I stated while subtly nodding my head in her direction.

"Richard Young?" she asked as she looked at my father.

He rose to his feet.

"Yes?"

"Glad to finally meet you. I'm Veronica Edwards. You work with my brother, Abel Roberts. He sent me over to work with Julie and keep an eye on you and your family."

"Well, I don't work with Abel, but I thank you for stopping by," my father held his composure and sat back down to his plate.

"I don't think you heard me correctly. I know all about this, Richard," she said. "I'm here to watch over you all and make sure you're safe. Julie knows me as a notorious analyst who knows her way around, but just trust me on this."

My father ignored her and spoke to Jacob to show her that he was ignoring her.

"Pass the salt, Jacob" he spoke.

"Miracle, here's my card."

She handed me a card and continued to speak, "I will continue to watch you all. Hopefully, you'll realize that I'm on your side soon enough." She walked away from the table and my father looked at me.

"Don't get involved with that woman," he spoke. "The fact that she knows that I'm still a cop puts us in jeopardy. I'll call Abel and ask him about this, but —"

One of Julie's security guards approached us, though she was nowhere in sight.

"Miracle, you need to come with us. It's time," the man spoke.

"Can we finish having breakfast first?" Uncle Jared spoke.

"You all may, yes, but Miracle has to come now. Julie doesn't need you all for today."

I stood up, grabbed my clutch handbag, and kissed my mother and father on the cheek, as well as hugged my aunt and uncle.

Jacob and Melanie each took one of my hands.

"We'll walk her to the door," Melanie stated to the parents as they walked with me.

"Be safe, Miracle," Jacob stated as we reached the front with the bodyguard.

"Yeah, girl, yesterday was crazy; we'll tell you about it later, but this stuff puts our lives on the line." Melanie gave me a hug and Jacob did the same.

"I'll be ok," I mentioned as the bodyguard and I exited the building.

He walked me to my car and I got inside. He got into the van in front of me and drove off. As I followed him, I was shaking as I was nervous as to what the day held.

I followed him to another car where he motioned his hand for me to pull alongside the vehicle. Quincy was inside of the next.

"Here's the deal. Julie won't be with us, and the guards will only drive us to the location. Take this," he tossed a gun into the passenger window of my car. "Some stuff may go down with the Jamaicans and the cars, so we gotta be ready. We have to follow them to the house," he stated as he pulled off behind the guard's van.

During the whole ride, my body shivered in fear.

Once we arrived, Quincy and I both walked up to the already opened door.

"Hello?" he stated aloud as we entered the home. "We're here for the cars; we were sent by Julie Wilson."

A machine gun began firing as Quincy and I both jumped behind furniture for cover.

The bullets stopped and a man spoke from behind the wall.

"We don't have any cars, man," the Jamaican spoke.

"Oh, now we both know that's a bunch of bullshit, considering we just saw the truck with cars as we pulled in," Quincy stood and didn't show any fear and held 2 guns in his hands.

"Just finish these bitches," another man stated as bullets started to fire again.

Quincy shot both of his guns in two different directions.

"God, don't let me die today," I spoke under my breath and crossed my chest.

The Jamaicans stopped shooting and we could hear them running out of the back door.

"Come on, Miracle." Quincy helped me up and we both ran outside.

"We're taking one car," he shouted and we both ran to his. "You drive!" he directed me.

As we got inside the car, the truck that held the cars pulled off.

"Keep up with the truck, Miracle."

As Quincy spoke, I could hear Jessie's voice in my head telling me to watch my back.

I disregarded the voice and I sped behind the truck onto the expressway.

The Jamaicans shot their weapons at the car until they were out of bullets.

"We can't let their asses get away," Quincy shouted to me, and I pulled up closer to the truck.

"*A la mierda*," I stated and almost bumped into the back of the truck; they started to release the cars from the truck.

"Oh shit!" Quincy shouted as he pulled out his gun and ducked his head down low.

I slammed on the brakes and the car hit the ground in front of me.

I pulled alongside the truck and Quincy shot at the driver. He attempted to drive us off the road.

"What does Julie have us into?!" I shouted as I braked and got behind the truck.

I pulled out my gun and shot at the Jamaicans on the truck; they continued to throw cars off the truck. I fired a shot and it hit one of the men, and they came rolling off the truck like a tumbleweed.

"Do that shit!" Quincy stated as his shot went through the window but missed the driver. "Miracle, I need you to get me closer; I'm going to jump onto the truck."

"*¿Estas loco?* Was this a part of the plan?" I asked him.

"No; now we're improvising," Quincy stated.

"Don't get killed," I mentioned as I pulled closer.

"Didn't think you cared so much," Quincy took off his seatbelt and opened his door. "Drive in front of the truck but stop hard so that it can knock off the door. Insurance will cover the damages to my car," Quincy was confident in his decision, so I followed his orders.

I sped to get in front of the truck and Quincy fully opened his door.

"Okay, stop!" he shouted and I hit the brakes.

The truck came speeding past and knocked the door off the car.

Quincy prepared to jump as I sped to catch up with the truck. As I was side by side, Quincy leaped from the car and caught part of the door as his legs dangled freely.

"Shit," I stated as I drove closer to the truck.

Quincy put both of his legs on the truck as he pulled himself up to get to the door. He used his gun to break out the window, completely, and he fought with one hand against the driver.

As he fought one-handed and I slowed down to try to shoot more Jamaicans off the back of the truck, more cars were thrown.

"Julie's not going to like this," I spoke aloud.

I couldn't believe what my father got us involved in by agreeing to work with Julie.

A woman on a motorcycle sped up and aimed her gun in the direction of Quincy.

"*Ay dios mio*," I stated as I drove faster and got behind the woman. I had no idea who she was or what her intentions were.

She fired one bullet and sped off it hit the driver in the arm. Quincy managed to get the door open and use his hand to pull the driver out as he climbed inside.

"Hell yeah!" he stated as he sat in the truck and started to drive. He called my cellphone and I answered.

"Phase two is complete; now we just need to get rid of the Jamaicans on the back of the truck."

"I'll handle it, since we can drive reasonably," I responded before hanging up.

I slowed the car down and positioned myself behind the truck. I fired a bullet at both Jamaicans and they both fell off.

Quincy exited the expressway and we both drove to where he was set to drop off the cars.

He got out of the truck once he parked, and I parked behind him before exiting his car.

He looked at me before speaking.

"You're shaking. You cold?"

"I've never done anything like that before in my life," I confessed. "I'm shaken up by it."

"At least you won't say you had a boring childhood," Quincy mentioned. "Your dad was one of the top police officers in the country; particularly, in Chicago and Puerto Rico; it's apparent where you get your bravery skills from," Quincy passed me his jacket and I rejected it.

"You don't need to keep pretending, Miracle," Quincy passed me the jacket once more. "You don't need to act like you don't like me."

"Don't flatter yourself," I replied while rolling my eyes. "This is only business." I put my index finger on the end of my hair and wrapped my finger in it.

"Whatever you say, Miracle."

Quincy's cellphone rang and he answered it. I walked over to his car. It now had bullet holes in the body as well as scratches, and the windshield was now cracked. The passenger's door was missing and his headlights were blown; his Nissan Roadster no longer resembled the Roadster.

He hung up and looked at me.

"That was Julie. She says that she's glad that we're safe and that she didn't expect things to turn so sour. She says that she deeply apologizes and regrets sending two teenagers out here alone."

I rolled my eyes at her apology.

"Did we really just do that?" I asked Quincy, ignoring her apology.

"We got the goods; too bad four of her cars were totaled." Quincy looked at the truck, looked at his car, and looked back at me.

He looked at the clock on his phone before speaking.

"It is 6:30 Miracle; you ready to go back to your car?"

"I guess it's now or never," I spoke as I got into the passenger side of the car and put on my seatbelt.

"Sorry about the door," he joked.

"Cute," I replied sarcastically.

He drove off and left the truck locked and parked. I placed my earphones in and started to tune him out.

"What you listening to, over there?" he joked as he reached for my iPod and grabbed it.

"Quincy! Come on now, stop playing!" I stated as I reached for my iPod.

"You so into this music and can't give me a conversation, so I wanna know what you listening to," he grabbed the auxiliary cord and plugged it into my iPod.

"*I shouldn't love you, but I want to/ I just can't turn away/ I shouldn't see you, but I can't move/ I can't look away.*"

"Is there any reason you're listening to this?" Quincy asked me and I snatched my iPod away.

"It's just a song," I added and blushed. "You shouldn't have taken my iPod anyway."

Quincy reached his arm in the backseat. When he pulled his arm back up front, he passed me his sweater. He could see I was slightly shivering.

"Here, put this on. We don't want you to freeze to death," he joked.

The temperature was 65 degrees, but it felt cooler, considering we were surrounded by water.

"Thanks," I stated with attitude

"Are you always this mean?"

"No, only around people who try to hurt me and think that they're the shit," I covered myself with the sweater.

"Just because I'm the football star doesn't mean I think I'm the shit; people praise me when I'm honestly no better than the average person."

"I know that and I'm glad you acknowledge that," I replied.

"Well, at least we both know that I'm average," he spoke as he continued to drive.

"No, you're below average," I corrected him.

"Oh, it's like that?" he chuckled.

"Yeah, it's like that." I focused my eyes back on the road and he turned on the radio.

I was surprised when I heard Double X-L. 'Don't Cry (I'm Right Here)' by Ari Love featuring Tiana was playing.

"Your father owns part of this station, correct?" he asked.

"Yes," I answered.

"My favorites are always playing. Limited commercials, interesting conversation, and great music all build for a great station."

"Well, I'll be sure to let him know he has a fan."

Quincy vocalized and sang with Ari, and I felt a slight chill run down my body.

"¿*Sabes qué*? You can sing." I spoke.

"I do a little something in my spare time. Many people don't think I can, but I practice things other than football."

The sun was setting and the moon was rising and we were pulling into the parking lot; Quincy put the car in park.

"Well, we're here. Make sure you give your father the compliments," Quincy smiled and revealed his pearly whites.

"Look, if you think you can win me over by trying to get on my father's good side, then—" Quincy interrupted me mid-sentence with a kiss on the lips.

I didn't fight back or retreat from the kiss at all, something in my body wouldn't let me resist. When he finally retreated about 8 seconds later, I leaned in for another kiss and we connected our lips for another extended amount of time.

I know it was wrong, but it felt so right. Once the kiss was finished, I exited Quincy's car without saying a word and got into mine.

I started the engine and drove off. He followed me to the hotel to make sure I was safe for the night.

9

Miracle

As I walked to the hotel room, I felt as though I were on cloud 9, but I knew that it was wrong.

Why was I having these feelings towards Quincy? If my father knew, I knew there would be hell to pay.

I adjusted my hair and pulled out my key-card. I entered the hotel room.

"Miracle, you're alive!" my mother shouted as saw me enter through the door.

"*Si*, Mami," I stated as I was confused at her statement. "Why wouldn't I be?"

"You're all over the news," my father stated. "You shot your first gun today, huh?"

I nodded my head as I hugged my mother.

"The news covered everything that happened. You all shot some Jamaicans, trashed some cars, fucked up a Roadster... major damage," Uncle Jared spoke.

"It wasn't our fault," I responded. "We wanted to keep everything simple, but things quickly escalated."

"Yeah, we saw Quincy jump from the car onto the truck," Jacob spoke.

"You all were almost killed," Melanie added.

"The only reason you didn't have the entire force on your asses is because Julie arranged it so that the cops wouldn't interfere," my mother spoke.

"Well, the most important thing is that you're okay," Aunt Madison spoke as she walked towards me.

The phone rang and my father answered.

"Young's room," he displayed a look of concern on his face before hanging up.

"All of the adults, we're needed downstairs. Miracle, Melanie, Jacob; be responsible up here."

The adults walked out of the room and I fell back on the bed and let out a big sigh.

"Damn, girl, looks like you're on cloud 9 and can't come down; or should I say, you don't want to come down. What's up?" Melanie asked as she sat down on the bed.

"This day was just... amazing," I replied.

"Girl, you are truly a daredevil. You were just almost killed."

"*No estoy hablando de eso*," I replied to Melanie as I sat up. "I'm talking about after all of that happened. The whole experience was a thrill ride, and once it was all over... I may have caught some feelings." I started to blush and Melanie got closer to me as Jacob looked out of the window.

"*Cuéntame lo que pasó*," Melanie whispered so that Jacob couldn't hear.

"Well, the whole adventure, I tried to give Quincy the cold shoulder, *y funcionó*, until it was time to go back to my car. Once we pulled into the lot, as I was shouting at Quincy, he leaned in and kissed my lips. I swear I felt as though I was going to explode, girl!" I excitedly told her.

"Wait, you kissed Quincy?" Jacob overheard us and walked over. "Are you stupid?"

"Yeah, girl, have you lost your mind? Why are you kissing the enemy?" Melanie quickly sided with Jacob.

"Damn, well if I knew you all would judge me like that, *yo huberia dicho mierda.*"

"It's not like that, girl, but do you realize what he has put you through?" Melanie questioned.

"*¿Tu sabes qué?* I know it isn't right. But I can't help how I'm feeling," I stated.

I got up from the bed and walked to the window. Melanie walked over and put her hand on my shoulder.

"Look, Jacob and I, we're just worried about you; we don't want you to get hurt, Miracle."

"You all are my best friends. Naturally, you're going to worry. And I appreciate that, but if something goes down, I will let you all know."

"Miracle, we don't want it to get to that point," Jacob mentioned. "I almost got thrown in prison for fucking that nigga up on the plane."

I could tell he was becoming furious.

"Jacob, I –," I started but he interrupted.

"It doesn't matter what you say, because now, Daddy's little princess, is in harm's way," Jacob glared at me. "And she may have put all of us there with her."

Jacob walked off.

"Come on, girl, think about it," Melanie stated before following behind Jacob.

I sat on the bed and pulled out my phone; a text from Quincy had come through. I read the message and placed my phone down before getting changed into my pajamas. I got back on the bed, laid my head down, and fell asleep.

∎∎

-*Richard*

As we reached the lobby of the hotel, Julie walked up to us.

"Richard!" she exclaimed and reached for a handshake. "Exceptional driving yesterday! Slowly but surely, I am reclaiming what's mine."

"You almost had my daughter killed," Jamie spoke hastily.

"Jamie," I motioned for her to be quiet.

"That's what I called you all down here for," she mentioned. "Follow me."

She walked into the casino towards the VIP section. Before sitting, Joey walked up to us.

"That's not necessary this time around," Julie spoke.

The men stepped back.

"Yeah, that's right. Get yo ass back," Jared chuckled and jumped at the man.

The man didn't laugh at Jared's joke.

"Damn man, smile. I'm just fucking with you," Jared stated.

"You a fool," I chuckled at Jared.

"Here's the thing," Julie stated once Jared and I finished. "Things are escalating very quickly."

She pulled out some more photos as the waitress brought her out a cigar and a glass of whiskey.

She spread the pictures on the table.

"Tomorrow's job consists of strength, determination, intelligence, speed, agility, and of course, stealth."

She pointed to one of the pictures.

"Brian Smith: he's the contact behind this job. Everything he has is mine. It was supposed to be a loan, but he's running a little behind on his payments, and so it's time for him to pay up— if you know what I mean," Julie blew smoke as Jared looked at me.

"So, what role do we play in all of this?" Jared asked her.

"Yeah, I mean, why does it seem like we need so much planning for this mission?" Madison asked.

"Seems like a scam to me," Jamie stated.

"This guy works with the police force," Julie spoke as she put her drink down.

"Yep, and there's the catch," I spoke.

"The job is to simply visit him and reclaim what's mine. I'm bringing this to the adults because I know how dangerous this may get," she continued.

"So, wait…. You want us to go to a police officer's home, pop his ass, take your shit, and roll out of there?" Jared spoke.

"You will have every cop on your ass when you leave his home," Julie added.

"Fuck this," Jared stated before walking off.

"Jared," I shouted as I rose out of my chair.

"Richard, fuck this. I'm not going down over no bullshit like this. And what am I to benefit from this?"

I got closer to him and whispered. "Jared, bear with us for everything. If we don't do what this woman wants, hell, we could all be dead by tomorrow morning." Jared looked over his shoulder and shook his head in disgust.

"Fuck it," he stated before walking with me back to the table.

"Blew off enough steam, Jared?" Julie asked.

He scoffed at her.

Madison took his hand and kissed his cheek as he sat down.

"So, what's the plan?" he asked her.

"Simple; as you said earlier: go to his house, take my shit, and bounce. Everything but straight-up shooting his ass. That," she sipped her whiskey, "that shit'll get you killed."

"Brian Smith, is he expecting us at all?" I asked.

"He's not. I'm not going to tell you all who's to play what role; you all have to figure that out on your own, but I will tell you to be prepared for anything."

"Do we at least have a window?" Jamie asked Julie.

"Your window is from the time you leave here tomorrow until he sees fit. Like I said, he's a cop and has connections all the time. These cops aren't on my payroll, so it's not much I can do to stop them," she admitted. "As far as planning out how it happens, you guys have to do all of that."

"You two," Joey spoke to Jared and me, "seem like you will be the brains of this operation. I don't trust you fuckers, but I'm just going to warn you not to do anything stupid."

Jared made a face at Joey and I spoke.

"What is it that we're looking for?"

"My cars. I have a white Bugatti, a yellow Lamborghini, and a dark brown Mercedes Benz. I need the cars," Julie responded before taking another sip of her whiskey.

"How do you expect us to drive out there in some cars and bring back three additional cars?" Jamie asked.

"Look, I don't give a damn about how you do it. I just want the shit done," Julie puffed her cigar.

"We could always take the kids with us," Jamie strategized.

"Yeah, but we don't wanna put them in harm's way," Madison replied.

"Again, I don't care how the plan is executed, as long as it's done and the results are what's expected."

"You are heartless," Jared mentioned as Julie put down her cigar.

"You guys can leave now. Take these blueprints with you: it's just a map of where everything is and how everything's supposed to go."

Once Julie spoke and handed us the papers, Joey and some of the other security guards started to escort us from the casino.

"Oh, and Jared," Julie called.

Jared turned slightly.

"I'm fed up, not heartless."

The men finished escorting us from the casino and we returned upstairs.

"Shit's getting out of control, Rick," Jared mentioned to me.

"I know, bro, I know," I shook my head in disgust as we turned to the room.

I saw Miracle was asleep and Melanie was sitting beside Jacob near the table.

"We're back," Jamie stated as we all walked in. "Why's she asleep so early?"

"We aren't sure," Melanie mentioned to us. "How was it?"

"Things are going fine," I lied. "Excuse us for a second," I told Melanie as all the adults walked into the second room of our suite and closed the door behind us.

"We don't want the children to worry about tomorrow, so we must plot it out in privacy," I told them.

Jamie placed the papers on the table.

"I see Julie went all out and is quite the artist," Jared mimicked her drawing of the stick figures.

Madison laughed as Jamie chuckled.

"You stupid, bro," I stated with a gentle laugh.

"Nah, for real though, it looks like she has everything outlined. She just has a few missing pieces."

"We just have to finish the puzzle," I mentioned to him.

"So lemme see if I can identify who's who," Jared joked again. "I'm guessing the stick figure with the curly hair is Miracle, long hair is Jamie, the five o'clock shadow is you, and Madison is this one with her hair in a ponytail."

"What about you, Jacob, and Melanie?" I asked him.

"Simple… I'm the one with all the muscle, Jacob is the gruff face, and Melanie is right here by Jacob."

"Yeah, you got all the muscle but I was whooping ya ass back in the day," I chuckled.

"Man, you would catch me off guard," Jared touched his soul patch.

"Will you two focus?" Madison asked.

"Just trying to make light of the situation," I spoke as we all directed our energy back on the project.

"Well, I can easily see that this is the crooked cop," I mentioned as I pointed out a guy with the word 'pig' on his head.

"We can easily determine what we're going to do. We need to figure out what the kids are going to do," Madison spoke.

"If they're even going to be involved," Jamie mentioned.

"Julie has them on this paper. Chances are, they're going to be involved," I responded with a look of concern.

"I'll have Jacob keep an eye on the girls during all of this. They will stay safe," Jared spoke.

"I hope so," I uttered.

■■■

Miracle

I opened my eyes and Jacob was sitting on the chair next to me, texting.

"Are my parents back?" I asked.

"Yeah, they're in the other room. Melanie stepped out to get some air," he never took his eyes off the phone.

I started to feel around for my phone and didn't find it.

I looked at the stand next to the bed and in the drawers. I then turned to Jacob.

"Jacob, have you seen my phone?"

"Yeah," he replied, never making eye contact with me, but continuing his text.

"¿*Donde esta?*"

"I have it," he replied as he locked the screen.

I quickly took my phone from him.

"What did you do?" I asked him.

"I texted your boyfriend and told him to stay away from you," he enunciated. Miracle, you're putting all of us in danger. The fact that Quincy is associated with Julie jeopardizes us all."

I quickly returned to the message and read what Quincy replied.

"Jacob, you're the worst for doing this." I felt like hurting him.

"I know you hate me now," he stated as he stood up, "but you will thank me later."

I got out of bed and walked to the bathroom and let out tears from the anger I was feeling.

"Come on, Miracle," Jacob stated from the other side of the door.

"Leave me alone, Jacob," I stated as I turned off the lights and sat in the cold and dark bathroom.

■■■

10

-Richard

"You know that truck that the kids used today?" I asked as we continued to plan.

"Yeah, what about it?" Jared questioned.

"What if the kids aren't involved until later? We can play it smart," I uttered. Jared looked at Madison.

"What do you mean, babe?" Jamie asked.

"Like we used to do with your aunt. Remember the situation at the Hancock building and she outsmarted us by calling the national database and avoided a connection with me? She played her cards right."

Jared picked up the basketball that Jacob brought on the trip and sat on the bed next to Madison. He tossed the ball in the air and let it come back down to his hands.

"So, how is that the same?" Madison asked me.

"Babe, the kids are gonna be Julie. That truck; the kids will have one like it and come by once we're inside," Jared spoke.

"And while we're talking to the officer, they'll load the cars onto the truck and leave. We can walk away nice and scratch-free." I finished.

"Well, we better go scope out the place," Jared suggested as he stood up. "If we're gonna plan like this, we need to know our routes. Come on Rick, you're driving," he tossed me my car keys and kissed Madison.

"We'll be back," I mentioned to Jamie as I kissed her.

Jared and I exited the room and took the elevator down to the lobby of the hotel. We asked the valet to pull the car around the front of the hotel.

Joey approached us.

"You all aren't thinking about making a run for it, are you?" his two partners surrounded us.

"Now where would we run to? You all have everything under your control: the cops, the airport, the pier... you control it all."

"Well, let me search you for weapons," Joey stated as he grabbed for Jared's pocket.

"Aye man," Jared stated as he stepped back and punched Joey in the face. "We don't need to be searched to go for a stroll around the city."

I grabbed Jared but Joey quickly tried to attack him. I let go of Jared and grabbed Joey's arms and pushed him back against the wall, making sure he was slammed against it. His partner grabbed Jared and put him into a headlock and Jared elbowed him in the stomach.

Jared and I ran outside and quickly got inside of the car. I quickly sped off.

"Search these nuts, bitch," Jared shouted out the window before tossing the GPS chip out of the car.

"Where did you find that chip?" I asked him as I drove towards home.

"I noticed it was sticking out of the glove compartment yesterday. Julie's daughter is just as conniving as she is."

"If not more," I mentioned.

I continued to drive until I reached Brian's home.

"Damn, it's dark out here," Jared shouted as he grabbed the flashlight from under his seat.

"Well, let's be glad this isn't a nighttime mission," I told him. "Shine the light on the house, but not for long."

Jared turned on the flashlight and revealed the front door to his house.

"Goddamn, these houses are expensive!" Jared exclaimed.

"Which is exactly why we can't fuck this up," I reported.

He shined the light on the driveway and revealed a black Ferrari and a yellow Lexus. A garage was also present, but it was closed and no windows were on it.

"I don't see Julie's cars," I added.

"Maybe they're in the garage," Jared suggested.

"Yeah, but that doesn't make our job any easier."

"We can always go scope out the garage," he added.

"I'm not trying to get out of this car at night. Bro, I don't know these people, nor do I care to know them," I turned off the car's engine and removed the keys.

"Well," he pulled out his gun, "I'm going to check this shit out," Jared opened the car door and held his gun firmly.

"Jared," I spoke before he got out, but he walked over, stealthily, to the garage.

"Damn it!" I pulled out my gun and ran over to where he was.

"You always getting us into something," I whispered.

"You'll be thanking me once tomorrow comes." He replied as he put his hands in the crease between the garage and the ground.

"Are you crazy?" I asked him. "You don't know what's in that garage."

"You're right, I don't know, but just help me lift it."

"If I die, I'm coming back to fucking kill you." I squatted in the same manner as Jared, and put my hands under the garage.

We lifted the door slowly, but the garage door went flying up and slammed as it reached the top.

"Shit!" I whispered. "Hide!"

We each ran for cover as the motion light on the back door turned on and the light turned towards the garage door.

We each hid by separate bushes and trees for about five minutes before coming out of hiding.

"That was close," Jared replied with a chuckle as we came out.

"Everything's all fun and games for you," I joked. "Well, now you see it. No cars are here."

"Just an empty ass garage," Jared reached up for the garage handle and slowly pulled it down.

We walked back to my car and we each climbed inside.

"Well, we've scoped out the outside of his home," Jared mentioned. "And no cars."

"Where could he be holding them?" I asked aloud.

"Circle the block, Rick," Jared spoke. "We don't want to draw too much attention to ourselves."

"Good idea." I started the car engine and drove down the street.

I turned down the alley.

"Get some pictures of the width of this alley," I spoke.

I continued to drive down the alley. There was a lot of activity in the alley, but behind Brian's home were the cars we were looking for.

"Bingo," I stated. "Get a picture of this, J."

"There's no way that truck would comfortably fit down here," Jared mentioned.

"We'll make it work," I spoke.

The men in the alley were smoking and drinking and each eyed us down as we drove past.

"Smells like weed," Jared mentioned.

"For this to be a cop's home, you'd think people weren't as stupid as they are," I turned the corner as we exited the alley and Jared started to record the street activity.

"Go around this neighborhood. We need more footage and to know what we can expect."

I drove around the city as Jared continued to record.

"There's the police station," I stated as I rolled past. "About three minutes away from the man's home."

"Maybe one minute if they're speeding," Jared uttered.

"I haven't seen that many police vehicles passing by," I noticed.

"Remember, it's nighttime. Things will be different in the morning."

We wrapped up our findings and drove back to the hotel. Julie was waiting for us at the door.

"Richard, Jared, I'm hearing that you all got into an altercation with my friend Joey," she began.

"Hey, your friend approached us on some bullshit," Jared retorted.

"My friend is here to be sure everything goes as smoothly as possible."

"So, why don't you face us yourself?! This is your operation, correct?" Jared was now shouting and I put my hand on his shoulder to tell him to calm down.

"Slow your goddamn roll, right now, Jared!" Julie shouted to him and Joey came closer to her side. "You need to learn your position, and stay in it."

Jared glared at Julie and Joey but spoke no words.

"Come on, Jared, let's go," I added.

"One more thing," Julie stated as we walked past her; she lowered her tone. "I've been hearing a few things about you, Richard, and for your sake, you better pray that they're not true and if they are, that I don't find out about it."

"Julie, you're a smart woman, right?" I asked.

Julie didn't respond verbally.

"So, let's let these rumors remain for what they are: rumors."

"Yeah, you better pray they're just rumors," she continued into the casino with Joey.

Jared and I walked towards the elevator.

"Does she know?"

"I don't know, and I don't want to find out. Things are getting thick real quick and I just want out for all of us," I stated.

"Then we need to just tell this bitch 'fuck you' and keep it moving," Jared responded.

"If it were just you and me, I'm sure we would take that angle, but we don't want to put anyone else in jeopardy. We do that, and there's no way out," I shook my head. "The boats, the planes; she has shown that she controls all of that."

We got off the elevator and proceeded to the room.

The children were asleep and we walked into the adjacent room.

"We're back," I took off my jacket and put my gun on the table; Jared did the same.

"Where the hell did you all get those?" Jamie chuckled. "And how did you get past Julie with them?"

"First rule of being police: serve and protect by any means necessary," I chuckled.

"We can't let her know *all* of our tricks," Jared laughed.

I directed our attention back to the mission.

"We scoped out the place. This mission is almost impossible," I spoke as I shook my head.

"Well, let's see what you got," Jamie mentioned as she got off the bed.

She and Madison walked over to the table and Jared pulled out his phone. I grabbed the marker and started to mark the map Julie had given us.

"What Julie didn't include is the police station three minutes away from his home," I stated as I drew a square and wrote police on it.

"Which only gives us a sixty-second window to get in and get out; considering the cops will be speeding to get to his place," Jared added.

"Sixty seconds is not a lot of time," Madison added.

"And the cars aren't in front of the house. They're in this tiny ass alley that truck won't even fit down, and if it does, they'll have a hard time getting it in and out."

"So, we're stuck." Jamie ran her hands through her hair.

"No baby, what we will have to do is buy time. We go into his house and make small talk, which would give the children, time to get in the cars and bring them out of the alley. Then, they will drive the cars onto the truck. Our sixty-second window begins once the cars are on the truck."

"He'll hear the car start, look to see what's up, and the rest pops off from there," Jared finished.

The door to the room flew open and we quickly grabbed the guns; Jared and I hid them in our belts.

Jacob stepped through the door as he stretched and yawned.

"Boy, didn't I teach you to knock?" Jared asked.

"Sorry, Pop," Jacob stated.

"It's actually good that you're up, Jacob," I started. "Can you go downstairs and find Julie? When you do, tell her I need to talk to her."

"What's this about?" he asked me.

"Tomorrow, there's going to be a huge mission and I need to speak to her about it."

"Should I take Melanie with me?" he asked.

"Take Melanie and Miracle," Jared answered.

Jacob disappeared from the room and closed the door behind him.

"We're going to ask Julie about the truck. If she gives us access to one, it takes the load off us having to take three cars and drive them individually to wherever Julie wants them."

My phone rang and I answered it.

"I hear you want to speak with me," Julie spoke.

"Yeah, Julie. You know the truck that Quincy and Miracle took over today? Is there any way you can give us access to it?"

"I can have it here by morning for you," Julie spoke immediately

"Sounds great. What time does all of this go down tomorrow?"

"3:00. You want to do it when the cops aren't at their peak. But I'm sure you know all about the peak times for cops, huh Richard?"

I ignored her comment and continued.

"Sounds good. That's all I needed to know," I stated before hanging up the phone and looking back at the plan. "So, Julie's gonna get us the truck."

"Makes part of our job easier. So, we just need to assign roles," Jared mentioned as he sat on the bed and held the basketball in his hands.

"Simple. The adults enter his home; we act as though we're selling a product. Something he won't and can't say no to."

"A vacation get-away," Jamie stated. "All cops want a break, right, babe?" she stood closer to me and hugged me.

I kissed her lips and proceeded.

"That's right, baby," I cleared my throat. "Do we all agree on the vacation get-away?"

"Sounds good to me, but where should we say we're sending his ass?"

"Somewhere tropical. That's where I'd wanna vacation," Madison answered.

"The Iggus Islands," Jamie thought.

"That's cool, I'm on board," Jared continued to toss the ball in the air.

"Well then, it's settled. We give him an offer he can't resist. We go into his home and just wait for the kids to come and load the cars on the truck."

"And the cops?" Madison was concerned.

"We have to do our best not to encounter them. We need to make that window count," Jared declared.

Jacob knocked on the door and he and Melanie walked into the room.

"Where's Miracle?" I asked.

"She's still sleeping," Jacob spoke.

"J, wake Miracle and tell her to come here," Jared told Jacob.

Jacob released Melanie's hand and walked into the other room.

"Melanie, be prepared to drive tomorrow," Jared stated as he caught the ball as it returned to earth.

Jacob entered the room and Miracle was behind him.

"Children, tomorrow we will all be a part of a very dangerous mission; we could either end up in prison or killed from what we're going to attempt," Madison confessed.

"So, we have to be very precise and do everything to the tee to stay out of jail." Jared returned the ball to the floor and looked at the children.

I explained the plan to them and we all retired to our beds and went to sleep.

We awoke the next morning and were eating breakfast when Veronica approached us.

"I saw what happened, Miracle," she started, "may I join you all?"

I ignored her, but Jamie spoke after rolling her eyes at me for ignoring Veronica.

"Please, sit," she glared at me.

"Thank you." Veronica sat down and proceeded. "Close call, huh, Miracle?"

"What are you talking about?" Miracle asked with an attitude.

"Watch your tone, young lady," I spoke.

Miracle sighed and spoke. "What do you mean 'close call'?"

"The trucker almost killed Quincy, but the trucker was shot and wounded, allowing you all to pull him out and take over the truck."

"How do you know all those details? It wasn't reported," Miracle was inquisitive of this woman's knowledge.

"I'm the one that shot the driver."

I looked up from my plate for a second as she said this, but put my head back down and continued to eat.

I told you, Miracle, I'm looking out for you all because I don't want anyone to get hurt."

Miracle looked up from her plate and I looked at Veronica.

"It's true. Not only do I want for you all to be safe here, but also, for you all to make it home safely."

"Ms. Edwards—" I started.

"Veronica," she replied.

"Veronica, I don't trust people very easily, as you can see. So, I don't plan on associating with you in any way, shape, or form, until I feel comfortable."

"Richard, that's all fine and well. I know my purpose, and I guess I just have to prove myself to you."

"Good luck with that," I mentioned as I put down the napkin I was holding. I rose to my feet and motioned for Jared to follow me. I extended my hand for a handshake. "Nice to meet you, Veronica."

She shook my hand and I walked off with Jared at my side. We decided to scope out the area one more time before we had to do the mission.

Miracle

"Sorry about that. My husband's been through a lot and so he has a hard time trusting people," my mother spoke.

Veronica chuckled, "that's fine. I have a husband myself, so I know how it is."

"I'm not going to reveal or say anything about my husband; I want to know who *you* are."

"Well, I've introduced myself to Miracle," Veronica looked around the table. "I'm Veronica and currently I'm under the 'employment' of Julie."

"So, why are you *here*?" Aunt Madison interrupted.

"Julie thinks I'm a master criminal. I work with my brother, Abel. You all may know him as Lieutenant Roberts. I'm just looking after you all."

I looked at the woman.

"Miracle *es mi todo*; family first."

Aunt Madison looked at me and I looked at my cell phone; it was noon.

"I understand all of that. I just wanted to let you know who I am and what I'm about," she looked at the clock on the wall. "I have to get going; Julie is expecting me in thirty minutes and who knows what kind of traffic I will run into. I wish you all the absolute best on today's mission and I hope you all stay safe."

Veronica shook Aunt Madison and my mother's hand and walked off.

"Miracle, do not tell that lady too much. It would risk all of our lives."

"As if we aren't already in danger," Jacob spoke and continued to eat his breakfast.

I looked at him and returned my focus to my plate.

***

11

-Richard

Time was winding down and it was almost time to do the mission.

The children all got inside of the tow-truck as the adults into their vehicles.

Jamie and I rode together, and Madison and Jared rode together. I opened the two-way radio app on my phone.

"Jared, keep everything smooth. When we get there, keep your gun out of sight. We should have it all planned out well enough to run smoothly. I don't even want to think about what happens if something goes wrong."

"I gotcha bro; we stick to the plan," Jared spoke.

"Jacob, you all wait behind for a little. No need for us to simultaneously arrive," I announced.

We arrived at the man's home at 3:08 and we each put on the festive masks.

"You all ready?" I asked quietly.

They each nodded in approval.

I rang the doorbell and he cracked the door.

"May I help you all?"

"Good afternoon, sir," I started. "We are here to present an excellent opportunity for you; it'll allow you to take a vacation to a tropical paradise. May we step inside for a second?" I spoke.

"Why are you all wearing masks if you're giving away a vacation?"

"They wear masks all the time on the island," Madison responded.

"We're just passing on the spirit of the island and would like for you to take a trip there," Jamie touched her hair.

"Nah, I don't need a vacation. If I want it, I would buy it," Brian started to close the door and Jared put his hand in the door to hold it open.

"But sir, we insist on showing you this opportunity. How often is it that someone comes to your home to give you an exclusive trip?" Jared insisted on getting inside the home.

"Never. That's why I don't want the trip," Brian was getting agitated at Jared's persistence.

"Sir, please?" Jamie spoke in a soft tone.

"No means no. Now look, I'm a police officer and I will have you all arrested on the charge of harassment and trespassing," he argued and looked inside of his home.

"Well, that's a chance we're willing to take. The department sent us over to bless you with this once in a lifetime opportunity," Madison argued.

We all knew that if we didn't get inside the home, the children wouldn't have enough time to work their magic with the cars.

"The police department?" he asked.

"Yes," Madison replied.

"Which department?" he asked to test her knowledge.

Madison was silent, but I didn't allow for it to be silent for too long.

"Look, we just need to give you this trip, okay Brian? If we don't do it, then Julie will fire us for not giving the trip away to you."

I quickly realized I made two crucial mistakes.

"First question: how the fuck do you know my name?" he asked. "Second question: did you just say Julie? As in Julie Wilson?"

"Did I just say Julie?" I asked trying to fix the mistake. "Nah, I said Jewel," I spoke.

I saw Brian reach over to the counter next to the door and Jared put his hand on his gun.

"Whoa, calm down now," I spoke to Brian and Jared.

Jared didn't draw the weapon.

Brian pulled out a radio and spoke into it.

"This is Officer Smith, shield number 9834; I'm requesting units to my home immediately," spoke in his radio. "Fuck off my property," he shouted and slammed the door.

"Shit!" I shouted as we all ran down the stairs. "Babe, you and Madison ride together. Do not follow us, we need to make sure the kids shake these cops, and then we will all meet at the drop-off point."

"Okay, babe," she stated as she ran to Jared's car.

Jared ran to the passenger door of my car.

The officer came out of the side door with a shotgun aimed. He fired a bullet but it missed both cars and we both sped off towards the alley. The children were loading the last car onto the truck. I sounded my horn repeatedly to inform the kids that the window was closed and it was time to get out.

"Oh my, shit!" Brian spoke as he ran to his back gate and saw the truck driving off with the cars on board.

He fired shots at the truck, and then, the men we'd previously seen in the alley, came outside. They were unarmed, but once they reached the alley, they started to chase the truck on foot.

"It figures. He's paying them for protection," I spoke to Jared as I shook my head.

I sped down the alley and police vehicles blocked off both exits to the alley. Brian shot the tires of the truck.

Miracle

The truck rumbled and Jacob continued to drive as the tires were quickly losing air.

"Plan B; climb out on the sides of the truck and get in the cars. I'm going to do the same for the final car. We're going to go bowling with these pigs," Jacob was confident in his plan.

I opened the door of the truck, although it was going at 20 miles-per-hour.

Melanie and I grabbed the rail of the truck and eased our way to the side.

We held on tightly and slowly crept our way to the cars; I got in the Lamborghini and Melanie got in the Benz. We each started the cars and reversed from the back of the truck. The cars hit the ground and we drove behind the truck. Jacob wedged down the gas pedal using the emergency toolbox and eased his way over to the Bugatti.

He seemed to get to the Bugatti with ease.

He reversed from the truck and the truck drove full speed at the officers. Once it knocked them out of the way, we sped past the officers flashing our lights.

"Strike!" Jacob shouted into the phone with a laugh.

We sped down the street with a few officers right behind us.

-*Richard*

"God damn!" Jared shouted as the kids had just evaded the police. "Yeah, these kids have got some serious explaining to do."

"Let's just make it out," I responded as I sped past the police.

My cellphone rang.

"Richard, it's Veronica. I'm viewing you all in the system."

"Veronica, get the fuck off my—"

"Richard, let me help you with this," she spoke.

I didn't have time to think. I let out a sigh and she continued to speak.

"You have a ten-second window and the cops are coming from the North," she stated.

"Dammit," I shouted as we didn't see any officers around us. "Jared, call the kids and let them know these instructions," Jared called Jacob; Jacob called Melanie, and Melanie called Miracle.

"Coming up, you have a left. Take it; there aren't any cops in sight," Veronica instructed.

Jared told the children the instructions and they all seemed to turn in unison. I made the turn and realized Jamie was driving behind me; there were officers now chasing her.

"Shit! Veronica, we have to split. There's too many of them," I told her.

My optimism was quickly leaving.

As we passed another intersection, a truck came speeding beside us and rammed the officers off the road.

Miracle

I became very antsy as the speedometer crept to two-hundred and the police were still on our trail.

We soon heard helicopters above us.

"Melanie, you holdin' up ok?" Jacob asked over the phone.

"Everything's just peachy, considering the circumstances," she replied. "How about you, Miracle?"

I hesitated to speak; I could tell Jacob was still upset with me.

"*Estoy bien*," I answered in Spanish.

"We have a helicopter on our asses and we can't seem to shake these cops. We're going to have to split up," Jacob was confident as I saw him make a right turn.

Melanie didn't make the turn, but I followed him.

"Hell no, we stick together. That's the plan. I'm sure if we drive smart we can lose these cops."

We continued to climb in speed; I looked at the speedometer and saw it approaching 220 miles-per-hour.

My mother and father drove behind us.

-Richard

"All units be advised; suspects are in a white 2012 Bugatti, a dark brown 1989 Benz, a yellow 2014 Lamborghini, a white 2010 Dodge Charger, and a black 2008 Jaguar s-type," I could hear the police scanner over my phone.

"You all don't have much time; since you all turned right, you have a whole string of cops coming your way. You have to get out of there," Veronica stated. "I've told Julie about what's going on, so she's having three of her truck drivers hit the expressway now. I'm going to guide you to them, so follow my directions," she insisted.

"Jacob, there is a string of officers coming in our direction," Jared stated over his phone to his son.

"Perfect!" we heard Jacob say as he could be heard calling for Miracle and Melanie.

They accelerated and quickly sped towards the oncoming police. The officers sounded their sirens and Jacob took the lead and drove directly at an officer. At the last second, the officer swerved from the lane and into the light pole.

The light pole fell and caused many other officers to swerve to avoid hitting it.

I continued to speed, and we drove past the officer that crashed.

More police sped in our direction with guns aimed and prepared to shoot. In an instant, Jacob and Miracle made a quick turn down the alley, but the turn was so sudden, I continued to drive straight.

"Guys, stop turning," Jared shouted. "We have to get to the destination," he instructed the children.

Officers shot at my vehicle and the bullets left holes in the body and crack the windshield.

"It's okay," Veronica answered. "As long as you shake them and move towards the expressway," I heard her typing. "Once you reach the overpass, there will be three large trucks that you will be able to drive into and you will lose the police for good."

"Let's do it," Jacob stated before accelerating more.

"Jacob, we've gotta shake these cops before we get to the expressway," Jared mentioned over his phone. "And we have to get on at least six miles before the exit to the hotel. There will be three large trucks waiting for all of us to drive into."

As I turned, I saw Jacob and Miracle driving ahead of us.

"You all don't have any police vehicles headed your way. Take advantage of this window that you've carved out. You guys have a helicopter trailing you, but once you reach the tunnel, you'll lose it," Veronica spoke a few moments later.

"Thanks, Veronica," I stated.

Even I was shocked that I just said that.

"I'll see you all on the other side," she stated before hanging up.

I noticed Jamie was still trailing me and I called her on my phone.

"Jamie, there will be three trucks coming up on the expressway that we will drive into. We will lose the helicopters that way. Just stay behind us."

"Julie has gotta be the most psychopathic bitch in the world," Jamie mentioned to me. "Crazier than my aunt."

"Not as crazy as these kids are gonna feel once we question them on their skills. This isn't regular racing or driving skills, it seems like they are experts on this," I thought. "Just stay behind us," I spoke before hanging up.

Miracle

Jacob let Melanie know what the plan was and she was soon turning the corner. As we all reunited, we each got on the expressway and swerved in and out of traffic.

My mother and father were behind us and sped to try to keep up with us.

Once we reached the overpass, we saw the trucks.

"Keep it lined up perfectly," Jacob spoke he took the lead and got directly behind the truck; Melanie got behind him, and I trailed her.

He drove into the trailer that the truck was pulling. As Melanie drove in behind him, the tunnel was ending. I drove in behind Melanie, and the driver lowered the back door to the trailer. I prayed that our parents were also safe inside of the other trucks.

The light inside of the trailer turned on and we each turned off our vehicle. Jacob got out and walked over to Melanie's car.

"We did that shit," he spoke as he helped her out of the car.

I got out of my car as they kissed and I leaned against my car.

Jacob retreated from the kiss and took Melanie's hand. They both walked over to me.

"Girl, why you shaking? It's done. We got the cars and it's over." Melanie hugged me and kiss on the cheek.

I didn't reply; a tear fell out of my eye.

"Come here, Miracle," Jacob spoke as he hugged me. "It's over," he assured me as he hugged me tightly.

"It's not even that," I spoke after a few moments. "I feel like things are different between us now. Like, I don't think you still see me the same."

"Miracle, you're my best friend. You may do things that I don't like, but it doesn't mean it changes my opinion of you. The most important thing to me is that you're happy." He wiped my tears. "I'm just looking out for you."

"Just let Quincy know that he will get fucked up if he hurts you," Melanie added with a chuckle, yet I could tell that she was serious.

"I'm just scared because I've never really experienced the fire I feel when I'm with him."

"They're just butterflies," Jacob spoke. "Just keep everything under control," Jacob stated as Melanie crouched and looked at the cars.

"What are you looking at?" I asked Melanie.

"Not a single scratch." Melanie stood up straight. "I guess we're better than we thought."

"I wonder what other crazy shit Julie has planned," Jacob mentioned. "I guess we just have to take it day-by-day."

I picked up the phone and called my father; he added my mother to the call.

"Hello?" my father answered.

"Papi, how are things?"

"We're here inside of the truck," he answered.

"¡*Estamos vivos*!" My mother joked on the other line of the phone as she and Aunt Madison laughed.

"I hope that was the worst of what we have to do," my father spoke.

"Things are fine over here, too. All we can do is sit, talk, and wait to get to where we're going," I twirled my hair as Jacob and Melanie spoke.

"I think we're almost at the destination," my mother spoke.

"I was just calling to make sure you all were safe over there. I will see you once we get there."

"We may be going to a different location than you since you all have the cars. We're probably going back to the hotel."

"Whoever may be waiting for you at the drop-off point, keep your composure," my father spoke.

"I will, Papi," I assured before hanging up the phone.

Jacob, Melanie, and I continued to speak until the truck came to a stop and the driver turned off the engine.

The driver turned off the light inside of the trailer and exited the truck.

Within seconds, the door to the trailer was rising.

"Ah, there my beautiful cars are!" Julie exclaimed.

"You almost had us killed," Jacob spoke as we all walked towards the exit.

"Yeah, if you thought what Miracle experienced was bad, maybe you don't know how dangerous it is to have helicopters and half a city's law enforcement on you."

"It was only half of the suburb's law enforcement. Trust me, it would have been a lot worse for the city," Julie chuckled while walking over to her cars. "You three, back my cars out of here," she demanded.

"Don't you think you've asked enough of us for the day?" Jacob asked.

Joey stepped from around the truck.

"No; you haven't done enough until I say you've done enough," Julie spoke.

I could tell Jacob just wanted to leave her cars inside of the truck but didn't want to risk mine or Melanie's safety.

"Come on, y'all," Jacob spoke as he walked back towards the Bugatti.

Melanie got in her car, but I didn't get in the Lamborghini.

I realized that neither Jacob nor Melanie could back out if I didn't.

"You gonna get in the car?" Julie asked me.

I rolled my eyes and got in the Lamborghini.

The leather seats within the car felt cold against my skin as I started the engine. I reversed the Lamborghini out of the truck and stopped it in the parking lot.

Melanie reversed the Benz and Jacob reversed the Bugatti; they both parked their cars beside the Lamborghini.

"Not a single scratch on them; that's what I like."

Julie walked up to the cars as we all got out of the vehicles. She inspected the cars and looked at Joey.

He nodded his head and Julie spoke again.

"Put 'em back," she directed.

"What was the point in driving the cars out of the truck?" Jacob asked.

"So, I could inspect my merchandise. I have to make sure there wasn't too much damage done."

"This is some bullshit," Jacob uttered before walking back to the Bugatti.

He started the car and drove into the truck, as did Melanie with the Benz, and myself with the Lamborghini.

We each turned off the cars and gave Julie the keys.

"How did you all get the keys?" Julie asked as we walked off the back of the truck.

"The cop had them inside of the car, and the doors were unlocked. All we did was have to load them and take them," Melanie spoke. "Maybe he'd left them there for the people behind his home, who chased us after we took the cars."

I remained silent.

Joey then approached me and handed me five hundred dollars and did the same for Jacob and Melanie.

"You all did good," Julie spoke as a van arrived. "Veronica will drive you all back to the hotel. Let your parents know everything is fine and the mission is a success."

"Will do," Jacob spoke as we walked to the van.

The door opened, and we climbed inside.

As the door closed and the van pulled off, Veronica spoke to us about everything that happened, but I couldn't get my mind off Jessie, Quincy, the fact that we just committed major crimes; my mind was all over the place.

I closed my eyes and took a nap on the ride to the hotel.

12

-*Richard*

"This bitch made us do this crazy shit in our personal vehicles. Now every cop in the D.R. has our plates and we can't even go out without having to worry about getting arrested!"

Madison was furious at the mission we just succeeded in doing. Jared took off his coat and hung it on a hanger and spoke.

"You know she's only doing this dumb shit for revenge."

"Revenge my ass! It's not worth getting our children killed over. If Julie has beef with me, she needs to take it up with me and leave my family out of her bullshit," I spoke as I sat on the bed.

Jamie dialed Miracle's phone number but did not get an answer.

"*¿Dónde está mi Milagro?*" she worried. I put my arm around her and kissed her on the cheek.

"Jacob promised to keep her safe, baby. I'm sure they're fine." I assured her.

"Fuck Julie, Joey, and whoever else she has on her payroll. Let's just bust this bitch and—"

"And what, bro?" I rose to my feet and asked him. "We're here in the D.R. and we're wanted ourselves. She knows the ins and outs of the city, and I know you've been hearing that she runs this shit."

"Run these nuts!" Jared shouted. "Julie can go and fuck herself. She's full of shit, and I'm willing to bet that if we left tomorrow, she wouldn't do shit." Jared added.

"And we don't even wanna take that chance, babe." Madison was now calm, and Jared wanted to punch a hole in the hotel door. "I'm sure Richard has a plan to get out of all of this."

"I want this to be over as much as everyone else. The stunt today put our children in major harm's way, and no one fucks with our children. But the plan is to just finish with Julie and bust her ass."

"Speaking of today," Jamie started to speak since she calmed down with worrying, "where did those kids learn to do everything that they did today?"

"They got some major explaining to do," Jared spoke. "But then again, children are smarter than we think." He directed his words to Madison. "You know how much time he spends in that garage. That boy is *obsessed* with cars."

Our guns lied on the table and there was a knock at the door. I quickly put the guns in the drawer and Jared opened it.

"You guys were absolutely amazing today," Julie spoke at the door with Joey behind her. "May I come inside?"

"Sure, come on in," Madison spoke.

Julie walked inside and Joey followed her.

"Actually Julie, come with me into the next room," I spoke as I rose to my feet. "I want to discuss something in private with you."

"This should be good," Jared chuckled.

I looked at him and raised my eyebrows to tell him to shut up.

Julie walked into the adjoining room and I followed.

I sat in the chair and I motioned for her to sit.

"So, what'd you want to talk to me about?" she asked.

"What is your beef with me?" I asked her.

"You know exactly what the issue is between us. But there isn't an issue as long as you do as I say."

"You put my damn daughter, nephew, and his girlfriend in harm's way today. Not only them, but you put my wife, bro, and his wife in harm's way," I slightly raised my voice. "If you have an issue with me, you need to take it up with me."

"Get off that bullshit," she spoke in a higher tone than me. "I told you that things would escalate during this job—."

"Yeah, but not enough to get my daughter killed over. We all felonies lingering over our heads right now," I told her.

"I have people getting in the system right now to clear your plates out of the system. We're taking a day or two off to lay low, but we're gonna get right back to work. Come tomorrow evening, the cops won't have a record of you at all."

I looked at her and she smirked at me.

"This shit better end soon!" I told her before opening the door.

"You'll have your life back really soon. And the best part: you won't have to worry about me," Julie walked out of the room. "That is, as long as you aren't trying to fuck me over."

We walked back into the room with Jared, Jamie, Madison, and Joey. I sat next to Jamie on the bed.

"Julie, you aren't worth the stress or bullshit," Jared spoke.

"Damn, I guess everyone's ganging up on me today," she replied. "Look, I know today got crazy. I'm sorry it happened. Everyone's safe and that's all we can truly thank God for."

"What God do you worship, Julie?" I asked her. "Because we surely cannot worship the same God."

"Why don't you ask my cousin?" she glanced at Jamie.

"Don't involve me in your twisted shit," Jamie spoke.

"I'm just being completely honest," Julie spoke. "I'll be out of your lives once this is all over and done with. But for now, I'm your boss," Julie rose to her feet and walked towards the door.

Joey placed two thousand dollars on the dresser and Julie spoke again.

"Five hundred per person for the work done today. I'll be in touch in the next few days. We're laying low tomorrow and maybe the next day to let the heat die down," she exited the room and Joey left behind her.

"I wanted to attack that bitch!" Madison exclaimed a few moments after Julie left the room.

"I think we're all glad and lucky that you didn't," I mentioned as there was another knock at the door.

Jared looked through the peephole of the door before opening it.

"Miracle," Jamie stated as she stood up and walked over to the door.

Jacob hugged his mother and father, and Melanie hugged Jacob's parents.

"We're safe," Jacob spoke as Miracle hugged Jamie.

"The cars were delivered to Julie and she's taking them somewhere in a truck. She said that everything was a success."

"Yeah, we know; she just left." Jared started as he closed the door. "But you all aren't off the hook. Where in the hell did you all learn to drive like that?" Jared asked the teenagers.

"It's not that hard," Melanie replied while rolling her eyes.

"Yeah, for a cop," I mentioned. "But for three teenagers, it should be very hard."

The teenagers were silent and Miracle's phone rang. Her cheeks instantly turned red as she looked at who was calling and answered on the second ring.

"Hey, you," she spoke on the phone and walked into the other room.

"Why's she so smiley?" I asked.

"You gotta ask her," Melanie spoke.

I noticed that Jacob was silent.

"Whoever it is, has your daughter happier than a fat kid in a bakery," Jared chuckled.

I laughed at Jared's joke, but I still couldn't get over the fact that these children drove like they do these kinds of jobs daily.

"What was the condition of the cars?" Jared asked.

"All were unmarked," Jacob spoke. "She gave us each $500 for bringing the cars back."

"Maybe you all won't be bugging me for money," I joked. "Jacob, you've collected almost 5 grand while here in the D.R. and the girls have each gotten $500. What you gonna do with yourself now that you're big ballin'," I laughed.

"All of this is going towards my garage," Jacob spoke. "Well, not all of it, but a lot of it."

"I'm glad that you have a plan in life, Jacob. If it's one thing I encourage everyone to do, it's to have a plan in life. Have multiple plans, though, just in case one plan doesn't work, you have a backup."

"Thanks, Unc." Jacob put his hands in his pockets and Miracle slowly walked out of the room; she was smiling from ear-to-ear.

"What's got you smiling?" I asked her. Her smile faded almost immediately.

"Nothing," she stated as she twirled her hair.

"Lemme find out a boy is making my baby smile and blush," I spoke. "Make sure he knows that I'm a cop," I spoke in a soft tone.

Jacob whispered something to Melanie and Jared continued to speak.

"Well, I think that after today, we all deserve to be treated." As he finished talking, the phone to the room rang.

I pressed speakerphone.

"Mr. Young?" the woman at the front desk spoke.

"Speaking," I answered.

"Ms. Julie Wilson would like to see you and your party downstairs in the casino."

"Will do," I responded before hanging up the phone. "Maybe that's our treat," I told Jared as we all walked out of the room and to the elevator.

As we got downstairs, Joey was waiting to escort us to the casino.

"Julie; she's expecting you. Follow me." His voice sounded as though there was more of an Italian accent than there previously was.

He walked over to the casino and we followed him before sitting down. Julie had a table cloth napkin unraveled in front of her. A cigar cutter was on the cloth, as well as an empty glass.

"Welcome, ladies and gentlemen," Julie spoke as we were all seated. "Amazing work today, and I am extremely grateful for it."

A waitress came out and brought out an envelope and laid it out in front of Julie.

Julie opened the envelope slowly and Jacob spoke.

"Lemme guess, Ms. Wilson, another Cuban cigar?" he adjusted himself in his seat.

She finished pulling out what was inside the envelope. "Smart boy," she remarked as the waitress lit the cigar. "Thank you," Julie stated to the waitress; she blew smoke to the side. "What is it that you all would like to drink?" Julie looked at me directly.

"Sprite, on the rocks for me and the 2 ladies here," Jacob stated; referring to Miracle and Melanie.

"*En realidad,*" Miracle started, "I'd like a raspberry lemonade. Trying to stay away from soda."

"That's understandable. You don't want all that acid in your system," Julie spoke and she inhaled on the cigar and held it in her mouth. "And for the adults?"

"I'll take some of that whiskey that you always have," Jared told her as Madison lay her head on his shoulder.

"Red wine," Jamie spoke. "For me and Madison."

"I'll take a glass of that whiskey, as well," I uttered and Jamie held my hand.

The waitress walked to the back and Julie continued to speak.

"Today's work was nothing short of spectacular!" She started as she put her cigar down.

Jared sat up in his seat.

"I've recovered three of my most prized possessions; undamaged," she finished.

"Well, we figured that's how you would want them," Jacob spoke.

"Although we went through hell to get them;" Melanie mentioned immediately after Jacob.

"That's exactly why I invited you all down here." Julie placed her cigar on the cloth. "Things took a hard left today and I didn't expect all those cops."

I looked at Miracle who was now looking at the television. A news report of what happened today was on.

"And we are live, reporting from Officer Brian Smith's home, where three cars, still missing, were stolen a few hours ago. Tell us what happened, Officer Smith."

"Well, to start, there were about 4 individuals who approached my doorstep trying to offer me some kind of getaway. I didn't accept and they were so persistent until one of the men said the name 'Julie'. I closed the door and called for backup. I shot at their cars but missed. All I know after that, is that I ran around to the back of my home because I heard a loud bump. There were three more individuals, teenagers I believe, that were loading the cars onto the truck. I shot at the tires of the truck, and the teens each eased around the side of the truck and reversed the cars off the truck and sped off."

As the reporter spoke, the camera went from video footage of her and Brian's face to the footage the helicopter recorded. It showed the three cars the children drove evading the police, as well as my car and Jared's car being pursued.

"On your television screen, you will see the three suspects as they drive and evade police, as well as two vehicles in which seem to be accomplices."

"You see that?" Julie spoke. "That's why I chose you all to do this for me."

"I thought it was because I killed your mother," I responded.

"Oh no, Richard. This is bigger than that. I will soon have everything I have once lost under my control, here in the D.R."

The waitress brought out the drinks.

"I propose a toast," Julie raised her glass. "To a job well done."

Everyone raised their glass, except for myself.

"You're not going to join the party, Richard?" Julie asked.

Jared nudged me under the table and looked at me. I reluctantly lifted the glass and we tapped them together. We lowered our glasses, and each took a sip.

"We're going to be taking a few days off. Things are still hot and we need to let them cool down." Joey spoke as he stood behind Julie.

I looked towards Miracle; she was smiling as she sipped her lemonade.

"Do you all mind if I join you?" Quincy stood there in a suit.

I remained silent and Miracle seemed to immediately light up.

"Everyone, I think you all know my nephew, Quincy," Julie stated as she rose to her feet.

I immediately felt a slight chill.

"So, that's the relationship," I spoke aloud.

"Have a seat, Q," Julie continued.

Quincy walked towards Miracle and took the empty seat next to her; she didn't seem to even flinch.

I saw Jacob whisper something to Melanie and Julie proceeded to speak.

"Today was an example of the world not working the way we want it to. The world doesn't revolve around our asses and so we need not act like it does and as though someone owes us something."

"How ironic," I uttered before sipping my drink.

"There something you feel you need to add, Ricky?" Julie held her cigar in between her two fingers.

"I mean, you're preaching about how the world owes you absolutely nothing, yet we're here in the D.R. because you feel I owe you something."

"That's right. The world doesn't owe me a damn thing…. But for the next few days, weeks, or even months, you owe me your loyalty," Julie was sure that her way was the right way.

"I don't feel that I owe you shit," I rebelled. "The only thing I owe you is—" I immediately stopped my sentence.

"What is it that you owe me, Rick?" Julie asked.

Jared stared at me and gave me a look.

I nodded my head and Julie continued to speak.

"I will shut all of this shit down," Julie stated. "I invited you all down to celebrate, not be hostile towards each other."

"Fuck this," I stated as I rose to my feet in disgust. "I enjoyed the drink, Julie. I will see the rest of you all upstairs."

"Richard," Jamie spoke. "Sit back down, baby," she pleaded.

I looked at Julie sternly, before returning to my seat. I held Jamie's hand in mine and Julie continued to speak.

"As people, we must all work together to succeed. Without a team, nothing would be possible."

***

As we each walked up to the room, I could sense that something was wrong. Jacob and Melanie were behind us, but Miracle waited downstairs to speak to Quincy.

She claimed she had a few questions for him; I knew that wasn't the reason she stayed behind.

Jacob and Melanie remained quiet.

"Mr. Young, we're going to return downstairs to keep an eye on Miracle." Melanie held Jacob's hand.

"Go on, and keep a close eye on my Miracle," I told them as I had an arm around Jamie.

The children disappeared downstairs and the adults walked into the room.

Miracle

Quincy was making me laugh as we both sat outside on the bench. No one was around. The sound of the waves crashing and the moonlight shining down on us was peaceful and relaxing.

Seagulls were on the far side over the beach and I was wearing Quincy's jacket.

"Come on, try it," he insisted.

"Okay, okay," I bowed my head down and quickly threw my head back, and attempted to flip my hair back without using my hands.

Quincy chuckled at my attempt, as my hair returned to its original position and not the way I wanted it to.

"Now you're looking like a poodle," he spoke and he moved my hair out of my face. "You're my poodle," he gently added.

I blushed, and he kissed me on the cheek.

Jacob and Melanie walked up beside us.

"There you are, Miracle," Melanie stated.

Jacob kept his hands in his pockets but never took his eyes off Quincy.

I stood up and hugged Melanie. Jacob walked over and hugged me before I sat back down.

"I'm sure you're aware that you better not do a thing to hurt Miracle," Jacob spoke in a tone to show he was serious.

"Calm down," Quincy looked at me and licked his lips. "Nothing will happen to Miracle."

Jacob continued to glare at Quincy.

"A few days off," Melanie spoke as she changed the subject.

"It's gonna feel good to relax," Quincy retorted after Melanie.

"What is it that you do while working with Julie?" Melanie asked him.

"Everything you can think of. I do the planning and production of everything. Julie and I brainstorm on how we're going to get things done, and she sends me out to make those things happen."

"So, what does she actually do?" I asked.

"Yeah, if she has people to do everything for her."

"She organizes. That's her position." Quincy spoke as he adjusted his hat to make sure it was cocked to the right and back.

"It's everyone else's job to make sure everything goes as planned. If it doesn't, Julie will cut you off."

"Julie sounds like a true bitch," Melanie spoke.

"My aunt is real cool. She just doesn't like to get fucked over."

"*Estas muy loca*," I responded.

Julie walked outside with a Cuban cigar in her hand and a glass of Hennessey in the other.

She had a large, royal blue mink coat around her shoulders; Joey and two other large men followed her outside of the hotel.

"What are you kids up to?" She asked as she inhaled on the cigar.

"Just talking," Quincy answered.

"Damn Julie, you must be ballin'. You have that big ass mink on your shoulders, stay lookin' fresh, got almost everyone and they mama working for you, and have your own security," Melanie touched the mink.

Julie chuckled. "I'm well off if that's what you mean," she sipped her drink. "Just like someone else I know," Julie looked at me.

I tried to change the subject.

"This weather is crazy," I stated nervously.

"Considering we're surrounded by water on all sides, you can expect the nights to be rather chilly," she replied.

Joey stood behind Julie and looked at Jacob, Melanie, and myself.

Melanie held Jacob's hand tighter and Quincy spoke.

"What brings you out here, Auntie?"

"Just wanted to enjoy the quiet sounds of the beach while I drank and smoked," Julie took a sip of the drink and a piece of ice went in her mouth. She chewed on it. "As I said, we're laying low for the next day or so, or however long it may take for things to die down."

"Can we get some insight on the next job?" I asked her.

"There's a pool party that's happening soon, I hope the heat has died down by then," she started.

"And I guess you want us to steal the pool or kidnap the guests?" Melanie interrupted.

"Bigger than that. No, it's not a cop's residence, but there will be camera crews there."

"So, we're going to be caught committing the crimes?" Jacob asked.

"Not exactly. You all will have to avoid those camera crews and bring back my jewels from the house. Last I checked, everything was upstairs in the room to the far East."

I looked down, nervously, and touched my hair.

"I'll have specifics later, but this will be all about stealth. You will need someone to distract, someone to be on the lookout, and someone to retrieve the jewels."

"What kind of jewels?" Jacob asked inquisitively.

"Diamonds, primarily. Got a few rubies, gold pieces, emeralds; it's valued at over 400K. Oh, and you won't be using cars," she spoke.

"Then how do we get away?" Jacob asked her.

"Bikes," she answered.

We all chuckled at this, except for Julie.

"Oh wait, you're serious?" Melanie asked.

Julie sipped the drink and proceeded.

"You'll get more details later."

She looked at her watch and made a motion with her hand. "I think it's time that you all start heading up to your rooms for the evening," Julie spoke.

I looked at my phone; it was 1:30 in the morning.

"Let us finish here, Auntie, and I'll walk Miracle up in a few minutes," Quincy spoke as Julie puffed her last breath of smoke and flicked her cigar into the ocean.

"You kids have a good night," she spoke before she walked off.

Joey and the other two men followed her.

"Yeah, we're about to head upstairs," Jacob spoke as he hugged me. "See you up there, Miracle."

"Yeah girl, don't stay too long. You know your daddy is gonna get that ass if you come in there at 3 in the morning," Melanie joked.

"I'll see you all in a bit," I laughed.

Melanie and Jacob walked into the hotel and Quincy moved closer to me.

As I turned my head from watching Melanie and Jacob inside, Quincy kissed me on the lips. It took me by surprise and I started to blush.

"My Puerto Rican mami," he spoke.

He leaned in closer to me and put his lips on mine, but this time, he slid his tongue in my mouth.

As we passionately kissed, I could feel my hormones starting to rage and I wanted to rip his clothes off his body, even though I wasn't sexually attracted to him.

Quincy slowly retreated and took my hand. We walked into the hotel and he walked me up to my room.

"Will I see you tomorrow?" he asked as we approached the room and I started to enter.

"Tomorrow, and the next day, and the next day," I spoke and we gave each other a quick kiss on the lips.

It was official, I was in love with him.

"Have a good night, Miracle," Quincy said.

"You too, Q," I closed the door completely.

13

Miracle

A few days passed by and everyone was sitting in the room and talking when multiple loud, rapid knocks interrupted our conversation.

My mother opened the door and Julie walked in. She gave no greeting; she just spoke.

"Okay, Jacob, I need for you to go outside and make sure the bikes are ready. Miracle and Melanie, I need you both to come with me," she was frantic.

"Mami, Papi, we'll be back a little later," I told my mother and father.

"Stay safe," my mother spoke in a soft tone.

"You know I'm only one call away," my father told me.

"I know. I'll be safe. We're just praying everything runs smoothly."

Jacob said goodbye to his mother and father, as well as my parents, and left the room.

I spoke to Aunt Madison and Uncle Jared before walking out with Melanie.

"Okay, so we're cutting it close," Julie spoke as we all power-walked to the elevator. "The camera crews are arriving at the party as we speak. If they get to the room before you all do, the mission is over. Once you all get there, designate someone to distract the crowd and someone to be the watch person, while the final person takes the jewels."

The elevator arrived at our floor and we all stepped inside. Julie pressed the button to the lobby and the doors closed.

"How are we getting there?" Melanie asked her.

"Bikes. You will ride over there, get the jewels, and then ride back and bring them to the rear entrance of the hotel."

Melanie and I looked at each other and the elevator doors opened. We walked out of the hotel.

"You all have about fifteen minutes to get there; here's the address," Julie passed Jacob a card.

I looked at the vehicles; I thought they would be motorcycles, but to my surprise, they were actual bicycles.

"*¿En serio?*" I asked her.

"I'll see you all in a bit," Julie stated as she ignored my question, and then walked back into the hotel.

"Well," Jacob stated as he put on his helmet and rang his bell twice. "Let's ride."

We all laughed, got on a bike, and rode until we got to the party.

"Ok, I'll create the diversion and lure everyone away from you and Miracle," Melanie stated. "I was born for this kind of attention." She flipped her hair.

I shook my head as we walked into the home. When we opened the door, we were instantly hit by the sound of loud music and the smell of marijuana.

"Shit," Jacob shouted as he fanned the air in front of him with his hands.

"Let's be glad my father isn't here," I answered as we walked towards the kitchen. "He'd have a field day because of what everyone's doing. Imagine all the citations and cops on the scene," I joked and Jacob chuckled.

"Let's be glad he isn't," Jacob stated. "I'll be the lookout. We need to get to the room upstairs," he shouted.

People were dancing and drinking while Jacob and I eased our way upstairs.

We looked out of the nearby window and saw the camera crews all beginning to surround Melanie; she made sure to keep her face out of the camera's sight. Jacob and I continued to walk up the spiral staircase.

"Okay, Miracle. You go get the jewels and I will stay out here and keep watch. If anyone is coming, I will speak to them so that you can hear me, and I need for you to hide."

"Got it," I spoke as I entered the room.

I checked the obvious places jewelry would be kept. The first place I looked was on the dresser. I heard a slight creak in the floor but thought nothing of it.

"What's taking so long?" Jacob asked.

"The shit isn't here," I whispered and I finally found a diamond under the desktop clock.

"Never mind, I got one."

"You need some help?" Jacob was joking with me and I chuckled a bit.

"Nah, *estoy bien.*" I continued to feel around and made my way to the bed.

I felt under the pillows and sheets; more jewels were in the pillowcase.

"They literally sleep on their money," I told Jacob as I also pulled out a stack of one-hundred-dollar bills along with the diamonds, rubies, and gold.

I looked over by the closet and started to look in shoeboxes. I opened one and found the final jewels. As I put the jewels in my pocket, I felt an object press against my side.

"Don't move," the voice whispered as the person came out of the closet.

I slowly put my hands up and I shivered in fear as I quietly tried to get Jacob's attention.

"Why the fuck are you trying to rob me? Who sent you?"

I didn't answer and the person pressed the gun deeper into my side.

"I'm waiting on an answer," the voice uttered slightly louder.

I threw my elbow back into the person's rib cage and turned to fight for control of the gun.

"J!" I shouted as I fought with the man over the gun.

He peeked into the room and saw what was going on. Jacob came in and kicked the gunman and helped me up.

I ran over to the door and Jacob was reaching for the gun.

Jacob and the man struggled for control of the gun and pulled the trigger; a shot rang through the window and it shattered. People started screaming and running.

The man gained control of the gun in his left hand.

"Little bitch," Jacob cursed as he punched the man in the face. The impact from the punch caused the man to lose the weapon.

Jacob and the gunman wrestled on the ground as people ran out of the house.

"Get out of here and go get help," Jacob shouted.

"I'm not leaving without you!" I exclaimed and ran over to try and help Jacob.

Jacob punched the gunman, stood up, and we both ran out of the room.

"Let's get the fuck up out of here," Jacob ordered as he tried to catch his breath.

The man stood up and grabbed another gun from his closet; he jogged out of the room and shot at us.

"Stay low, stay low!" Jacob shouted as we ran down the spiral staircase. The bullet hit the head of the statue next to us and it shattered.

"Shit," the man stated as he followed us.

"I can't believe this dumbass has us on bicycles," Jacob huffed as he referred to Julie.

"Let's just make it out of here alive," I rebutted.

As we ran outside, I bumped into my father and he asked what we were running from, but held me in his arms. The man ran outside with his gun aimed and my father quickly drew his weapon from his pants. Before my father could fully pull out his gun, the man fired a bullet and it hit my father on the right side of his chest.

"Papi!" I shouted as my father fell to the ground.

The man tried to fire another shot, but the gun clicked.

He quickly reached in his pocket to grab another clip.

"Come on, M!" Jacob shouted as he carried my father on his shoulder.

I cried softly as we ran over to Melanie. She was now sitting atop a red Kawasaki ZX-14 motorcycle.

Two other motorcycles sat beside her; both were red.

I got on one motorcycle; tears were still falling from my eyes. Melanie got off her bike and held my father up as Jacob climbed on the motorcycle. She sat my father behind Jacob on the motorcycle. They put on his helmet and Jacob made sure my father's hands were interlocked around his waist.

"Let's bounce!" he stated as he sped off at top speed. Melanie immediately followed him and I followed her.

The man finished loading the clip in his gun and continued to fire shots at us. Jacob immediately swerved into oncoming traffic with my father on his back.

"Where are we riding?" Melanie shouted as we all continued to speed.

"Back to the hotel," Jacob shouted.

"No! *Tenemos que ir al hospital,*" I retaliated.

"Miracle we have to get back to the hotel," Jacob stated as he sped faster and turned down the alley.

I let out more tears as we all sped back and within minutes, we were pulling around the back of the hotel.

"Julie, we're downstairs," Jacob spoke over his phone as he held my father up.

Jacob hung up the phone and walked my father over to the bumper of a car. He then dialed his father and my mother to inform them that my father had been shot. My father held his hand over the bullet wound; the bleeding had slowed down.

I ran over and hugged him. "¿Papi, *como es?*"

"Bleeding has slowed down but I can still feel the blood rushing," he spoke as he coughed. "Get Aunt Madison down here, she'll know how to slow it down. She went to school for this and has helped me before."

"They're on their way," I answered, fighting to hold back the tears. "Hold on, Papi."

Julie walked out of the door with Joey behind her. She saw my father and cringed a little.

"Joey, get some paramedics over here!" Julie shouted.

Joey quickly dialed 9-1-1 on his phone as Julie walked over to a van and climbed inside. She pulled out her phone. Jacob's hands and shirt were covered in blood as my father slowly closed his eyes.

"Papi, stay awake," I cried as Melanie hugged me.

"Miracle, I love you," he uttered.

"Unc, don't do this," Jacob let out a tear.

Jacob's parents came out of the doors, as well as my mother.

"Richard!" my mother shrieked as she ran over to my father and she instantly started to cry.

"Shit, shit, shit," Uncle Jared spoke as he ran over.

Aunt Madison quickly took off her sweater.

"How long has he been bleeding?" she asked Jacob as she balled up her sweater and put it over my father's wound.

"Jacob, tell me exactly what happened," my mother managed to speak regardless of her tears.

"Give him to Jamie," Uncle Jared spoke to his son.

Jacob passed my father to my mother; his entire upper body was covered in blood.

They all continued to ask him questions at once and I could tell he was becoming bothered by it.

Jacob let out a sound of disgust.

"We got the jewels for Julie, and we ran outside. Uncle Richard was out there, and the man shot him," Jacob let out more tears and balled up his fists.

"Everybody, stand back," Uncle Jared spoke.

He knew that Jacob was hurting and knew exactly how his son would project his anger.

Jacob rose to his feet and wiped the tears that accumulated.

Jacob instantly turned and swung his fist.

He hit the van Julie sat inside and left a dent. Julie got out of the vehicle.

"Jacob, stop," Melanie spoke as she stood up.

She wiped the tears from her eyes and walked towards him.

He punched the rear window of the van and broke it. He then proceeded to pick up a brick and walk towards the car.

"Whoa, Jacob," my mother spoke as she continued to hold my father.

"Stop, baby," Melanie jogged to him.

I rose to my feet and everyone except my mother and father walked over to restrain Jacob.

"Jacob, don't do it," I spoke as I walked up to him with my hands out.

His father reached up and opened Jacob's grip, allowing him to take the brick from Jacob. He let out tears on Melanie's shoulder.

Melanie put her hand on his head as he cried and I let out a few more tears.

The ambulance came speeding through the parking lot and paramedics jumped out of the back. They lifted my father and put him on a stretcher. The paramedics put IV tubes in his arm and connected him to a heart monitor.

"*Lo estamos llevando a la sala de emergencia del Centro de Medicina Avanzada,*" the paramedic spoke.

"I want to ride with Papi," I spoke, wiping away a few tears.

"Papi will be fine," my mother spoke as she tried to remain strong. "He's a Young: a fighter, a provider, and more importantly, he wouldn't let us down," my mother's voice started to crack as the paramedic closed the door.

He immediately left the lot after closing the doors.

"Yes, Miracle. Daddy will be okay," Julie spoke. "I need for you guys to—"

"No, fuck you!" Aunt Madison retorted as she was furious that Julie wanted us to do another job.

"Do it your damn self," my mother added.

"Excuse you all?" Joey spoke.

"Joey, don't try to get all tough," Uncle Jared spoke. "We're not doing any more jobs at the moment."

"You all will do whatever I want you to do. Because if you don't…" Julie started to speak.

"If we don't, what?" my mother asked her. "My husband has been fucking shot in the chest and all you can care about is your damn self."

"Cuz," Julie took off her sunglasses, "in this world, all you have is yourself. You came into this world alone, and you will leave alone."

My mother ran and tackled Julie to the ground and her sunglasses flew out of her hand.

"¡*Chinga cabrón*!" my mother cursed and she started to hit Julie.

Joey quickly grabbed at my mother but Jacob punched him in the nose. Joey stumbled and fell back to the ground.

Aunt Madison and Melanie both jogged over and both took ahold of one of my mother's arms. They lifted her to her feet.

"Mrs. Young, calm down." Melanie pleaded.

"Mami,*"* I stated as I took her hand.

Joey threw his body at Jacob and pushed him back into the van. Jacob hit Joey in the back, but Joey hit him in his stomach.

Uncle Jared grabbed Joey behind his head and slammed it hard against the door of the van. Jacob got from against the van and hit Joey in the stomach.

"Jacob, stop!" Melanie shouted.

Julie stood back up.

"You just issued yourself a death wish," she stated as she wiped the blood from her lip.

My mother cried on Aunt Madison's shoulder. Aunt Madison glared at Julie.

Julie picked up her sunglasses and Joey got back up.

She spat out blood before speaking again.

"You know what? Players fuck up sometimes," she chuckled. "You *are* family so I'll give you 24 hours to think over what you've just done and make a final determination on if you don't want to do any more missions. It's your life— er, choice."

Joey and Julie disappeared into the hotel and we all stood there in tears.

Jacob and his father both sat on the van's bumper.

Without my father, we knew that everything was turning sour and going downhill.

14

Miracle

"What are we going to do now?" Jacob questioned aloud.

"I don't know about you all, but I'm going to see my husband," my mother mentioned as she grabbed her keys from the dresser in our hotel room.

"Well, that's a given." Aunt Madison answered. "All of this other shit is irrelevant."

"That's my fuckin' partner," Uncle Jared spoke gruffly.

"Well, before we jump to conclusions on God's plan," Melanie started, "let's go check on him."

I put on my coat and I heard my father's voice in my head.

"*Miracle.*"

"Papi?" I spoke aloud.

"*Tell your mother that I love her, but she needs to apologize to Julie. I am still alive; well, my soul is… my body, as you could probably tell, is lifeless. I am still living in my body to get better for you all.*"

I walked to the bathroom. Surely, everyone would think I was crazy if they heard me having a conversation with no one.

"*Things are falling apart since I've been shot, but I need for you to step up in my place, at least until I'm better.*"

"Papi, I can't do anything without you by my side," I let out a tear as I whispered.

"*This is NOT the Miracle that I've raised. You are a strong, beautiful, and bright young lady. You can do anything you put your mind to. I haven't raised you to say, 'I can't'.*" My father was speaking to me, and I was listening, but I wished he was physically with me.

"I know, Papi," I answered. "I'm going to try to do it."

"*There is no such thing as 'trying' to do something. Try to open the door,*" he told me. I opened the door. "*No. you opened the door. You didn't try to open the door. I want you to TRY to open the door.*"

This time I thought and I was confused.

"I can't try to open it," I told him.

"*Correct. You can't try to do anything, because it will never get done. It's either going to happen or won't.*"

"I'm sorry, Papi, I will step up in your place and keep you proud."

"*Thank you, baby. Let your mother know that I love her. You know I love you with all of my heart and let everyone else know I love them as well, and I will do my best to protect you all.*"

"Ok, Papi. We are about to come to visit you. Please get better."

"*I will do my best, Miracle,*" my father's voice faded and I slowly exited the bathroom, tears forming in my eyes again.

Everyone else was putting on their coats. I eased over to the dresser, reached inside, and pulled out my father's handgun that we brought up to the room.

I hid it in my coat.

"Is everyone ready to go?" my mother asked as she stood at the door.

"Papi told me to tell you all that he loves you and to remain strong," I spoke and awaited the questions. Surprisingly, none were asked, but tears were shed.

"Let's go," Aunt Madison spoke.

A loud clap of thunder shook the hotel and rain started to pour out of the sky. We all got inside of my mother's vehicle and she drove to the hospital.

"So, I guess you really can hear dead people," Jacob spoke.

"He's not dead," I replied. "He told me."

"So, he's in, like, a coma?" Melanie questioned.

"*No estoy seguro*," I uttered. "I didn't think to ask him where he was, but he said his soul was still in his body."

My mother slowed the car down because the rain was now pouring. Lightning struck the lightning rod of the building ahead of us and my mother applied the brakes.

"I think your father is warning us about something, Miracle," my mother spoke.

"*¿Mande?*" I asked.

"Evil must be ahead," she stated as she tried to make light of the situation.

She drove a little faster and we were soon pulling into the parking lot of the hospital. I slid the gun, without anyone noticing, from out of my coat and stored it under the seat of the car. Everyone got out and we all ran to the hospital.

"Richard Young?" my mother asked the lady at the front desk.

"Your name?"

"Jamie Young, I'm his wife. And this is our daughter, Miracle Young," my mother spoke.

"I'm sorry Mrs. Young, but only two people can go back at a time. You have six people."

"Well, that's okay. My daughter and I will both go back, and once we return, two more people can go."

"Sounds good," the lady mentioned as she wrote out two passes. "Go straight to the back and make a left."

"*Gracias,*" my mother spoke.

We both walked to my father's cubicle in the emergency room. As we were walking, I felt a chill run down my body.

We slowly walked into the room. My father was connected to many monitors and machines to pump fluids into his body. He looked peaceful as he laid there, yet I could tell he was going through more pain than any of us.

"Richard," my mother spoke as she gently touched him.

"No use in even trying, he's in a deep coma," the doctor spoke.

My mother covered her mouth and teared up as she heard the word 'coma'.

"What are his chances of survival?" I asked the doctor.

"I'm not sure," he replied before jotting down some notes.

I looked at what appeared to be my father's lifeless body. A tear formed in my eye and fell on his cheek.

"Doctor, can you make a huge exception for me? I know the rules are two visitors per patient, but I think it's very important for all of us to be in here." My mother was still teary-eyed but was now able to speak.

The doctor looked at us sternly.

"Mrs. Young, I will be willing to make an exception in this case, although it is strongly against hospital rules and regulations. How many more people did you have in your party?"

"Four more," my mother replied.

"I will go and get them from the waiting room."

"*Gracias*," my mother spoke before the doctor left the room.

I grabbed a chair and put it behind my mother.

"Mami, *siéntate*," I spoke.

She sat down and held my father's hand.

The entire room was quiet, except for the heart monitor; with every beep, we were thanking God for keeping him with us. The doctor returned with the other four members before speaking.

"His condition is very good considering he is in a coma," the doctor spoke. "He's still physically living on his own; no breathing tubes, no machines to keep his heart pumping. The bullet entered his chest and penetrated the wall that protects his heart. As it ripped the tissue, the heart responded in a manner that put Mr. Young into a deep coma."

"Doc, do you think he's gonna pull through?" Uncle Jared asked.

"If I had to give a guess, at this moment, I would say yes. His readings are good and his body is functioning on its own."

My mother kissed my father's hand.

"What's the chance that he wouldn't come out of this coma?" Aunt Madison asked as she teared up.

"Honestly, these are tricky situations. It is really hard to say the chances of pulling through a coma. All we can do is pray."

The doctor's pager vibrated and he looked at it.

"If you all would excuse me. I have an important call that has come through."

"Thanks, Doc," Uncle Jared spoke as the doctor exited.

The next few minutes were silent in the room until my mother finally spoke.

"I'm starting to regret that we roughed up Julie."

"She got what was coming to her," Uncle Jared spoke. "You mess with Richard, you mess with all of us."

"I was once told, 'family may turn on you, but it's up to you to not do the same to them'. In the end, all we really have is family; that includes every person in this room right now," my mother included Melanie.

"What are you thinking, Jamie?" Aunt Madison questioned.

"I'm not sure whether we should continue doing these missions or not."

"*Now or never,*" I heard my father's voice tell me.
"Mami," I spoke.

"Yes, Miracle?"

"Papi is speaking to me. He told me to tell you to apologize to Julie and that you have to do the right thing."

She looked at me, then around the room, and finally, her eyes landed on my father.

"It's hard going back to that life, Miracle," my mother stated.

"What life?" I asked.

"Before your father and I met, I was a good girl but with bad morals. I know he's told you about your aunt—."

"Julie," I stated.

"Your Aunt Julie was notorious and very successful in what she did. She controlled most of Chicago, and everyone knew who she was. However, what was more important than what she did, was me. She raised me from the beginning; she raised me to be a good girl, but do *estupideces.*"

"If Aunt Julie cared so much about you, why did she try to kill you?" I asked her.

"Julie wasn't so fond of your mother dating your father," Aunt Madison started. "So, when she found out they were working against her, Julie felt she was in danger, so she had to try to put an end to the threat."

Jacob and Melanie continued to hold hands and they were both looking out of the window, but I could tell they were both listening.

"And the reason we're here now is that Julie, your great-aunt's daughter, wants for us to regain her property for her. Consider it a price for killing her mother," Uncle Jared shook his head as he looked at my father's body.

"So, can someone tell me why she was killed?" I asked.

"We couldn't take it anymore. She tried to kill your father and me, attempted to kidnap you, and raise you as her own. Your father did what he had to do to save his family." My mother looked at my father. "He's always done that. My hero and protector," she started to cry some more and grabbed a tissue. "That's why your name is Miracle. You were literally, our miracle baby. You were a month early and I was under so much stress during my pregnancy with you."

"So, we're here because some *puta*, excuse my French, wants revenge for her mother's death?" Melanie asked. It was clear that she was getting irritated.

"Ultimately, yes. That is why we're here."

"*Es stupido*" Melanie added.

"*Pero*, the question *ultima* is, do we continue to do these jobs for Julie? With Richard being in a coma, it'll be harder," my mother held my father's hand tighter. "Plus, you can count me out because I'm going to be by my husband's side."

"I think we should continue to do the jobs, for the sake of all of us. Right now, since we don't have Richard, we're left with two men to fight for us: Jacob and Jared. Now, while my men are extremely talented and gifted, it's not the same as having Rich as an addition to stand against Julie." Aunt Madison sounded worried, yet confident.

"So, this narrows it down to five of us doing the missions. I can tell it will only get harder," Jacob stated.

"Who knows what could be next." I shuddered.

***

As we drove back to the hotel from the hospital, I slid the gun back under my coat. I honestly couldn't stand the thought of my father being in a coma; he appeared lifeless, yet I knew he was still alive.

My mother drove to the front of the hotel and we all exited the vehicle; the valet guy drove the car away.

"Now, to find Julie," my mother led us into the hotel and the casino.

"Where's Julie Wilson?" Jacob shouted and everyone looked at us.

Murmurs instantly started to circulate.

"That's them."

"They're the ones who fought Ms. Wilson."

"I heard Joey got his ass, whooped!"

We walked to the back and Joey walked up to us. His lip was red.

"May I help you all?" he asked, still angry.

"We're here to see Julie," my mother spoke.

I remembered I had the gun on me and I knew he was going to search me. I quickly ran to the elevator.

"Miracle, *¿adónde vas?*" my mother shouted.

"*Me vuelvo*," I replied.

My mind was all over the place as I put the gun back in the hotel room.

As I opened the door to leave the room, Quincy was standing there.

"I heard the bad news, Miracle," Quincy spoke, sounding sympathetic.

He reached his arms out for a hug.

I hugged him back and a few tears left my eyes.

"It'll be okay, Miracle. God works miracles every single day. Your father will pull through for you and your family."

"It's just hard to even think of him in that state."

"I know, Miracle. But let's put it in His hands."

He kissed me on my forehead and continued to hug me.

"Where are you rushing off to?" he asked.

"I'm going back downstairs to my family," I spoke.

"You're just coming from the hospital?"

"Yes. My father's still in a coma, *pero* my mother is going to stay with him."

Quincy didn't speak for a few seconds and touched his scruffy chin hair.

"What did the doctors say?" He asked as I closed the door to the room. I put the key card in my back pocket.

"The doctor wasn't too sure if my father was going to make it. Comas are tricky things."

"It will all work out," Quincy assured me before putting his arm around me. He kissed me on the forehead, again.

We walked into the elevator and I pushed to button for the lobby.

As the elevator descended, Q turned on his iPod and hugged me from behind; I could hear 'The Finer Things' by B. Smoove playing through his headphones.

"*¿Realmente te gusta* Smoove, huh?"

He chuckled and kissed my cheek. "This dude is the shiznit."

"*Me gusta* Kai-G. I really feel he's been through a little more than Smoove, and so has more of a story to tell."

"I respect that," Quincy chuckled as he put a hand in my hair.

The door to the elevator opened and Quincy released his hug from behind me. He walked beside me towards my mother. She was now speaking to Julie.

"Julie, I've done some thinking and I want to apologize for what happened earlier."

"You know, Jamie, apologies typically are not valid for me.... But considering that you are family, I will make this exception."

"And in addition to the apology," my mother hesitated, "we will continue doing the jobs for you."

"Excellent," Julie spoke.

She walked to the back table. Joey motioned for us to follow her.

"Now look," she turned around and sat down. "I am truly sorry about what happened to Richard," she spoke as the waitress brought her a cigar. "But no matter how sorry I feel, I cannot change what happened. From here on out, we need to have a better plan going into these missions. Some are much easier than this, and some will be much harder. This next mission, for example, is harder; well, it can be, depending on how you do the job," Julie chuckled. "You will be destroying my vehicles at a gang hangout."

"Gangs?" I asked.

"Yes, Miracle, gangs. 5 letter word, the plural form of 'gang'," Julie spoke.

I stared at her and rolled my eyes.

"Just know that there may be a shootout and the five of you will be shooting against multiple gang members. I will be sending you all to my seller; he's going to hook you all up with a few weapons and armor to protect yourselves."

"Why the hell are we going to destroy cars?" Aunt Madison asked.

"They've been doing some illegal shit in those cars," Julie inhaled and exhaled on her cigar. "Do you really think I will have much of a use for them?"

"So, why are we even dealing with them?" Uncle Jared asked.

"Insurance can do a hell of a job." Julie blew another cloud of smoke.

"You must practice that," Jacob spoke after Julie she blew the circle of smoke.

She chuckled.

"I need to have a report that they've been destroyed by tomorrow night. Once you arrive at the hangout spot and you destroy the cars, you will be on the run from the gang members, if they spot you."

"So, no preparation. You're just throwing us into another suicidal mission… after my father ended up in a coma after today's mission?"

"I can't change what happened. I wish I could, but I can't. Preparation is key, and so I'm giving you all until tomorrow evening to have my shit back. Quincy will travel with you all and will direct you all to my seller for the weapons and armor."

"Don't fuck this up," Joey stated in a gruff tone.

We each looked at each other.

"What are you all thinking?" Julie asked.

"It's just a very high risk, Julie," Aunt Madison spoke.

"I'm fully aware of this. You will be suited and ready for the mission as the time approaches."

"So, we have until tomorrow evening to be damn near killed?" Jacob asked.

"Jacob!" Uncle Jared spoke.

"Quincy will take you all to my guy to get everything." Julie took another puff of her cigar. "Quincy, take them up there in the van. My colleague, Veronica, will be riding with him." Julie put her cigar on the tray and walked away.

"Come on, everyone," Quincy spoke as he walked towards the exit. '

We all walked in silence until we got outside.

"This is just stupid. Something bad is going to happen," Melanie spoke as we reached the van.

"I wish there was something I could do," Quincy spoke, "but all I can do is follow her orders. I can reduce the risk by doing a little planning of my own, but ultimately, it's in her hands."

I was the last one to enter the van and Quincy put his hand on my back.

"I'll make sure all of you are safe," he whispered to me.

I entered the vehicle and Quincy closed the door.

Veronica was sitting in the back of the van.

My mother spoke in a whisper as Quincy started the van and drove off.

"I thought you were here to help us," my mother asked.

"Jamie, I am here for you. It hurt me more than anything when I found out that Richard was severely injured."

"So, how could you let it happen?" Aunt Madison asked.

"Julie had me working on a programming job for her. Richard wasn't even supposed to arrive at the home."

"I guess it's a learning experience for all of us," Jacob added.

"It's the slightest thought that we could lose him forever," I stated as I held my head low.

"Veronica, if you want my trust, you need to promise me one thing, and one thing only." My mother cleared her throat.

"What do you need for me to promise you to gain your trust?"

I looked around the van and observed how we were sitting. It was similar to the back of a paddy wagon.

"Miracle *es mi todo*," she began. "Other than Richard, she's all I have…"

"You have us," Aunt Madison spoke.

"You all are family, but you can't compare to Richard and Miracle; you all know that," my mother responded. She redirected her focus to Veronica, "protect her from all harm. I don't need to hear that something has happened to my flesh and blood."

Veronica extended her hand to my mother.

My mother denied her handshake and embraced Veronica.

"I promise," Veronica spoke.

My mother slowly sat back in her seat and I put in my earphones for the remainder of the ride.

***

As we pulled up to Julie's weapons supplier, Veronica spoke in a low tone as we stepped outside the truck.

"Control what you say as we get inside. This guy is extremely dangerous and keeps a very low profile. If he even suspects that law enforcement has entered, he will shut it all down and it puts all of us in jeopardy."

She paused and looked at Jacob.

"This means you, Jacob. Do not enter the store being tough with him."

"I'll control him," Melanie spoke as she held Jacob's hand.

"I'll behave," Jacob replied to Veronica.

"Alright, everyone, let's set some ground rules," Quincy spoke as he walked in front of us. "The guy in here, his name is Xino. He carries heavy artillery and military-grade weapons and protection kits. If you so much as to look suspicious to him, that's your life. Why do you think he's camped out here in the middle of nowhere?"

"Maybe no one likes him," Uncle Jared spoke and he tried to lighten the situation.

We all chuckled at the joke.

"Nah, he likes to remain under the radar. This way, if something goes down, it can't and won't be traced back to him. Let me do all the talking because he is familiar with me. I can talk us into getting some very good items. Do not reach for a gun, keep your hands out of your pockets, stay off your phones, and stay vigilant!" Quincy warned us before turning around and walking to the entrance.

He walked through the double doors, and the first thing audible was loud rock music.

"Xino," Quincy stated as he shook the man's hand.

"Q, my man, what's going on?" Xino turned down the music.

"Chillin'. Julie wanted me to bring these people down for a few pieces and some protection. Something's gonna go down tomorrow and they have to be well equipped."

Xino walked up to us.

"What's the deal? You bitches look like cops," he smelled of liquor and his sleeveless shirt revealed his numerous tattoos.

"On the contrary," Quincy spoke, "They're clean. Julie performs inspections. Plus, do you think Julie would allow them to work for her if they were dirty?"

My body shook a little as I looked at Xino. I was not receiving a positive vibe from him.

"Yeah, you're right. With these pretty ass lips, there's no way she's dirty." He walked closer to my mother. "Unless she's dirty in another way," he touched her chin.

"I'm married," my mother stated as she gently moved his hand and raised her left hand to display the wedding ring and band.

"That's cool. I like married women. It makes the relationship easier," he spoke as he put his hand on the wall.

"With all due respect, I think you should take two steps away from her," Uncle Jared spoke.

"Are you her husband?" Xino asked.

"No, he's *my* husband," Aunt Madison spoke.

Xino took steps towards my uncle.

"So, how are you going to tell me what to do with this woman?"

"Because her husband is my brother," Uncle Jared retorted.

"That's my problem?" Xino questioned.

"Xino, we really need to keep it moving and get the stuff. Shit goes down tomorrow and they still need to prep," Quincy spoke calmly as he could see the tension was rising.

Xino looked back at Quincy and returned his focus to my mother. He smirked and walked away.

"So, what's the focus?" he asked Quincy. "Looking for manuals, automatics, semi-automatics, handguns; let me know."

"It's gonna vary per person. You know me, I'm an automatic guy, so you can give me a Micro-Uzi with the extended clip."

Xino passed Quincy the weapon from under the counter. He walked from behind the counter with a shotgun in one hand, and a pistol in the other. He walked up to me, and fear filled my body.

"Hold this," he stated as he passed me the pistol. I took it from him, and he watched the way I held the gun. "Aim it at Quincy. It's not real, I'm trying to fit you for a weapon."

Quincy stood against the wall. I aimed the replica at him.

"Begin moving around, Quincy. Follow him with the gun," Xino spoke to me as he watched me handle the gun. "Yeah, you're definitely a 'handgun' kind of girl. Would you prefer an automatic?"

"Um," I didn't understand nor have a preference.

"Hook her up with an automatic," Quincy spoke.

Xino passed me an Uzi with an extended clip.

"Think you can handle that?"

I shrugged as I held the gun.

"Give me two pistols," Uncle Jared spoke. "Two automatic pistols are all I need with extra clips."

"A man who knows what he wants. My nigga," Xino stated as he passed Uncle Jared the pistols.

Xino walked up to my mother, Aunt Madison, and Melanie.

"Have you all ever even held a gun?" he asked.

The three looked at him.

"Wanna find out?" my mother asked with a sarcastic smile

"And you're a feisty woman. I like. I'm gonna hook you up with this baby, right here." He handed my mother an SIG Pro handgun.

Xino looked at Melanie.

"You don't even look like a 'gun' kind of girl. Something about you is telling me that you're sassy."

"And classy.... Never trashy," Melanie added.

"I'm gonna hook you up with this police-grade handgun, but I'm going to give you more tactical supplies. Grenades, flash-bangs, etc."

He walked behind the counter and pulled out an empty duffle bag.

"I'm putting your stuff in here," he told Melanie. "The rest of you all, make sure your guns have the safety on and place them in here."

He left the bag on the counter and walked out with a shotgun. He handed it to Jacob.

"My man, you think you can handle this?"

Jacob held the shotgun and aimed it. He looked through the scope.

"Be careful though, it's got a little bite to it," he warned Jacob as he walked back towards the counter.

"I got this," Jacob retorted.

"Miss Lady, do you have a preference?" he asked Aunt Madison.

"Something that won't get me killed," she spoke.

"That depends on how you can shoot. Tell me, what your strengths are." He flipped through a catalog.

"Well, I'm fast and stealthy." Aunt Madison looked at Xino.

"All I needed to hear was stealthy…. I'm gonna set you up with a sniper."

"We gotta travel light," Quincy spoke. "A big, heavy sniper will slow us down tomorrow… there will be a lot of movement."

"Well, I've already decided I won't be doing tomorrow's job. I'm going to spend the day at the hospital. So, Madison can handle my handgun."

"Then it's all settled. Everyone has guns, now we just gotta get you all some armor and ammo."

Xino walked from behind the counter with a vest. He walked up to me.

"Try this on," he spoke to me. I was a bit confused at how to put on the vest, considering I'd never put on one.

"How does this go?" I asked.

"Here, put your arms towards me; I'll help you get it on your body." Xino walked towards me.

"Negative," Uncle Jared spoke. "I'll help her put it on." Uncle Jared walked towards me and held the vest. He put it over my head and I immediately felt the weight of it. He tightened the two side straps.

"Perfect fit," Xino spoke. "Throw this in the bag."

He tossed the vest in the bag, and fitted everyone else, before putting the extra ammo into the bag. He also put earpieces in the bag for easy communication during the mission

"Iight, Q, now if y'all get caught…"

"I'm already knowing." Quincy grabbed the bag.

"Good luck tomorrow," Xino added. "And, uh, Ms. Fiesty…"

My mother turned and looked at Xino.

"I'll be looking out for you." He smirked, licked his bottom lip, and my mother walked off.

15

Miracle

As we reached the van, Quincy opened the back door for us, and we got inside.

"Tomorrow is going to be crazy," Uncle Jared spoke.

"Whatever you all do, please be careful." My mother spoke.

Veronica had been silent for most of the trip and was finally speaking again.

"Jamie, I will watch over Miracle and everyone for the next mission."

I could tell Veronica was trying her hardest to earn my mother's trust.

"Whatever Julie may have me working on, I'll let her know that I want in on the mission."

"Thank you, Veronica, but I don't want you to put yourself at risk."

"It's the least I could do," she added. "I promised to look over you all, so that's what I will do. But I do have something to tell you," she whispered.

"¿*Qué es?*" my mother asked.

"My brother is on his way down here."

My mother let out a sigh.

"He can't come down here," Uncle Jared spoke. "If he does, all of our lives are over."

Everyone spoke in a tone so that Quincy couldn't hear.

"Well, what am I supposed to do?" Veronica whispered.

"Tell him not to come," Aunt Madison spoke.

"He's boarding the plane as we speak."

A sense of hopelessness fell upon us.

"He's aware of the situation and has agreed to not show any signs of him being law enforcement so that Julie won't have any suspicions."

"This is all becoming a bit much," my mother spoke.

"Hopefully, it will all be over soon," Veronica added.

I put in my earphones, and the rest of the trip to the hotel was silent to me; I couldn't hear anything but my music.

***

The next afternoon, everyone was frantic and scrambling, including my mother, although she wasn't going to partake in the mission.

"Will we be under the fucking radar?" Julie shouted on her phone. "Look, I don't give a damn what strings you have to pull. I'm paying you big money for this, so I don't want a sign of a cop there, you hear me?"

She hung up the phone and walked over to us.

"We may have run into a tiny problem," she began.

"What kind of problem and how tiny?" Uncle Jared asked.

"We are currently not going to be under the radar. Cops could be all over your asses."

"What the fuck?" Uncle Jared asked. "You can't possibly want us to continue with this."

"Yeah, Julie, this is risking more than just our lives," Aunt Madison began.

"I know, I know. Well, I was just talking to a guy who's a hacker, and he's supposed to be hacking into the servers and putting us under the radar. However, he currently has not done it yet."

"So, what are we to do?" Jacob asked.

"We follow the plan. You all have to figure out how to execute everything, but I'll give you a run-down." Julie pulled out a map of the area. "Can someone bring me a Cuban?" she asked.

One of her security guards brought her a cigar. She put it in her mouth and he lit it.

Veronica approached us.

"Why, it's my lovely assistant, Veronica." Julie seemed delighted to see her.

"Permission to tag along on today's mission?" She asked Julie.

My mother seemed a little relieved that Veronica had arrived.

Julie looked at Veronica.

"Permission granted," she stated, seconds later.

Veronica took a seat next to my mother.

"When you all get to the area, I can't say if the gang members will be visible or not, but Joey is there and called me a few moments ago. All of the cars are in the lot."

Veronica took a seat next to my mother.

"Remote explosives will be of good use, during this mission. This way, you can plant them on the cars and detonate them from a safe distance."

"So, what was the point in getting all this heat?" Melanie asked.

"Because once you blow up the cars, or before you do, you all may be in a war against the gang members."

I could see Aunt Madison and Melanie fill with fear.

"You would think we were past all of these gangs, wars, violence," Uncle Jared spoke. "It's a sign of the times."

"I'll be the first to admit, our generation is screwed up," Jacob replied.

Quincy walked through the door with the bag of weapons, armor, and ammunition.

"Obviously, we cannot pull the guns out here, but you can each head to the washroom and put on the armor underneath your shirts." Quincy passed each of us a vest. "Once you all get them on, we will take Jamie to the hospital and drive to the lot where the cars are being held."

As everyone, except for my mother, Julie, and Quincy, walked away, Julie spoke.

"You're going to the hospital, Jamie?"

"Yes. I'm spending the day with my husband. Maybe, I'll pray for a miracle to happen."

"You are very lucky that we do not need you to help out with the mission... Or else, I wouldn't permit it," Julie added authority to her statement.

"My husband is in the hospital. A little sympathy would be appreciated," my mother replied with an attitude.

Julie's cellphone rang and she quickly answered.

"Talk to me." She was hoping that she would get good news. "Really?"

My mother stared at Julie in disgust.

"Fuck. Okay. No, it's chill. Alright. Hey, look, I'm going to have to pull back on a cut of your pay. I knew you'd understand, bye." Julie hung up the phone and we each came back to the front.

"*Que pasa?*" my mother asked.
"We got bad news. Cops may also be on your asses after this. Q, go remove the license plate and tags from the van."

Quincy walked away and Julie shook her head.

"Shit!"

"So," I began to speak, "no longer are we only worried about being murdered today, but we also have to worry about being thrown in jail for life."

"Sounds like bullshit to me," Uncle Jared spoke.

"It's too late to pull back. All I can ask is that you all are stealthy with this mission."

It was apparent that Julie wasn't going to change her mind about the mission, although there was a high risk for us.

Quincy walked back inside, moments later. "Plates and tags are off the van."

"Great. Alright, I'm wishing you all the best and praying for a safe return. I'll call my guy and see if he can touch into the system to at least assist you all with this."

Quincy hugged Julie and we all went outside to the van. Before climbing in, we each got our guns and put the ammunition inside the pockets on the vest. Once we each held our guns, we got in the back of the van. Quincy got in the front seat and drove to the hospital.

We were all silent. Even once we arrived at the hospital, my mother exited without saying a word. She gave everyone hugs and kisses on the cheek but left without uttering a word.

She disappeared into the building, and Quincy drove off.

"So…" I stated, attempting to break the silence and start a conversation.

"Shit's about to get real," Uncle Jared spoke as he held his guns.

"I've learned not to stress so much over it," Veronica stated. "When you stress, things only get worse."

"It's already bad. And we may have the entire police force of the D.R. on our asses once we leave," Aunt Madison reminded us. "Can't your brother do anything about this?" she lowered her tone.

"He's at the hospital with Richard and Jamie. Plus, if we all want to keep surviving, he isn't even supposed to present the image of a cop. Here, no one knows his face or name. He doesn't have any representation that shows he's a cop," Veronica spoke. "Well, I'm sure he has his badge and weapon, but it's all secured and hidden."

"Yeah, it would be extremely hard to escape if Julie suspected anything. She controls everything; the air, the sea, land… there wouldn't be anywhere to run or hide," Jacob answered.

Quincy pulled near the lot.

"This is it, guys," he spoke as I got out of the van, followed by Melanie and Jacob. Veronica, Uncle Jared, and Aunt Madison waited behind in the van.

"It's cold as shit," Jacob spoke as we walked towards the cars and placed one of the remote detonators between two of them. "Julie owes us for this."

"Yeah, right. You really think she would pay us for this?" Melanie asked as she placed the explosive near a car on the opposite end.

A man approached the lot.

"Uh, guys, we have a man approaching us," I stated as he came closer and spoke.

"Can I help you all with anything?" he asked as he stared at us.

"This is not good," Quincy spoke through the headset; he had driven the van around the corner.

"Hell no, it's not," Uncle Jared stated.

"We wait," Quincy spoke.

"Like hell we do," Veronica stated as she opened the van's door.

"Veronica, where are you going?" Aunt Madison asked.

"I promised Jamie I would look after Miracle. She already has one family member in the hospital… I won't let that happen with Miracle," Veronica closed the van's door.

The man stepped closer to us and flashed his gun that was in his pants.

"Can I help you bitches with anything?" he asked louder.

"We're just over here checking out these cars," Jacob spoke. "We're trying to buy a new one, so we're trying to see what's out here."

"This ain't no damn dealership," he spoke as he saw the remote to detonate the explosives in my hand.

I heard Quincy through my headset. "Okay, Julie, it's about to go down."

The man quickly drew his gun and aimed it at us.

He prepared to shoot.

"What the fuck are you all doing over here?" He aimed his AK-47 at us.

Veronica aimed her gun from the top of the office building on the corner and shot a bullet at the man; killing him with the sniper.

We quickly ducked and Melanie grabbed the AK-47. Other gang members quickly ran out with their guns aimed and began shooting. Jacob, Melanie, and I quickly got behind different vehicles.

"Miracle," Jacob shouted as a guy crept up behind me.

In an instant, Jacob shot the shotgun and the bullet struck the man in the chest. I ran over to Jacob's car.

"Miracle you gotta constantly watch your back," he spoke. "This is the real deal."

My heart was racing; maybe even more than when Quincy and I were stealing the cars.

"On the count of three?" I asked Jacob as we were both squatted behind the car.

"Pass me the AK that the man held," he asked as he nodded towards the guy he had shot.

I reached over to the dead man and grabbed the gun; I passed it to Jacob.

"One," I stated.

"Two," he replied.

"Three," We both blind-fired at the men.

"Miracle!" Melanie shouted through the earpiece.

I turned my head and looked ahead of us. A grenade lied about 30 feet ahead of us. I quickly pulled Jacob close to me, and the grenade exploded.

Jacob and I were both blown back by the impact of the blast, and I couldn't move my body.

I laid beside Jacob and I saw some gang members running over to us with their guns aimed.

"Jacob," I stated out of fear; our lives were about to be over.

As they got closer, they were halted by bullets flying through their bodies, and they immediately fell to the ground. I looked up and saw Uncle Jared and Aunt Madison shooting at the gang members. They both reached out a hand to help Jacob and me.

They held us on their shoulders and walked us towards the van, but they were still firing shots.

"We can't leave Melanie," I stated as I tried to stand on my own; my legs would not permit it.

"We're taking you all to the truck," my aunt insisted. "You all cannot proceed like this."

"We'll go back for Melanie," my uncle spoke to me. "We cannot have anything happen to any of you."

Quincy opened the door to the van, and they put Jacob and me in the back.

They closed the door and walked back to Melanie.

"Jacob," I started.

"Yes, Miracle?" he asked.

He had been silent the entire walk back to the van.

"I don't know what I would have done if you had been killed a moment ago. You're my rock; always there and looking out for me."

"I would have been killed if it wasn't for you." Jacob looked at me as he held his hands over his stomach."

"*Mande?*" I asked.

"If you hadn't pulled me closer to you, that grenade could have killed me. Because of you, I'm experiencing a few scratches and bruises. Nothing more."

"*¿Sabes qué?* I think it's my father looking out for us," I stated.

Quincy got in the back of the van.

"Miracle, let me look at you." He shook his head in disappointment. "I'm sorry."

"You didn't do anything. Why are you apologizing?"

"Because I wasn't there."

"*¿Sabes qué?* You can't control the dumb shit your aunt has us doing."

"Yeah, but I could have at least been there to pop them fools."

"You've done enough," I told him with a kiss on the cheek.

Jacob reached his hand out and shook Quincy's hand.

"I may not like you," Jacob started, "but I have to respect a guy who cares so much about this lady. Watch her back."

"No doubt. Much respect."

The back door to the van opened and Veronica was the first to get inside; Aunt Madison, Uncle Jared, and Melanie followed her. They were all rushing to get inside.

"Quincy, get us out of here!" my uncle shouted. Quincy climbed in the front and started the van.

Melanie pulled out the remote and quickly detonated the explosives. The explosives exploded, as did the cars.

Quincy pressed his foot down completely on the accelerator as gang members got in their vehicles and chased us.

Uncle Jared picked up the AK-47 and aimed it at the window. Veronica picked up the sniper and Melanie grabbed the pistols.

"Fire at will," my uncle shouted as he shot the gun at the cars behind us.

"Y'all hold on, we're coming to a wide turn," Quincy stated as he came to a wide turn.

The van drove on 2 tires as Quincy took the turn, but returned two four as he completed. I reached out and held Jacob's hand.

"The tires, get their tires," Uncle Jared yelled.

"I'm trying," Melanie shouted back as one of her bullets shot through the gang member's car and hit the driver.

Their car swerved off the road and into the ocean.

Quincy sounded his horn to alert pedestrians and other drivers to clear the path; very few drivers switched lanes.

Melanie grabbed the few explosives she had left.

"I only have three more and there are four of their cars. I cannot afford to miss," Melanie thought aloud; something she tended to do when she would become anxious about something that was going to happen.

"Mr. Hubbard, I need for you all to break these windows completely," Melanie mentioned as she prepared to throw the bombs.

Uncle Jared and Veronica both smashed the windows with the ends of their weapons. My aunt continued to keep her head low and cover Jacob and me.

Melanie looked out of the completely smashed windows and threw an explosive; it landed and stuck on the hood.

Melanie grabbed another explosive and prepared to throw it. Quincy drove over a bump and made her throw the device onto the road, missing the vehicles.

"Fuck," she cursed. "I'm sorry," she apologized to my aunt and uncle.

"Do you have another explosive?" My uncle asked.

"I have one more. When we hit the bump, the other one flew out of my hand."

"Oh shit," My uncle stated.

"What now?" Aunt Madison asked.

"We have to blow up the one that stuck to the car," my uncle improvised.

"What we have to do is time it correctly. When they're beside one another, Melanie I want you to trigger the explosives," Uncle Jared was confident in his decision. "Madison, Veronica, you all get down by Miracle and Jared."

As Veronica and Aunt Madison got down beside us, my uncle yelled to Quincy.

"Q, take us to the expressway. I need for you to punch this shit to the max."

"I got you," Quincy spoke as he accelerated.

"Alright, Melanie. You've always wanted to shine; here's your chance," Uncle Jared stated as he and Melanie continued to watch the gang members trail us.

Quincy sped faster in the direction of the expressway and Melanie began to sweat.

"Don't get nervous," my uncle spoke to Melanie.

"What if I press it at the wrong time?"

"You won't. Let's just focus. Once he gets us to the expressway, you will blow them all up."

The gang members shot at the van and shot the back tires out.

"Damn it!" Quincy shouted. "We're on 2 flats. Plan B," he spoke as the truck rumbled.

"What the hell is 'Plan B'?" Uncle Jared asked as he crawled towards the front of the van.

"We're not going to make it to the expressway. There's a river coming up. We're going to have to ditch the truck and blow it up before we hit the water."

"This is some crazy shit," Aunt Madison answered. "So, you want us to jump out of a moving vehicle?"

"Unless you all have a better idea, yes," Quincy spoke.

I gained the strength to sit up; Jacob did as well.

"We have about half-a-mile to go before we reach the river. The unfortunate part, it is half-a-mile from the police station. So, if we're going to do this, we do this right," Quincy wedged down the gas pedal and rigged the steering wheel before putting his belongings in his pocket. He opened the side door to the truck.

"Melanie, use that last explosive," my uncle spoke. "Attach it to the van," he uttered.

"Okay," Melanie followed his directions.

"We all jump at the same time, and as soon as we jump, we blow up the vehicles. Let's not even give them a chance to pursue us any further."

"I'm on board with it," Jacob stated.

I could see he was regaining his strength.

"The van is going about sixty-five miles-an-hour right now, so it will not be an easy landing, but we have to do it," Quincy stood in the doorway.

The gang members continued to shoot at the vehicle and we noticed we were approaching the river.

"You all ready?" Quincy asked.

"Just call it," Uncle Jared shouted.

"3" he shouted. We all jumped from the van in the direction of the river.

The gang members sped up to ram the van and cause it to spin out to prevent us from jumping.

Melanie triggered the explosives as she jumped.

The cars and the van exploded, and we each landed on the grass; a few feet away from the river.

"Shit," Quincy stated as he got up, slightly upset that we didn't reach the water, but happy we survived.

The water would have made the landing more tolerable.

"Let's be glad there aren't any cars around to see this explosion." Uncle Jared stated as he stood up. "Is everyone okay?" he asked as he helped Aunt Madison stand.

"Just a little shaken up; a few cuts and bruises," Aunt Madison replied, "but still living."

"We better get the hell out of here," Quincy spoke. "Before anyone shows up and notices this mess," he helped me up.

Jacob rose to his feet and helped Melanie and me stand, followed by Veronica.

"There go the weapons," Jacob joked.

"Cool," Quincy chuckled. "At least we don't have to worry about destroying the evidence."

I lowered my head and we started to walk.

***

"*And, it keeps getting worse. Crime in our beloved country seems to be getting worse and worse as the days go by. A few weeks ago, we reported a heist that involved the robbery of three vehicles and a police chase that left half of the city, in shock.*"

As we arrived back at the hotel, Julie was watching the news.

"I can't believe we just walked all the way back here," I complained.

"Put a smile on, M," Uncle Jared spoke.

I smiled sarcastically.

"When the pain leaves, you'll get a real smile," I spoke in a low tone.

"*And as the crime gets worse, the police are upping their arsenal to keep the city safe. However, with the latest crime, officers are at a standstill in developing a motive or suspect list.*"

Julie turned and notice us in the hotel lobby. She whispered to Joey and he walked over to us.

"*It has the city shaken up, as investigators try to find out what occurred that left many civilians murdered and many vehicles destroyed.*"

The newscast switched to a witness and Julie spoke to us.

"You all are safe," she stated as she hugged Quincy.

"Yes, we're fine, Auntie. We had to ditch the van."

"What do you mean?"

"We had to fucking jump from it towards the river, which we missed," Melanie shouted.

"Watch your mouth, young lady," Aunt Madison spoke.

"The news is covering everything," Julie spoke as she faced the television.

"*It has the community wondering 'why?'. Police are finding empty bullet casings and they appear to follow a trail. They will see where they lead, but so far, they have no leads or tips, with the exception that they believe this to be gang-related. Reporting live from Santo Domingo, I'm Julia Rodriguez.*"

"Everyone has everything, correct?" Quincy asked.

We each reached in our pockets.

"Everything is good," Jacob stated.

"We're going to lay low," Quincy spoke. "The heat is extremely hot right now, and we have to let things cool down a bit."

"Well, we're going to head to the hospital to visit Richard," Uncle Jared reached in his pocket, felt the gun, and removed his hand from his pocket.

"You all are dismissed," Julie spoke.

We walked towards the elevator.

"My back is killing me," Uncle Jared spoke as we all walked onto the elevator.

"Maybe Julie knows a nice masseuse to rub you down," Aunt Madison joked.

"Things are escalating very quickly," Jacob mentioned; "it's not long before one of us ends up dead."

"Don't speak like that," Melanie told him.

She looked at me and noticed I was crying.

"You haven't said much of a word since we've been back," Aunt Madison spoke. "Why are you crying?"

"My father... I'm worried, honestly. I can't help but think something bad is headed our way... Something worse," I silently cried.

"Don't cry," Jacob stated. "We're all right here and everything will be fine."

"I hope so."

16

-Richard

I slowly opened my eyes; I heard footsteps near me. I turned my head slightly and saw Jamie. My entire body was weak, and I could barely move my arms, but I was alive.

"Well, I just have it in the event that Young wakes up, today."
I could hear Abel's voice, and I wondered why he was here in the Dominican Republic.
"And these are tapes of...?" Jamie asked as she held my hand.
"Richard's been working with us for a long time," he spoke. "This is a DVD containing evidence of a case that we've been working on for years. It needs to be reviewed."
Jamie released my hand and picked up the DVD.
"What is the review for?" she asked.

"Jamie, I hate to be the one to tell you this, but a case that Richard's been working on for years was closed, and it's just re-opened. We need to go through the DVD and review the evidence."

Jamie held my hand again and I tightened my grip on her hold. She looked up at me; she was shocked to see that I was looking at her.

"He's awake," she spoke as she moved closer to my face.

Abel walked over to me.

Jamie let out a tear and kissed me on the cheek.

"Richard," Abel spoke.

I tried to speak, but the words would not come out. Jamie called for the nurse and Abel continued to speak.

"Can you sit up?" he asked. "Blink once for yes, twice for no, and three times for maybe."

I blinked three times.

"Jamie, let's try to sit Richard up," he spoke. "You hold his upper body up, and I'm going to raise the head of the bed."

Jamie reached and pulled my upper body close to her and he raised the upper portion of the bed.

Jamie placed my body back on the bed and the nurse came into the room.

"Someone's awake," she stated. "How are you feeling?" she asked.

I tried to speak, but I couldn't.

"He can't speak, yet," Abel spoke. "I've been having him blink to tell me 'yes', 'no', or 'maybe'."

The nurse wrote down some notes on her clipboard.

"Sir, who are you?" she asked him.

"Abel Roberts," he spoke.

She wrote on the clipboard again.

"We may need a therapist to come in," she spoke.

"Do you need a therapist?" Jamie asked me.

I blinked twice.

"That won't be necessary," Roberts spoke.

"Sir, I'm sorry, but I'm a highly trained nurse, and you're just a civilian. If we don't have a therapist, how will he be able to fend and learn?"

Abel sighed and spoke in a low tone.

"Officer Abel Roberts, Chicago Police Department." He pulled his badge out of his pocket. "I can request a therapist to come over for Richard Young," he spoke. "My unit will pay for it," he spoke.

The nurse put the clipboard on the table and approached me.

"I'm going to take your vitals, Mr. Young," she spoke as she put the stethoscope to my chest and listened.

Abel made a call on his phone and Jamie sent out a text, letting everyone know I had awoken from the coma.

"You're quite the soldier, huh?" the nurse asked as she wrote down my blood pressure on the clipboard.

I looked at her but didn't show any emotion. I reached for the pen and paper she held.

"You want the pen?" she asked.

I tried to speak again.

"Yes," I spoke in a raspy whisper.

She passed me the pen and paper.

'How long was I in a coma?' I wrote.

"Well, Mr. Young, you've been in a coma for about four months." The nurse answered.

"Babe, everyone's on their way up: Jared, Madison, Jacob, Melanie, and Miracle."

'What about Julie?' I wrote. 'Doesn't she have them doing anything?'

The nurse saw that I wrote Julie's name.

"Miracle said that they were free today. Julie isn't coming by," Jamie walked next to me and held my hand.

"Julie... As in, Julie Wilson?" the nurse dropped the clipboard.

"What's wrong, Miss?" Abel asked.

"Oh my God," the nurse became weak in her legs.

He grabbed her and held her up.

"Let's have a seat," Abel spoke.

"She's always around," the nurse spoke.

"How do you know her?" Abel asked, curious about her comment.

"I just got out of a three-year contract with Miss Wilson. About six years ago, this hospital was tried for malpractice against a few hundred patients."

"How was Julie associated with this?" Jamie asked.

"Some of the hospital staff members were pointing fingers in my direction since I was the manager," the nurse spoke as she slightly rocked back and forth. "They claimed that I called for certain procedures to be done. Anyway," the nurse sat up, "I had to find an attorney to represent me and prove that I was innocent. And I found Julie. She said she didn't need payment. Instead, I could work off my debt if she won the case," the nurse shook her head. "She had the case dismissed, I got to keep my medical degree, and had to work for her.

The worst three years of my life; she had me doing things that could get me killed. Not necessarily illegal, but dangerous," the nurse spoke.

I closed my eyes.
"Richard," Jamie spoke as she touched me.
'Resting my eyes', I wrote.
She kissed me on the cheek.

"I'm sorry, but I must go now. The patient up the hall has a bad case of laryngitis," the nurse rose from the chair as she picked up the clipboard.
Abel rose to his feet.
"Let's not mention any of this to Julie," he spoke.
"You don't have to worry about me saying a word. I don't even want to ever see Julie again."
The nurse walked out of the room.

"I guess Julie's gotten around," Jamie spoke.
"Maybe a little too much," he responded.
Jamie held my hand tightly.
'What's this?' I wrote on the pad as I referred to the disc.
"Young, you know the case you'd been working on?" he asked. "The one where about thirty people were killed in Millennium Park and the case closed because no evidence connected any suspects to the crime?"
I sat up in the bed.
"The suspect has since been on the move: Chicago, New York, Philadelphia, Puerto Rico, and the Dominican Republic."
I thought for a moment.
'Julie?' I wrote.
"It fits," he responded. "We have to review this tape of the pieces of evidence and we'll have to go back to Chicago for a few days."
"Do you think it may have just been her mom?" Jamie questioned.
"Her mother may have started it, but this woman finished it. The case was closed about 7 years ago… her mother was dead by then."
Officer Roberts put the DVD in the player and pressed play on the remote.
■■

-Miracle

Over the next few days, my father's body was slowly healing, and he was able to speak.

He was now able to walk and jog on his own. I was sitting in the car with Jacob as he drove my father and Lieutenant Roberts to the airport.

"So, Julie still thinks you're in the hospital, Unc?" Jacob asked.

"Yes, Jacob. I will only be gone for a few days, so I need all of your help to keep Julie off our asses."

"The District has sent over a helicopter to take us back to Chicago, so that we aren't seen on Julie's radar," Lieutenant Roberts spoke.

My father's phone rang.

"Young, speaking," he answered.

"What if Julie starts to ask questions?" I asked with slight hesitation.

"Keep us covered," Lieutenant Roberts replied.

"Alright, bye," my father hung up the phone. "Jacob, take us to the field a few blocks from the airport. There were no available hangars for the helicopter so the department had to improvise."

Jacob made a left turn at the intersection before the airport's entrance.

He drove onto the field that was a few blocks ahead of us.

"Miracle, avoid conversation about me with Julie. She still thinks I'm hospitalized, so let's keep it that way until we come back with a solution."

"Why are you all going away?" I asked.

"Hopefully, to get a lead on this situation with Julie," Lieutenant Roberts spoke.

My father opened his door. He kissed me on the cheek and shook hands with Jacob.

"J, watch after my little girl."

"I'm not going to let her out of my sight," Jacob replied.

Jacob shook hands with Lieutenant Roberts.

"*Te amo, Papa*," I spoke as I kissed my father on the cheek.

"I love you, too, Miracle," my father answered as he stepped out of the car.

Lieutenant Roberts hugged me, and they both climbed into the helicopter.

Jacob and I sat in the car and watched as the helicopter began to levitate.

"Let's just stay out of Julie's way," Jacob spoke as he put the car in gear and drove off.

"J, how come I don't see you with Melanie like that, anymore?" I asked as he drove to the hotel.

"You want the truth?" he asked.

"Are we going to start lying to each other at this age?" I asked him, rhetorically.

He let out a sigh.

"Melanie and I are on the verge of breaking up," he replied.

"¿Como? ¿Porque?" I asked.

"Things are really rocky, and I can tell she just isn't into me, anymore," he stated, never taking his eyes off the road.

I didn't want to upset Jacob, so I quickly changed the subject.

"How are we to keep my father being gone, a secret?" I asked.

"We will just have to find a way," Jacob spoke. "They'll be back within the next few days. We just have to lay low."

Jacob arrived at the hotel and we exited the vehicle and walked inside. We walked towards the room and Joey approached us.

"Jacob, Julie needs to see you, immediately."

"What is it?" Jacob asked.

"Our hacker, or should I say, sorry excuse of a hacker, can't break into the grid to allow the next mission to take place."

"So, what does that have to do with me?" Jacob asked as we followed Joey.

"You're smart," Joey started. "This mission has a relay race involved, and 30 minutes after the race, there's a very large delivery of cash, about $1.5 million, and ecstasy being delivered to the science laboratory, which is all the way on the other side of town. We need brains to hack into the system for a clean escape," Joey spoke.

"What do you mean, 'escape'?" Jacob asked.

"We're taking that shit."

I looked back towards the elevator; with every step we took, the more it seemed we were moving deeper into a deep pot of danger.

"Jacob, so nice to see you," Julie shook his hand. "Have you ever done any hacking work before?"

"Freelance, just to mess around, but never anything professional," he uttered.

"Do you think you can get into the D.R.'s main grid to mess with traffic lights, cause blackouts, and disrupt police communication?"

"What's in it for me?" Jacob asked.

"How's the tune of 4500 sound?" Julie asked.

"5,000," Jacob negotiated.

Julie looked at him sternly.

Jacob slightly shrugged his shoulders.

"I am risking it all by hacking into government databases for illegal activity. Either 5K, or no deal," he spoke.

Julie thought for a moment.

"You are quite the negotiator," Julie spoke. "Fine, five-thousand if and only if you can successfully pull this off."

"When do you need this done?"

"Everything goes down in five days. There's going to be a major relay race 30 minutes before the mission. You're racing for money and cars, so brush up on your driving. You all keep the money from the race and split it however you'd like, but the cars are mine."

"And what about the other 1.5 million and the drugs?" Jacob asked her.

"How do you know about the money and drugs?" Julie raised an eyebrow.

"Well, you want us to help you take it, and I'd assume that you want it done correctly."

"Okay, let's do this," she spoke. "In this game, it's all about the moolah. You all can keep the money from the race, and from the heist, you pocket 10%. Therefore, your portion of the heist is equivalent to $150,000," she explained. You would have to put up 3,000 a piece: that's 9,000 for the race. So, your total earnings, considering everything is successful, will be $168,000."

I was shocked at the amount of money Julie was offering.

"Are you sure that this is something you can pull off? We are dealing with a lot of money, and if you can't handle the pressure, I'll understand," she explained.

I remained silent, but I watched as Jacob extended his hand for a shake.

"Do you know who I am?" Jacob asked with a smirk. "Let's do business."

***

Jacob sat at the desk on the laptop Julie provided him with.

"Jacob, how's the work coming?" his father asked.

"Well, I was able to get into the electrical grid, so I do have access to the traffic signals and the city's electricity."

Melanie sat on the bed and looked at Jacob; a sign of irritation was on her face.

"So, everything should be set for tomorrow?" my mother asked.

"Yes, it should be," Jacob replied.

"What about Richard? Have you all heard anything from him?" Aunt Madison was walking from the adjoining room.

"He called earlier," I answered. "The helicopter should be arriving tonight, and we're going to make it seem as though we're picking him up from the hospital."

"Then we're all good."

My uncle walked to the mirror and adjusted his bow-tie.

"Reminds me of our wedding," Aunt Madison joked as she put her head on his shoulder in the mirror.

"Don't forget, I was nerdier back then," Uncle Jared chuckled.

The sound of an alarm emitted from Jacob's laptop.

"Uh, guys," he spoke.

I could hear in his tone that something was wrong.

"What's wrong?" Melanie asked as she stood up.

His mother and father walked towards him.

"I have got some good news and some bad news," Jacob rapidly pressed keys on the keyboard.

"Lay it down," Uncle Jared spoke.

"The good news is that I'm able to take complete control of the network and control anything I want. To make it easier, I'm integrating all the functionality into an app that I can put on my phone," he slightly bragged.

"And the bad news?" I asked.

"Police have detected an intrusion into the data's grid. They are attempting to trace the signal."

"Shit!" Uncle Jared paced the floor.

"This is bad," Aunt Madison spoke.

"*Todo la razón*, and it's about to get worse," my mother spoke. "That was Richard. Medical documents were released, and Julie may know that he's out of the hospital. They will be arriving in about 30 minutes, so we need to be there before she finds out for sure."

Jacob shook his head.

"The field where they will land is about a good hour out," I replied. "There's no way to make it there in under 30 minutes."

The alarm emitted a faster tone.

"They're getting closer to tracing my IP," Jacob responded.

"Have you gained access to the main grid?" my uncle asked.

"Yes."

"Tell you what. Go and get Richard, and we will close the laptop and hide it if the police show."

Jacob rose to his feet and grabbed his car keys.

"I'll ride with you," I stated as I grabbed my wallet.

I hugged my mother, while Jacob hugged his parents, and we walked out of the room.

"Time to test my driving skills," Jacob stated as the elevator lowered.

"Let's just pray Julie hasn't gotten access to the leaks," I replied as my heart started to beat faster.

"It will be fine. We'll be there in about twenty minutes, with my driving, and we'll get your father. We'll bring him back to the hotel, and we will all be rested for tomorrow's mission."

Jacob and I got into his Charger, and he revved the engine. He drove in the direction of the airfield.

My phone rang as he drove.

"Hello?" I asked.

"Hey, beautiful," Quincy spoke over the phone.

"Hey, you," I replied.

"What are you up to right now?"

I had to lie.

"I'm just here in the hotel room. About to watch a movie and relax before tomorrow's mission."

"Tomorrow is going to be the biggest mission yet. You have to be prepared mentally and physically."

"With all the money on the line, I understand we have to all be on point. Which is exactly why I'm relaxing," I chuckled.

"Julie has told me the breakdown of tomorrow's mission," Quincy explained. "You, Jacob, and Melanie will be doing the relay race. During the heist, everyone is going to play a part."

Jacob approached the expressway and I knew I would have to hang up, otherwise, Quincy would hear the wind.

"Q, let me call you back," I spoke. "I have to do something for my mother."

"Alright, well I'll call you later," he replied.

"Okay," I hung up the phone.

Jacob merged on the expressway and swerved between lanes. I looked out the window and random thoughts were running through my mind. Jessie's voice came to me.

"There's danger ahead, Miracle. Keep your eyes open and watch your back at all times." Her voice left as quickly as it had arrived.

Jacob got off the expressway and turned down the street. He continued to drive until he reached the airfield; we waited for the helicopter to land.

"Hello," I answered my phone.

"Miracle, we are entering the D.R. now. Who's at the field?"

"Jacob and I are here, waiting for you to arrive. There's been a leak in the hospital documents," I answered. "We're not sure if Julie's been alerted, but we're trying to lay low. Once you touch down, we have to head back to the hotel." I rushed through my words, as I was getting extremely nervous now.

"Baby, slow down," my father spoke. "We're about to land now."

I could hear the helicopter approaching.

My father hung up the phone and Jacob got out of the Charger.

The helicopter landed, and Jacob gave my father and Lieutenant Roberts a handshake-hug.

They all got into the car and Jacob quickly drove in the direction of the hotel.

I provided my father with the details of the mission.

"Seems like Julie's been hard at work," he stated. "Let's just pray everything goes according to the plan."

17

Miracle

"I got the app finished," Jacob stated the next afternoon.

"Great, now you don't have to stay behind a hotel computer," I joked.

"Julie told me that she's also going to have her hacker behind the computer to make sure it runs smoothly. Which, I feel is stupid," he stated. "If the broad couldn't hack into the grid, why are they monitoring the result?"

"Who knows the reason for anything that Julie does," my father stated as he sipped his coke.

There was a knock at the door.

"Richard," Julie stated as my father opened the door. "How are you feeling?" she asked.

"Doing a lot better, thanks," my father replied.

"That's a good thing. I was thinking about letting you stay in the hotel."

"Negative," he instantly replied. "I have to look after my family. I've heard all about what's going down today."

"Who's the snitch?" Joey asked.

"Joey, chill," Julie started. "Well, we can put you in for today. We need all the help we can get with the heist. You all have the weapons, correct?"

"They're in the trunks," Jacob spoke.

"Great," Julie clapped her hands together. "You all need to get going. The race starts in about 45 minutes. And you know the heist is about 30 minutes after."

She reached in her pocket.

"Jacob, here's the 5,000 I owe you."

Julie handed Jacob a wrapped stack of hundred-dollar bills.

"Be sharp and precise. I will be watching you all today," Julie spoke as she left the room.

My heart raced as my father put his gun in his pants. My mother and Aunt Madison helped each other make sure their outfits looked nice, and Jacob turned on the laptop.

"Why are you leaving it on?" I was inquisitive.

"If it isn't on, I won't have a connection with my phone. The computer is acting as the grid and my phone is the hacker."

"So, if it turns off or dies?"

"Then we're pretty much screwed," Jacob spoke as he grabbed his car keys and laptop.

Melanie grabbed her keys from the table and I got mine.

Our fathers each grabbed their keys before we left the room.

Jacob walked over to the casino and gave Joey the laptop.

"The point of no return," I replied as I got in the car.

Jacob led the way and drove to the race.

***

"My star racers!" Julie exclaimed as we arrived.

"Julie, so these are the children you have us racing against?" the guy laughed. "They're amateurs!"

"Let's just see how amateur we are once the race is over," Melanie exclaimed.

"Yeah, yeah, yeah, do you each have the money to put up?" The race coordinator interrupted.

"Right here," Jacob stated as he pulled out a stack of bills. "9-K."

"And we each understand the rules, correct? Winner gets money and cars. Cars are to be raced as is, no further modifications can be made to your vehicles. The first racer will race to reach the second racer, who will then drive to reach the final racer, who will bring it all home."

I let out a sigh.

"If you all decide to chicken out of the race at any point, it will be considered a forfeit, and you will lose your money and cars," the man looked at Jacob.

"Yeah, but how would you be able to catch a fleeing driver, especially if they're skilled behind the wheel?" Jacob returned the glare.

"Here in the D.R., you won't get very far if you owe any debts." The man looked around and nodded towards several cameras.

"Racers need to take their positions!" the coordinator spoke.

"Alright, Melanie, just do everything we've ever worked on, and I know you got this in the bag," Jacob stated as he embraced Melanie, followed by a kiss. She returned the kiss and got in her vehicle.

"Good luck, M," I stated to her.

Melanie was the first racer, so she drove to the starting line. Jacob drove to the second checkpoint, which was about half-a-mile away, and I drove to the final checkpoint, which was a mile-and-a-half away from the start.

I looked at the monitor above me; it would show me what was going on in the race until it was my turn to drive.

"Ready," the coordinator started.

Melanie revved her engine.

"Steady."

Her opponent did the same.

"Go!" The coordinator shouted as he shot a starting pistol in the air. The audience cheered loudly.

They both sped away from the starting line.

"Come on, M," I stated as I watched the monitor.

The opponent drove ahead of Melanie and was determined to keep her behind him by any means necessary.

He slowed down a bit and let Melanie get on the side of him. He instantly swerved into her lane, attempting to hit her car and knock it off the road, but she hit the handbrake and turned her steering wheel to the right.

As her car stopped, so did her engine.

"*Pinche cabrón*," I shouted.

It took Melanie about five seconds to restart her engine, and she performed a U-turn.

"Come on, Melanie," I spoke as she drove at top speed to reach Jacob.

She reached Jacob about 10 seconds after the other racer had driven off.

I couldn't watch the race anymore; I just needed to focus on winning.

I closed my eyes for a few seconds.

As I opened my eyes, my opponent was driving off, although I could see Jacob in my rearview mirror, quickly approaching me.

He flashed his lights at me and honked his horn. I sped off as Jacob reached me, and quickly switched gears.

"Come on, baby," I spoke to my Mustang as I approached my opponent.

We approached a railroad crossing and the arms began to lower. The lights flashed, and I could see the train approaching in the distance.

I used the nitrous boost, and I sped ahead, slightly passing my opponent.

We both reached the railroad and drove across. The train was centimeters away as we crossed, but the train hit the side of his car's rear bumper and caused him to spin out.

I sped across the finish line and performed a 180-degree drift.

Jacob and Melanie exited their vehicles and ran over to me.

"Miracle!" Melanie shouted and she embraced me.

I could hear cheering all around us and I saw my mother and father.

"That was beautiful," Melanie added.

"Alright, alright, alright, y'all, settle down. That race was outstanding," the coordinator spoke.

He walked up to me. He handed me the money.

"18 thousand. Go on, smell it," he put his hand on my shoulder.

Jacob and Melanie both walked up beside me.

I passed them both six-thousand.

"And, the keys to the vehicles."

The man passed me 3 sets of keys.

Julie walked forward with my aunt, uncle, mother, and father.

Jacob and I embraced our family members, and the coordinator spoke.

"Now that's what I call a race! Anybody up for another one?" he chuckled.

"We gotta get going," I stated.

I passed Julie the car keys.

"Let's get moving," she spoke. "Great job out there, kids," Julie assured us. "The delivery is about to go down. I need for you all to have the same focus."

"You come at us with a job, and we're just here to deliver," Jacob replied.

Jacob and Melanie got into their vehicles and I got in mine.

"Here's the address to the laboratory." Julie passed Jacob a card through the window. "The delivery is in route."

Jacob held a finger out the window and twirled it. We all revved our engines and drove off.

I looked in my rearview mirror.

Julie pulled a cigar out of her pocket and lit it. She blew smoke and walked back towards the crowd.

We were switching from lane-to-lane to arrive at the laboratory before the truck got there.

"Alright everyone, we're about five minutes out," Jacob spoke over the earpiece. "Let's do this nice and clean. The hack is still holding the connection, so that's a good thing."

"Test it out, just to be sure," my father spoke.

Jacob came to a stop at a red light. We pulled up next to him.

He pulled out his phone and tapped on the screen; our light turned green seconds later, while the opposing traffic light was still green.

My father let out a chuckle.

"Let's do it," Uncle Jared spoke as he drove forward.

Moments later, we were pulling into the driveway of the laboratory.

"Stay in the car. We can't risk facial recognition catching us and logging us into the system," Jacob stated. "It's a good thing Julie removed our plates."

"Can you all hear me?" a voice transmitted through our headsets. A strain of feedback also transmitted.

"Damn!" my father shouted. "Loud and clear, who are you?"

"I'm Julie's hacker, Andre. I have a location on you all based on your vehicles and the nearby cameras."

"So, what do you suggest we do?" I asked.

"Wait until the truck arrives, and just go for it."

"Negative," Jacob stated. "Can you disable the cameras for a few moments?"

"It's a bit above my pay grade," Andre spoke.

"Julie makes all this damn money but can't afford to get a decent hacker?" my father questioned.

"I'm taking a risk here. I persuaded Julie to give us 10% of the money collected from the job; that's about 150K. Let's back out of this lot, but keep your heads down," Jacob put his Charger into reverse and eased out of the lot; the rest of us followed.

We parked our cars on the street and each of us got out of our vehicles.

"Dumbass," I could hear Jacob utter under his breath towards Andre, as he walked past me.

"We attack hard and fast," Jacob spoke as he got the vest from his trunk.

A van pulled up next to us.

"That's what she said," Quincy joked as he got out of the van that he drove.

He'd heard Jacob over the earpiece.

"Alright, guys, that truck will be here in T-minus 5 minutes," Andre spoke over the headset.

"I guess you can see that, too," Melanie stated sarcastically.

"The truck has a GPS chip in it, so yeah I can," Andre returned the attitude that Melanie gave.

"Alright y'all, calm down," my father spoke. "Jacob, this is your call."

I gripped my gun tightly.

"We have the weapons as a threat, but we are not to use them unless we need to," Jacob announced.

"Getting ready to turn down the street," Andre spoke.

I could hear buttons being pressed.

"Uh-oh," Andre spoke.

A row of street lights turned off.

I saw the truck stop in its path.

We all squatted behind our vehicles, aiming our weapons.

"No use in asking you to connect me to the radio within the truck, especially after that stunt," Jacob stated as he pulled out his phone with the free hand. He opened the app and pressed a few icons.

The audio from the truck's radio transmitted to our earpieces.

"All the lights just died, but only on the right side of the street."

"Someone is messing around. Abort!"

"We are rerouting to the backup location."

The truck began to move but quickly turned down the street.

"Dre, right now I need precision. Tell me where the truck is at every intersection. We're splitting up and have to know exactly where to take these people down," my father announced as he rose to his feet and got inside of his car.

"I can do that," he spoke.

The rest of us got in our vehicles.

"Miracle, Melanie, you all come with me. Pop and Unc, you all follow the truck."

We each drove off.

"The truck is traveling down Expreso 27 de Febrero," Andre spoke.

"We'll travel down Av Rómulo Betancourt to cut him off," Jacob spoke over his earpiece.

"Papi, keep us updated with where the truck goes," I said.

"I gotcha, baby girl," my father spoke.

Jacob sped some more, as did Melanie and me.

"They are turning at the intersection of Av Doctor Fernando Arturo Defillo," my father announced.

"We got them," Jacob turned down the street.

As we drove down the street, the passenger got out with a pistol. He aimed the weapon at us.

We all stopped moving.

A few more men exited the back of the vehicle with automatic weapons.

"¡*Identifíquense!*" one of the men shouted.

"Oh shit," Andre spoke in the headset.

"Play it cool," Jacob whispered.

No one said a word to the men, that is until my mother opened her door and spoke.

"*¿Qué quieres decir? Sólo estamos camino a casa,*" my mother spoke loudly.

"*Perdone, fue nuestro error. Podríamos haber jurado que nos seguían y que todos ustedes eran los perpetradores. Lo siento,*" The passenger apologized and climbed back in the truck.

The guards also lowered their weapons and got inside of the truck.

The truck started moving again.

"I had no idea that they would be packing so heavy," Andre mentioned.

"They have over a million fucking dollars and over one hundred pounds of ecstasy in the truck. What in the hell did you think?" Uncle Jared was disgusted, and it was no secret.

"Calm down," Jacob stated. "Dre, we are going to pull back. Tell us when the truck stops and where it stops."

"10-4," Andre spoke.

My father drove into a nearby gas station and we each followed him.

"So, 1.5 million is worth having automatic weapons aimed at you, huh?" my father asked.

"Everything will be okay, Richard," my mother assured him.

"What did that man say, anyway?" my father asked

"He told us to identify who we were. I just told him that we were just on our way home. He thought we were following him, but he apologized and left."

"Julie is fucking crazy," Uncle Jared spoke as he came from the trunk of his car.

"The irony of all this," Melanie spoke as she shook her head.

Aunt Madison spoke as she got out of the car.

"Let's just be ready," she began. "Andre can be letting us know of a location at any moment."

"Our approach is going to be based on how they respond. If they wish to respond with the shoot first approach—."

"Then that's our approach," my father uttered.

"I studied the lab and backup location. Whether or not they are going to the one I researched, I don't know."

Jacob pulled an old envelope from the car, as well as a pen. We all crowded around.

"The lab has five entrances, and the backup location only has two. Now, they have heavy weapons at both locations, because the deliveries are always worth a lot of money, starting at 500-thousand and up." Jacob wrote on the paper and spoke. "So, we have to get the money before they begin transferring it into the building because once it's in, that's it. Attacking the building would be a suicide mission."

"I've seen these guys in action before," Quincy started, "they don't play. No matter the route we take, we're going to have to play it smart."

We all looked at one another.

"Remember, J, they have cameras on all corners of the buildings," Quincy reminded him.

"That's where Andre comes into play. He's at the computer, so it's quicker for him to shut down the building's power. Hopefully, he can do it fast enough for us to get the stuff off the truck and get out of dodge."

"They roll deep," Quincy stated. "The best way to do this is the clean way."

"Guys, the truck has stopped at the 'San Bernado Laboratory'. About 3 blocks north of your location," Andre spoke.

"Let's move," my father directed.

We each got in our vehicles and drove out of the gas station. We drove to the laboratory and saw many trucks; we waited across the street and turned off the engines, except my father.

"No turning back, now," Jacob spoke through the earpiece.

"Which of these trucks do you think has the cash and drugs?" my aunt asked.

"We wait it out. We wait for someone to come out and guard the vehicle. Right now, everything is locked," Quincy spoke. "Whichever one they guard, there's our answer."

"There's going to be a lot of blood loss," my father mentioned.

We each sat in our vehicles until we saw a man come out of the building.

"Is that him?" I asked.

"Yeah, that's the guy," Quincy repeated.

"Alright, Dre, it's time. Kill the power to the building, including security cameras," my father finally turned off his engine.

We could hear Andre pressing buttons on the computer.

"Got it; there's no power to the building. I don't know how long it will hold out, but use the window."

"Melanie, go up to the guard. No weapons or anything. We need to distract him and get him away from the truck," Jacob instructed Melanie.

I could hear their tones were different towards each other.

"Gotta have me doing the hard work, huh?" she spoke as she exited the vehicle.

"Excuse me, sir?" Melanie shouted as she ran up to the guard.

He pulled out his pistol and aimed it at her.

"Whoa," she stated as she slowed down.

I started to take off my seatbelt.

"Miracle, wait," Jacob spoke. "He's not going to shoot her," he saw the hesitation in the guard's action.

"I was going to ask for your help," she spoke. "You see..." Melanie began to walk away from the truck with the security guard.

"Switch over to the building's radio system," Jacob stated. "No input, just output so we can hear what's going on."

"I just got a time on the outage. You all have 2 minutes until the power is restored," Andre spoke.

I could hear the guards speaking and panicking about the outage as we each got out of our vehicles with our weapons and bags.

We each ran stealthily towards the truck.

Once we reached it, Jacob raised the door of the trailer, and revealed the mountain of cash; Andre spoke.

"Silencer, Richard you have a guard coming your way. Take him out."

"We aren't killing anyone," my father spoke. "I'll just knock him unconscious as he turns the corner. This shit isn't worth it," my father watched the side of the truck.

"Rick, I'm going to cover this side of the truck," Uncle Jared spoke as he walked to the opposite end of the truck.

Jacob, my mother, my aunt, and I quickly started to put the money in the bag as my father hit one of the guards and laid him on the ground.

"A minute, 15," Andre spoke.

"We've got about a third of it in the bag," I spoke.

"We're not going to get everything in a minute and fifteen seconds," Jacob spoke. "You have to disrupt the power for longer."

"Can't do all of that," Andre spoke. "They will be running power off a generator."

We continued to throw the money in the bags and were mostly finished.

"Julie wants the drugs too, right?" Andre reminded us.

"Fuck me," my father spoke. This is operation suicide. There's no way we can get all of this back to her."

About 30 seconds later, I heard the generators powering up and we put more money in the bags quickly.

"You all have to get out of there," Andre shuddered.

"You're the hacker, get us out of this," Jacob spoke.

"You all have a set of guards coming your way," he spoke franticly.

"Should we abort?" my aunt asked.

"I'm not sure," my mother answered.

The guards arrived at the truck and saw us with the bags. As soon as they saw us, Quincy came crashing through the gates with the truck he drove, and sparks went flying.

The guards pulled out their pistols and shot at the truck. We zipped the bags of money and pulled out our weapons.

We ran towards the gate while blind firing in the direction of the guards.

Melanie ran back towards us and grabbed a bag of money.

Quincy got out of the truck and shot his machine gun.

"What are you doing?" Jacob asked through his headset.

"We need the drugs. This truck is going with us," Quincy spoke as he got inside of the truck.

One of the guards climbed up the side and tried to open the door.

The man began to hit the window with his weapon.

Jacob looked back and shot the guard in the leg with his weapon.

"Come on, Q," Jacob stated as he walked back while firing his weapon.

Quincy put the truck into reverse and backed the truck out of the driveway.

Security guards shot at the truck and us; alarms sounded.

We each reached our vehicles and climbed inside.

Flying bullets hit our vehicles and we sped off.

"Julie's not playing any games," Jacob shouted through the headset. "Dre, disrupt any police communication. The last thing we need right now is a bunch of cops.

We could hear Andre working quickly, but also becoming irritated.

"How do you want me to do all of this?"

"Never mind!" Jacob shouted. "I'll do it."

I sped alongside Jacob and saw him pull out his phone.

"It's trying to hack into it now. Andre, I just need you to watch the computer screen and make sure it doesn't fail. If it does, I need for you to manually override it with the dummy administrator password I created, 'DR321!'. If you can't do something as simple as that, Julie should really consider removing you from her payroll."

"Alright man, goddamn," Andre was offended.

Jacob sped faster towards the hotel.

"Communication has been interrupted," Andre confirmed.

"It's only a temporary disruption," Jacob added. "Once the disruption is finished, an officer can get on us and we will have to escape them."

Quincy honked his horn.

"Follow me," he spoke as he turned and drove through the expressway railing.

We each did the same until all the cars were following behind one another on the expressway.

Sirens were behind us, and a helicopter flew overhead.

"Q, where are you taking us?" my father asked.

"I know these streets inside and out," Quincy told us as he continued to swerve in and out of traffic.

"Fuck it," I could hear Jacob whisper as he took the exit to get off the expressway.

I could tell there was a lot on Jacob's mind; more than just what was currently going on.

I followed behind Jacob as everyone else continued to follow Quincy.

"Andre, switch to Jacob and Miracle's GPS and keep an eye on them."

"Jacob, where are you going?" I asked him.

"We're losing these cops, but we can't do that if we're all together, and we damn sure can't do it by following Quincy," Jacob spoke out of disgust.

"J, we're both carrying about 214 thousand in our cars. If we get stopped by the police…"

"Who said we were going to get caught?" he asked, curiously. "Just follow my lead, baby girl," Jacob stated as he sped faster.

"Excuse you?" Melanie was offended.

Jacob ignored her and continued to drive.

He drove towards oncoming police officers at full speed.

Some of the officers aimed their weapons out of the windows and shot at our vehicles.

"Keep your head low, M," Jacob shouted.

The bullets hit my car.

"Miracle, hit your lights; all of them. Put on the night vision glasses you have," Jacob stated as he continued to speed. "Got a care package for they ass."

I turned off my lights. Although I was scared and worried, I trusted Jacob, so I stayed right behind him.

"Enjoy," Jacob spoke.

Suddenly, all the lights went out, and the primary lights I saw were police headlights and siren lights.

"Oh shit!" I heard on the radio; it was police chatter.

"The power's out! We have no visual of anything."

"Andre, how long do we have for this blackout?"

I could hear Jacob's car driving swiftly. I also heard police cars crashing around me; using the night vision glasses, as well as the police headlights, I was able to avoid colliding with them.

"You have exactly three minutes before power boots back up, but then you can kill the power at the electrical grid again if needed."

"No need," Jacob mentioned. "Miracle, stay with me," I could hear him turning and speeding.

"I'm right behind you," I spoke.

"Dad, how are you all doing down there?" Jacob asked his father.

"Quincy has led us to a tunnel, so we're safe. We're going to head to the hotel from the tunnel, now."

"It's a good thing we got under the tunnel before the blackout," Aunt Madison spoke.

"You would have been fine," Jacob joked. "We're about five minutes out," he let out a chuckle.

"You kids be safe," my father answered.

"We'll see you at the hotel," my mother spoke.

"Muah," I kissed into the Bluetooth earpiece.

The power was restored to the city, and we slowed our driving to normal. We were right around the corner from the hotel.

We arrived and stepped out of our vehicles, but we left the engines running. I walked over and embraced Jacob, tightly. We both took our earpieces out and placed them on the car's hood.

"I'm very impressed with your driving, Miracle," Jacob spoke. "You've definitely improved."

We could still hear police sirens in the nearby area.

I couldn't say a word. I just looked at him and smiled.

A police vehicle sped past us and it felt as though my heart was going to stop.

"Calm down, M," he spoke. "It's over. No plates, no tags, and there's no sign of this pointing back to us."

Quincy arrived with my parents, Jacob's parents, and Melanie behind him.

They each got out of their vehicles.

"Jacob, we definitely wouldn't have been able to pull this off without you," my father spoke as he shook Jacob's hand.

"Come on, guys. Before we get too friendly, let's get this money to Julie." Uncle Jared reached into his trunk and grabbed the bag of money.

"1.5 million dollars," my mother spoke as we all held our bags.

Quincy got back in the truck and drove off.

"You know we could just bolt right now," Melanie laughed.

"With illegal money, I don't think so," I chuckled. "Besides, the quicker we finish with Julie, the better."

"Agreed," my father spoke.

██

-*Richard*

We put the bags on the table for Julie.

"The sweet smell of success," she spoke. "Excellent work, guys!"

She opened the bags.

"All 1.5 million is there," Jamie mentioned as she held my hand.

"How can I be so sure?" Julie questioned. "How do I know that I can trust Richard or Jared?" Julie looked at us and chuckled.

"Maybe you can, or maybe you can't, but I know for damn sure I'm not about to help your ass count that out," I retaliated. "So, you can take the money or leave it."

Julie looked at me sternly.

"Nah, I don't have to check behind you. You know better," she spoke.

"Yeah, I know better. I know better than to put my foot so far up your ass that—" Julie rose to her feet and I grabbed her by the collar.

Everyone seemed to jump in an instant.

Jacob grabbed me by the shoulders while Jared stood in between Julie and myself, forcing me to remove her collar.

Julie's bodyguards now had weapons aimed at me.

"Everybody, let's calm down," Jamie spoke.

I could tell she was nervous and feared for me.

Julie slowly sat back down. A few minutes passed before any further words were spoken.

"Take a bag," she replied. "It's your cut from the job. There are even amounts in each bag, correct?"

Her bodyguards lowered their weapons.

"Yes," Miracle answered.

"I thought you said we get 150 K," Jacob replied.

"How much is in here?" Joey asked.

"Maybe a little over 214 K per bag. They had the money separated in the truck into seven different piles, go figure," Melanie shrugged.

"Lucky number seven," Julie spoke out loud. "Make sure you don't have any marked bills, but go crazy with the extra," Julie inhaled on her cigar. "Where is Quincy?"

"He's in the truck with the drugs," Madison replied.

"He must be dropping them off and removing the evidence." Julie sipped her Hennessey. "We're done for the day," she stated.

Joey walked from behind the table and escorted us to the door.

"Have a good one," he replied as he shut and locked the door as we left out with the bag of money.

"Rick, you gotta control that temper," Jared mentioned.

"I know," I stated as I shook my head.

18

Miracle

Three months later, we were still in the Dominican Republic working for Julie. Since the ecstasy heist, all our jobs were small. Julie couldn't risk the heat potentially tracing back to her.

"There you are, Beautiful," Quincy stated as he got into the car. "I could have sworn you would have tried to jet out of here," he chuckled.

I chuckled. "Why would I do that?" I asked him.

"That's what princesses do," he joked. "How's your father doing?"

"He's doing much better. I'm glad that Julie's allowing us to take a break. It lets him rest up, you know?"

"Yeah, he deserves it. We all deserve it." Quincy turned on the radio as he sat in the backseat with me.

"Julie's got us doing some crazy shit, huh?" he asked.

"Well, besides the fact that we were almost killed multiple times, it's all great," I replied sarcastically.

"Yeah, sometimes my aunt can get a lil' crazy."

"Ha! A little?" I chuckled.

"Okay, she's insane," he replied with a laugh. "But at least we're getting our exercise."

"Yeah, the typical way to get exercise is to be in a shootout against gang members, or stealing 1.5 million dollars and some ecstasy from a science laboratory," I laughed.

"Now you're getting it," Quincy joked. "I'm going to go get us something to drink, he replied before getting out of the car.

"I'll be waiting right here," I answered.

I pulled out my cell phone and texted Jacob to start heading over to pick me up.

Miracle: Jacob, I am at Quincy's, but you can start heading over here to pick me up. Text me when you're outside. Te amo.

I sent the text and put my phone on the chair next to me and I sat in the garage by myself. A text came through about three minutes later, and I read it.

Jacob: I'll be there shortly. I may have a tight car, but it'll do lol. I love you, too.

I replied to the text Jacob sent.

Miracle: You're so silly. :) I will be waiting for you. We're just chilling in the garage and listening to some music.

Seconds passed and Jacob replied.

Jacob: Yeah, that's ALL you better be doing. I'll see you soon.

I put my phone under my thigh and turned up the radio a little bit. "We Can't Be Friends" by Deborah Cox was playing on the radio.

Quincy got back in the car with two glasses.

"I know you don't drink, so I got you some apple cider," he joked as he handed me the glass.

"You got jokes, I see." I chuckled as I sipped the juice.

"Plenty," he replied as he took a sip from his glass. "So, Miracle, things are getting kind of serious between us," he added.

"Who knows? It could just be because of the adrenaline of everything that's going on," I replied.

Quincy chuckled.

"So, what's the next step in our relationship?" he questioned as he held the glass in his hand.

Jessie's voice came to my head.

Miracle, watch what you do! I'm telling you, it's all a front. The feelings aren't real, and he's responsible for my death.

I instantly froze.

"Miracle?" he asked.

"*Perdoneme,*" I replied. "I'm not sure where that takes us. Where should it?" I asked.

"Well, we definitely need to be together more once you leave here. I mean, we go to the same school and don't even speak."

"Well, you're a football star. And all football stars are assholes," I retorted.

"Is that what you think?" he asked. "Am I an asshole?"

"You were!" I exclaimed. "But now you're not being one," I spoke in a softer tone.

"Thanks," he chuckled. "Well, how about we begin with this?" he stated and got closer.

He put his lips on mine and started to touch my body.

I kissed him back, and he slowly tried to slide his tongue in my mouth. I moved his hands away from my body.

"Not right now; I don't want that," I stated as I retreated from the kiss.

"Really?" he asked. "I could have sworn you liked it when I did this to you." He reached his hand behind me and grabbed my butt.

I slapped him across the face. "I think you need to stop," I replied.

"Girl, stop playing." He mentioned as he slapped my butt, once again.

"Quincy, *hablo en serio,*" I mentioned as I moved his hand.

"That's why you're getting turned on, right?" he asked me. "You better stop playing with me and give it up." He grabbed my butt once more, and I hit him in the penis. I quickly tried to open the car door.

"Little bitch," he stated as he grabbed at me and pinned my arms against the car door. "You're going to give me some, today," he began kissing my neck and he ripped open my shirt.

I began to scream.

"Who's going to hear you?" he asked me.

"*¿Sabes que?* You *are* an asshole," I exclaimed to him.

"An asshole with a great body," he mentioned. "Yup, I'm a cocky muthafucka," he continued to kiss on my body and began to put his hand in my pants.

"Get the fuck off me," I told him.

"If you make another fucking sound, it is going to be a problem."

"So, you're going to rape me?" I asked as a tear fell.

"You can either do this voluntarily or involuntarily. Take your pick," he replied.

I screamed at the top of my lungs, and Quincy slapped me. Once he slapped me, a car came crashing through the garage.

The windshield and passenger windows of the car broke, and the glass shattered and fell on us.

"Shit," Quincy grunted as he looked up.

He could see the front of his car was completely damaged and the car was pushed further back into the garage.

Someone opened the door and pulled Quincy out.

"Son of a bitch!" Jacob stated as he punched Quincy in the face repeatedly. "Didn't I tell you not to fuck up?" Jacob slammed Quincy to the ground.

The door on my side of the car opened.

My father and Uncle Jared helped me out of the car. I began to cry.

"Daddy's here," my father stated as he held me.

Jacob kneeled and continued to punch Quincy; Quincy fought back.

"I fuckin' told you to leave her alone."

Quincy reached up and grabbed Jacob's neck and quickly flipped him over.

"I've been waiting a long time to do this." Quincy tightened his grip around Jacob's neck.

Jacob grabbed at Quincy's collar and tried to hit him in the throat.

"That's right —struggle— you fuckin', little bitch." Quincy lifted Jacob's head and slammed it against the ground.

Uncle Jared ran over to Quincy and grabbed his arms. Quincy elbowed Uncle Jared, and Jacob got up and hit Quincy in the stomach.

Quincy keeled over due to the hit, and Jacob slapped him.

Jacob grabbed Quincy and rammed Quincy's head into the body of the car.

Sirens could be heard approaching the house and Jacob continued to fight.

He punched Quincy in the face before letting him fall to the ground.

Uncle Jared grabbed Jacob's arms and my father continued to hold me. Jacob broke free from his father's hold and kicked Quincy in the stomach.

"Jacob, stop," his father shouted as Jacob continued to kick Quincy. "He's had enough," Uncle Jared spoke.

Jacob ignored his father and kicked Quincy in the face.

"Hold on, Miracle," my father whispered to me as he walked over to Jacob and Quincy.

Uncle Jared grabbed Jacob's arms and held him back. Quincy lifted his head and my father slapped Quincy with the back of his hand. My father pulled out a gun and aimed it at Quincy's throat.

"Move again, and I will blow your brains out," my father stated to Quincy. "I warned you not to touch my daughter, correct?"

Quincy coughed up blood.

"Answer me, punk ass bitch," my father remarked.

"Her tight ass was calling for me," Quincy chuckled. "She's not a fuckin' angel like you think. Hoe ass."

My father hit Quincy in the throat with the gun.

"I don't give a damn if she had feelings for you, I never did like or trust your punk ass," Jacob shouted as he spat at Quincy.

"I will kill you right now, you know that?" my father spoke.

Jacob walked over to me and I immediately hugged him. He held me in his arms, but never took his eyes off Quincy.

"You're forgetting one thing," Quincy stated, trying to catch his breath. "My aunt," he smirked.

"Fuck you and your aunt!" my father exclaimed.

"She's already been notified about a disturbance here at my house; get killed if you want to."

Quincy gave a devious smile.

Police quickly surrounded the garage and unloaded from their vehicles; guns drawn and aimed.

"D-R-P-D, let me see your hands!" They screamed at us.

My father got off Quincy and police ran into the garage and grabbed at my father.

An officer ran over to Jacob and me, and a few officers went for Quincy and my uncle.

"You all have it wrong. I'm a cop!" my father shouted. "This man tried to rape my daughter!" he stated as he pointed to Quincy.

Another car pulled up to the garage; it was Lieutenant Roberts and Veronica. Lieutenant Roberts saw police holding my father and walked over.

"Stop, these two men are with the Chicago Police Department; under-cover. Authorized to carry a firearm," he showed his badge.

Officers released my father and uncle.

"Stay on his ass, though" my father referenced to Quincy.

Veronica walked over to my father, and he looked at her.

"Richard, this is bad," she spoke.

"What do you mean?" he asked.

"Julie's on her way. I've already called your wife and told her to pack up, but we have less than 24 hours to leave the Dominican Republic before something bad happens."

"Aye, Rick, what she say?" my uncle asked; he wanted to be sure he heard her correctly.

"Fuck!" my father shouted.

Veronica ran back over to the car to place a few phone calls.

Suddenly, an AK-47 started firing and we all ducked for cover; officers started to fall.

"Yo, Richard!" Julie shouted.

She shot the gun again and killed the few police officers who were still alive.

"Jacob, take Miracle in the house and get out to the car." Uncle Jared shouted over the bullets. "We'll be out shortly."

Jacob and I ran into Quincy's home and could still hear Julie.

"I fucking told you, no cops! And you've brought two cops?"

"Julie…"

"And, what's crazy, is that your bitch ass is a cop yourself." Julie looked over to Quincy.

"You okay, Q?" she asked.

We heard Quincy cough.

"I'm fine, Auntie."

■■■

-Richard

Quincy rose to his feet and walked over to Julie. He reached down and grabbed the gun from one of the deceased officers.

Jared, Abel, and I stood there with the AK-47 and handgun aimed at us.

"You just don't get it," Julie started, "this shit isn't a game that you can press 'reset' on. I gave you specific instructions before you came here," she wiped her forehead clear of sweat. "And you broke the primary rule; you brought cops in my presence."

"Julie, this is all fucked up," I stated to her.

"What's going to be fucked up, is that you all are going to die right here in this garage. You're not leaving the D.R." Julie stated as she dropped the empty clip to her AK.

She loaded a full one; Quincy picked up magazines for his handgun from the ground.

"You have pissed me all the way off," Julie stated. "So, now, you can join my mother. Maybe you can tell me how terrible death is."

Julie aimed the gun at me.

"Make it easier and let's not even move."

Jared looked and saw a chair next to him. As Julie put her finger on the trigger, he pushed the chair towards her.

We quickly got down behind Quincy's car, and Julie fired her AK-47.

"Shit, Rich. Where do we go from here?" Jared asked me as he pulled out the pistol he had.

Abel pulled out his handgun as well.

"Roberts?" I asked.

"This is your case. You're in charge, Young," Abel held his handgun and turned the safety off.

I pulled out my phone and called Jamie.

"Hello?" she answered on the first ring.

"Jamie," I stated. Julie continued to fire the AK-47.

"Richard, where are you? Madison, Melanie, and I are packing to flee. Veronica said we had 24 hours."

"Damn all that," I stated. "Look, we have a few hours to get out of the D.R., and you know Julie controls everything."

"Baby, where are you?" she asked. I could tell she was worried and could hear the gunfire.

"We're at Quincy's garage. We're about to head that way," I told her. "I love you and we'll be there soon." I hung up the phone.

"Follow my lead," I stated.

Bullets stopped flying; we were assuming it was because she had to reload.

We ran for the door and Julie shot her gun again.

We ran through the house.

"Don't make this hard, Richard," Julie stated as she walked into the house with Quincy.

We ran past the kitchen, where Julie resided, and she shot the gun at us.

The bullets missed us and hit the walls.

"This way," I whispered as we ran to the door. We opened it and heard more sirens approaching. We ran to the car, and Julie came to the door.

"Go, go, go!" I shouted to Abel.

He sped off.

Veronica's phone rang, and Julie was on the other end.

Veronica put the phone on speaker.

"Veronica! I need for you to call the airport and shut everything down, pr Julie Wilson. Call the docks and shut down the boats. Shut everything down!" Julie was frantic.

"Calm down, Julie. What happened?" Veronica asked as she remained in character.

"I'll explain it later. Just have everything shut down."

Before Julie hung up the phone, she spoke to Quincy.

"These bitches are not making it out of here alive."

Veronica put her phone down.

"Apparently, Julie still thinks you're working with her," Jared spoke.

"You heard the woman, shut it down," I joked as Abel continued to speed.

■■■

Miracle

Veronica chuckled.

"On a serious note, Richard, I've called and arranged for a boat to take your cars back to Puerto Rico. I have a plane being fueled to take all of us out of here."

"When will everything be ready?" my father asked.

"They're going to give me a call when they have everything set. The important thing is that you all are packed and ready to go. Call your wives," Veronica adjusted herself in the chair and put her hair in a ponytail.

Jacob continued to hold me in his arms; I cried quietly and let out a few tears.

"Stop crying, Miracle," he mentioned.

"I'm sorry, Jacob," I responded.

More tears fell from my eyes.

"Miracle, are you okay?" my father asked me.

I didn't answer him. Instead, I continued to cry harder.

He put his hand on my head.

"You will *always* be daddy's little girl. No matter how much you may grow up or how many mistakes you make. I love you, Miracle."

My father's voice soothed me, yet I couldn't stop crying.

How could I have been so stupid?

Uncle Jared looked at me and saw a few cuts on my arms.

"You thought shit was real before," Uncle Jared spoke as he passed me a towel, "shit's about to get real."

"Jacob, Miracle," my father began. "You all need to be on your 'A'-game now. We have a few hours to get everything and to get out of here. We may have to split up and meet up the hangar."

"I'll keep Miracle at my side, at all times," Jacob stated. "I promise, I will keep her safe."

"Rick, do you think that now's a good time to split up?" Uncle Jared asked.

"We have to," my father began. "If Julie catches us together, we're all dead."

Lieutenant Roberts pulled the car over.

"Jacob, you and Miracle head towards the airport. Take this," my father handed us a gun. "Do not enter the airport," he stated. "Wait for us to get there."

I hugged my father.

"*Te amo, mucho,* Papa," I stated as I tightened my hug.

"I love you, too, Miracle. Jacob, watch over my little girl," my father released his hug.

"Will do, Unc," Jacob stated as he held my hand tightly.

"Jacob, we'll see you all at the airport. Don't talk to anyone once you get there, and keep a low profile, son. I love you," Uncle Jared adjusted himself in his chair.

"See ya, Pops," Jacob spoke. "We'll be fine."

My father closed the door and Lieutenant Roberts sped off.

The streets were quiet; a few people were walking, but nothing major.

"I thought it would be a lot crazier because of what just happened," I spoke.

"Yeah, well let's not hang around for it to get crazy. Come on, M." Jacob walked towards the bus stop, holding my hand.

The bus going in the direction of the airport arrived minutes later and we stepped aboard.

"*Siete dolares y cincueta ciecentavos.*" The bus driver spoke.

"Seven-fifty," I told Jacob.

He pulled the money out and inserted it into the slot.

I walked to a seat near the rear of the bus and sat down.

An older woman looked at us.

"Are you all okay?" she asked as she saw my clothes were ripped and the blood on Jacob's clothes.

Neither of us replied; we looked at each other.

"*¿Necesita un doctor?*" she asked.

"We speak English," Jacob answered. "But no, Miss, thank you for your concern."

"Are you all sure that you're okay?"

"We'll be fine," I responded. "Thank you."

The lady shrugged off her concern and focused her attention back on the front of the bus.

"Jacob," I started.

"Yes, Miracle?" he asked in a soothing tone.

I laid my head on his chest. I could hear his heart beating.

I let out another tear; so much had happened so quickly, I couldn't help but let the tears fall.

"Don't cry, M," he replied.

"Thank you for being there for me," I stated.

"It's my sworn duty," he replied with a chuckle.

I looked into his eyes and picked my head from his chest.

Don't do it, I could hear my conscious talking.

I leaned in and kissed Jacob on the lips. He didn't fight back or retreat from the kiss.

He held me tight as we kissed, and we retreated seconds later.

Neither of us could believe what just happened and instead of speaking, he wiped the tear from my eye.

I laid my head back down on his chest. We were silent for a long moment until he finally spoke.

"Get some rest, baby."

I felt a slight chill run down my body as he called me his baby.

∎∎

-Richard

"We have to make it quick. Julie's men will be swarming the hotel; we need to get our stuff and go."

"What's the word?" Jared asked me.

I stopped and thought for a second.

"Shoot if prompted," I replied.

Jared and Abel looked at me, then at each other, and nodded in approval.

"I'm going to stay back. Julie still thinks I work for her, so I have to lay low until it's time to depart. I have to make sure the plane and boat stay fueled and ready to go," Veronica mentioned.

She began to get out of the car.

"Veronica," I stated.

She turned around.

"Thanks, for everything," I stated as I extended my hand to her.

"It's been a pleasure working with you, Richard," she spoke as she shook my hand.

She left the vehicle and walked to the bus stop.

"Stay safe, Sis," Roberts spoke. "I'll see you soon."

"Will do," she responded.

Abel drove off and continued towards the hotel.

"Damn, we've all split up," Jared stated as he drove towards the hotel.

"We gotta do, what we gotta do. We need to stay alive, and if we're all together, we all go down if one gets caught." I spoke.

Abel pulled up to the hotel and we each pulled out our guns.

We took the keys out of the car and parked it across the street.

We ran inside the hotel.

We ran to the elevators and I pressed the button, rapidly, numerous times.

"Come on, come on, come on," I mentioned out loud.

No one in the hotel seemed to be panicking, so I figured Julie hadn't contacted the men yet.

The elevator door opened, and Joey stood there with several other men.

"Shit!" I stated.

Joey threw his body at me and tackled me to the floor.

Jared and Abel aimed their guns at the other men, and they got on the ground. I started to wrestle with Joey, but he had a weight advantage over me.

Everyone in the hotel lobby started screaming.

I punched him in the face twice and he put his hands over my nose and mouth. Jared walked up to Joey and hit him in the back of the head with the gun.

"Little bitch," he asserted.

I shoved Joey onto the floor.

I gasped for breath. "I couldn't breathe under there," I spoke as we walked to the elevator.

"Wasn't even that heavy," Jared chuckled.

Abel pressed the button to our floor and the doors closed. As the doors opened, we each eased our way out of the elevator.

"There they are," some men shouted as they ran towards us.

I shot two of the men as Jared shot some men coming from the opposite direction. Abel took the lead towards the room as we covered his back.

I swiped my key card and opened the room door. I was almost knocked to the floor by an object being swung at me.

"Woah, shit!" I exclaimed.

"Baby!" Jamie exclaimed. "I am so sorry," she had a slight chuckle.

"At least my baby can defend herself," I joked. "Are you all packed?"

"Everything's ready," Madison spoke.

Jared and Abel both grabbed a suitcase and I grabbed the final one.

Melanie walked out of the room.

We all ran to the elevator and walked inside. Once it reached the lobby, we all ran outside to the car. Abel tossed me the keys.

"Young," he stated. "Get us to the airport."

We loaded the bags into the trunk of the car and we each got inside.

"First, we have to go to the dock and drop off these bags," I responded.

"Well, you better speed like you've never sped before," Abel spoke.

"What about the kids' cars?" Madison asked.

"Veronica is going to handle all of that," I spoke. "Jared, call Jacob and see how he and Miracle are doing."

Jared dialed Jacob's number and got an answer.

Miracle

Jacob answered his phone.

"Hello?" he stated as he put the phone on speakerphone.

"Jacob, how are things going with you and Miracle?" his father spoke.

"Things are okay," he stated as we walked off the bus. "We just made it to the airport."

"Any sign of Julie or her people?"

"So far, it's quiet."

"Okay. I'm going to call Veronica and see where the plane is located. I will call you back," his father hung up the phone, and Jacob looked at me.

"Will security let us on the plane with this gun?" he asked with a slight laugh.

"I'm sure your father will have all of the answers when he calls back," I assured him. "I'm just praying we make it out of here safely. You know Julie controls all of this."

"Just pray," Jacob reiterated.

His phone rang and he answered.

"Hello?"

"Jacob, do not go into the airport until we get there. We actually don't have a reason to enter the airport because the plane is on the field. We will be there in about five minutes," Uncle Jared sped through his words.

Jacob hung up the phone.

"Now I know, shit's about to get real," he replied. "My father never speaks that fast unless something is wrong."

"What about our cars?" I asked.

"Fuck; you're right!" Jacob exclaimed. "I'm sure they have it all handled," Jacob assured me.

My father pulled up in the car about ten minutes later. Jacob and I got in the backseat, although it was a tight squeeze.

My mother kissed me on the cheek, and Aunt Madison did the same to Jacob.

"Hold on," my father stated as he drove forward towards the gate that separated the main road from the runway.

Security approached the window.

"May I help you?" he asked.

"Yes, we have a plane to take us back to Puerto Rico on the runway. I am approaching the gate because it isn't scheduled as a regular takeoff." My father spoke to the security guard with no hesitation.

"I need authority approval to let you all on the runway. Do you have any evidence of this flight belonging to you?" he asked.

My father and uncle looked at each other. They knew that if they gave certain information to the security officer, it would get back to Julie.

Lieutenant Roberts spoke.

"I have my badge, which authorizes entrance to the runway. I'm a police officer," he pulled out his badge and the security officer examined it before lifting the gate.

"Sorry for the delay," he mentioned. "Have a great and safe flight."

My father drove onto the runway.

"Veronica said it was to the left. She said as soon as we enter the runway, we should see it," Uncle Jared spoke.

"There it is," I spoke.

My father drove over to the plane and we each got out.

We surrounded the plane and Veronica pulled up next to us.

"Okay guys, we have to make this quick," she spoke as she got out of her car. "This plane is a straight shot to Puerto Rico, but the biggest thing will be breaking the air to get out of here. Every plane that flies in and out is on the radar; you all know I'm supposed to have everything closed, so I've instructed the pilot to fly under the radar. Once you all land, I'll catch the next flight out."

"You're not going with us?" my father asked.

"I can't leave right now. I have to make sure some things are settled here, first." Veronica slightly shrugged her shoulders.

It was silent for a moment.

"Then I'm not going," my father spoke.

"You *have* to go," Veronica insisted.

"Veronica, you've been here for us since day one. You've had our backs through it all and kept watch over us. Even though I didn't believe in you, you didn't turn your back on us," my father spoke. "You have kept us safe; I'm not boarding that plane to leave you here with Julie," my father declared.

"*Yo tampoco voy a ir,*" my mother agreed. "Veronica, you're like family to us now, and we can't just leave you behind."

"That's right," Uncle Jared spoke. "Either you go with us…"

"Or none of us go, at all," Aunt Madison finished.

Veronica looked at each of us.

"V, we're not leaving without you," Lieutenant Roberts spoke.

Everyone was silent for a moment, but all eyes stayed on Veronica.

She let out a sigh.

"Let me make a call," she finally replied.

She pulled out her cell phone and dialed a number.

"Hello? Yeah, it's Veronica. Have you all gotten the cars to the docks yet? Tomorrow? And they'll be shipped off to Puerto Rico, correct? Got it, thank you."

She looked at us.

"I'm going with you," she spoke.

Lieutenant Roberts hugged her; it was followed by a handshake from my father.

"The men will be getting your vehicles loaded on the boat, tomorrow. But we have to get out of here."

"Well, let's get on the plane," Jacob stated as we walked to the plane.

Melanie stayed behind.

"You coming, Melanie?" my father asked.

She didn't answer.

"Come on, Melanie!" Jacob shouted as he turned around.

Melanie glared at him.

"I don't know why you're mad, you broke up with me!" he stated.

"I'm not mad," Melanie stated with an attitude.

"Come on, Melanie," I told her.

"Melanie. I need for you to board this plane," my father stated from the steps of the plane.

"Why don't you all just leave me here with Julie?" she asked.

"Because we're not just going to leave you here," my father spoke.

"Why not? It's not like I have anything left back in Puerto Rico to go to. I'm living alone and have basically raised myself from a young age since my mother died when I was 5 and my grandparents passed away when I was 14," she teared a little. "Nah, just leave me here."

Everyone boarded the plane, my father stood in the doorway talking to Melanie.

"Melanie, we *are* your family, and we will not leave you here with Julie," my father was sympathetic.

"I don't want to be on the same flight as Jacob," Melanie mentioned.

"We will sit you far away from him," my father answered. "But we have to get out of here," my father tried to reason with Melanie.

She finally walked onto the plane.

My father walked to the front to talk to the pilot with Uncle Jared.

Veronica and Abel closed the door to the plane.

After a few minutes, the pilot spoke over the intercom.

"This is your captain speaking. I'm Pilot Whitfield and I will be ensuring a safe trip to San Juan, Puerto Rico. I've been informed to fly under the radar, so we will not be as high in the air, as we typically are.

We are looking at a flight time of about 50 minutes, so I will be attempting to get you all there are smoothly and quickly as possible. We shouldn't experience much turbulence, but over the water, the air will become much cooler and a bit rougher. This plane is not pressurized in case of a need for emergency evacuation. It's currently about 87 degrees in San Juan, Puerto Rico, so sit back, and enjoy our brief journey."

The plane took off, and five minutes into the flight, three men came from the back of the plane.

"Where do you all think you're going?" one of the men asked us.

I'd never seen these men before.

Neither of us answered.

"Papi," I called for him.

"Looks like we got some individuals running home," the second man spoke as he walked towards the front.

"Jamie Young... married to Richard Young. Speaking of which, where is he?" the first man spoke as he looked at my mother.

The third man pulled out a gun and started to walk past us.

"How many of you all know what this is?" he asked. "Come on, I know you know," he was looking at Lieutenant Roberts. "You're the cop."

"Fuck!" Jacob spoke under his breath.

The door from the cockpit creaked open; my father and Uncle Jared walked out of the room and noticed the men. They stopped in their tracks.

"There he is," the man turned around. "Let's give a round of applause for the man of the hour."

"Julie thought you bitches would try to run," the second man answered. "So, we took it upon ourselves to figure some things out."

"Yo, where's Veronica?" the third guy asked. "She was supposed to shut this shit down a long time ago."

Veronica slumped down in her chair.

The first guy spoke into the microphone on his shoulder.

"We got 'em, boss. They're on an aircraft headed to Puerto Rico."

"I need you to tell me what the number is to the aircraft. It's located in the cockpit by the controls; close to the windshield."

Julie sounded extremely angry.

"Hold on boss," the first man stated. "Vic, toss me a gun."

The third man pulled a gun from his pocket and tossed it.

The first man walked towards the cockpit, and my mother jumped out of her seat onto his back. She started to attack him.

He fell to the ground with my mother on his back.

My father grabbed at the man, picked him up, and slammed him against the wall. The other men walked forward.

Jacob and Lieutenant Roberts both rose and started to fight the men.

Melanie, Veronica, and I all got on the floor. Uncle Jared ran over to my father.

My father punched the man, but the suspect continued to hold the gun firmly. The man moved his arm and aimed the gun at my father

"Rob, kill his ass," Vic shouted as he scuffled with Jacob.

My father grabbed Rob's hand, and they fired a shot in the air.

Uncle Jared pulled out his gun and aimed it at the man.

"Jared, do that shit!" my father shouted.

Uncle Jared shot Rob in the arm; it instantly seemed to weaken him.

My father punched Rob in the face three times, before grabbing his shirt and slamming him against the wall once more. My father released Rob, and he fell to the floor.

My mother rose to her feet and walked over to me.

"Miracle, I just want you to know that I love you… just in case," she cried a little.

"Mami, *no hablas de esa manera*. We will make it out of this. We just need to keep our heads and think," I hugged my mother and kissed her on the cheek.

I looked up and saw Jacob slam the final guy against the wall.

"David, tell me what's going on there," Julie spoke over the radio.

"You son of a bitch," my father spoke over the radio.

"Ah, it feels good to hear your voice, Richard," Julie replied. "Where's Veronica? I know that she's working with you."

"Bye Julie," my mother stated in a sing-song voice.

"Before you go, guess what?" Julie questioned.

"It's over, Julie. What the fuck do you want?" My father was getting annoyed.

"I've found your plane," she whispered.

We were all stunned.

"Yeah, your pilot messed up and flew above 30,000 feet. I've detected your plane." Julie chuckled. "You know, if only he stayed at 29,999 feet, I wouldn't have been able to locate you."

"Julie, don't do it," my father spoke.

"In five…" she started to countdown.

"Julie," Uncle Jared stated.

"Four…"

"Shit, shit, shit. What are we going to do?" my mother asked my father.

Julie continued to countdown.

"You know you got your own men on board. You fire a missile, they're dead as well."

"One. Goodbye Richard," Julie laughed, and we heard static on the radio.

"Julie!" my father shouted.

The pilot spoke over the intercom.

"Ladies and gentlemen, I apologize for the interruption. Do not panic and remain seated, but the plane's engines have stalled. There is absolutely no control over the aircraft. Brace for impact."

We were all speechless.

"We are currently gliding through the air, but are losing height. A nosedive will soon commence."

"Okay, guys, look. I have some parachutes in the back of the plane. Jacob, go grab them from the top shelf." Veronica spoke.

Jacob walked to the back and my heart was pounding.

"Have you all ever been sky-diving?" Veronica asked.

"I am not trying to die from jumping out of a plane," my uncle spoke.

"We have no choice but to jump. If this plane crashes, it will explode. I've made sure that the parachutes were flawless and we will land safely."

Jacob came back to the front with the parachutes.

"Thank you, Jacob," Veronica spoke.

She passed each of us a parachute.

My father paced the plane. My mother walked over to him.

"Baby, come on," she spoke. "Once we jump, hopefully, all of this will be over."

"Yeah, but baby, what if it's not? We're about to jump out of a plane because of this bullshit," my father was disgusted.

Each of us put on our parachutes and made sure they were secure; everyone except for my mother and father. The plane's alarms began to go off. Everything hurdled towards the front of the plane and we each grabbed on to a chair while the plane dived nose first

"Ladies and gentlemen, we are currently in a dive. Evacuation procedures are commencing. Head towards the emergency exits and prepare to climb on the wings of the plane."

"Richard, Jamie, put these on!" Veronica shouted as she tossed the parachutes at my parents.

My uncle opened the door to the plane.

The air pressure sucked the parachutes from the plane.

"We're over water," my uncle shouted as he looked down; he noticed the parachutes hurdling towards the water.

We all looked at my parents.

■■

-Richard

Jamie and I looked at each other, wondering what to do. Our parachutes were hurdling towards the water and the plane was quickly falling.

Jared looked at me and spoke.

"We have to jump, Rick. All of us," he told me.

"We don't have parachutes," I spoke.

"Baby, we have to do something," Jamie added.

"Here, Mami," Miracle took off her parachute and gave it to her mother.

"Miracle, I couldn't take your parachute," Jamie retorted.

David stood up and grabbed the gun from the floor.

"Looks like we got company," Jacob spoke as he saw the man.

He cocked his gun.

"Go!" I shouted.

Abel and Veronica jumped out of the plane, followed by Melanie.

"Rick, come on, man," Jared shouted.

"Just go," I replied.

Jared and Madison held hands as they jumped from the plane, leaving Jamie, myself, Miracle, and Jacob on the rapidly descending aircraft.

Jacob stood behind Miracle and pulled her closer. He hugged her waist.

"Put on that parachute and come on Unc," Jacob shouted as he prepared to jump.

The man shot the gun; Jacob jumped off the plane with Miracle.

The bullets penetrated the parachute that Jamie held.

"Can't use it now," I stated out of disgust as I took Jamie's hand.

"Baby," she stated.

It was obvious she was scared.

"Forever and ever?" I asked her.

"Forever, babe," she let out a tear.

I took her hand as the man reloaded his gun. We walked to the edge and jumped off the plane without a parachute.

We freefell and Jamie screamed as we fell.

I held her hand tighter and would not let it go. I saw everyone land in the water, but I knew our landing would not be as smooth as theirs.

The plane continued to fall and landed in the water onto some jagged rocks. It exploded and caused waves to form.

Seconds later, Jamie and I hit the water.

■■■

Miracle

We frantically searched for my mother and father. We couldn't be positive if they'd jumped or not.

"Richard!" Uncle Jared shouted as he swam towards where the plane landed.

"Mami!" I shouted as I dove into the water.

I returned to the surface, with no sign of my parents. I flipped my wet hair out of my face with my hands.

"I'm convinced they didn't have a parachute," Lieutenant Roberts spoke.

"Why do you say that?" I asked. "I gave them mine, and I jumped with Jacob."

"If they jumped and had a parachute, they would probably still be on the way down, and we would see them floating through the air."

"But since we don't see them, and we don't want to fear the worst, we're going to assume they jumped without a parachute," Aunt Madison responded.

We sat there and thought the worst for a moment; not that we wanted to, but it was involuntary.

My father swam to the surface with my mother; they were holding hands.

"Papi!" I shouted as I swam over to him. I hugged him and let out a few tears. I, then, embraced my mother next.

"Rich," Uncle Jared started. "Think it's over?" he asked.

"Honestly, I couldn't even begin to tell you," my father stated out of disgust.

I noticed he was bleeding on his left shoulder.

"Papi, you're bleeding," I spoke.

"I know. The fucker shot me as jumped," my father spoke. Hitting the water from that height is no joke," he breathed heavily.

194

We floated in the middle of the water before Veronica spoke.

"Let's get out of this water," she spoke.

A boat approached us with a bright light shining from it.

We all swam in a crowd and the boat came closer to us.

The rescuers extended hands to help us on board.

As we each sat on the boat, we were handed towels to dry off, and they gave us three large blankets.

"Are you all alright?" one rescuer asked. "We received a signal from the plane that it needed assistance."

"We're okay," my mother stated.

Another rescuer came out of the boat with a first aid kit to treat my father's wound.

"Tell us what happened," they spoke.

Jacob and I shared a blanket, and he held me tight. He kissed me on the forehead.

"Well, we are leaving the Dominican Republic to go back home to Puerto Rico," my father spoke as they patched his shoulder.

"And this woman, Julie Wilson, killed the plane's engine," my mother finished angrily.

"Calm down, baby," my father held her hand.

"Any fatalities?" the rescuer asked.

He took a cotton ball and dabbed my father's wound with it.

"4, including the pilot. We don't believe he made it. The plane exploded once it hit the water."

"He could have jumped," Uncle Jared spoke, trying to sound hopeful.

"Slim chance of that, considering he was trying to get the plane under control," Lieutenant Roberts spoke.

"Can we think positive for a moment?" my aunt asked.

"Positively speaking, we're all safe," Veronica emphasized.

"That's right, and I live to be with my wife and baby girl," my father continued.

The door to the boat opened, and Julie walked out. The rescuers stepped into the cockpit.

"What the fuck?!" Uncle Jared exclaimed as he jumped to his feet.

"Richard, Jamie!" she began. "Jared, Madison. And the kids: Jacob, Melanie, and, of course, little Miracle."

I could tell the feeling of relief left everyone's body as Julie spoke.

"Veronica," Julie added. "Oh, and I don't think we've formally met," she spoke to Lieutenant Roberts. "Julie Wilson," she introduced.

"You've got some nerve showing your face," my father spoke.

"You know, people have had many different approaches towards me, but no one has ever had the balls that you have shown when approaching me," Julie sat down in the chair. "Is this how you're going to treat the woman who just rescued you from the water?"

"Rescued us?" my mother asked.

"We wouldn't have ended up in the water if it wasn't for you," I spoke.

"As far as the media outlets are concerned, I rescued your asses from the water. Do not fuck with me right now," she spoke. "I'm taking you all back to the D.R. to get cleaned up. And rather than kill you all, you all will continue to work for me."

"You must be out your fuckin' mind," my uncle spoke.

"To even think we're doing anything else for you. Your goddamn, punk-ass nephew tried to rape my daughter, and you think we're going to keep doing this? Gonna have to kill me first." My father stood by his word.

"I didn't give you a fucking choice," Julie raised her tone. "Quincy did something bad, I admit. But I specifically told you 'no cops'. And, well, here you are... a damn cop, who has brought along another cop, and another cop flies out later. Do you take me for a fool?"

"Not a fool, just stupid," I snickered.

Everyone chuckled, but Julie.

She walked over, slapped me, and Jacob stood up.

"Julie you little..." he started.

A man emerged from the cockpit as Jacob was about to grab Julie. He aimed his gun at Jacob.

"Sit yo' ass down," Julie growled.

Jacob glared at her, before sitting back down next to me. He held my hand.

"Now that we're all on the same page," Julie spoke again, "I think it would be best to talk about what's going to happen next."

"There is nothing else," my father asked. "You don't get it, do you, Julie?"

He stood up and got in her face.

"It's over. Everything is done."

"Can I let you in on a secret?" she asked. "Out of everyone here, I have the most respect for you. Your courage is why I chose you."

"No, let's try that you're most intimidated by me. No one else has ever stood up to you, and no one else here has done so. So, it's not just about respect."

"It's all about respect. You think I'm scared of you? No, it's not over for me, but for you, you've reached the final level. Time to shut down the game."

My father stood in front of Julie and stared at her. He didn't back down, although a gun was aimed at him.

The boat reached the docks, and Julie chuckled.

"We're here."

She and my father were still staring each other down.

She walked away.

"Follow me," she ordered us.

"Stay behind Jared, me, and Abel," my father spoke in a whisper.

"We've rescued these individuals from the water. You all know the plane that crashed? These are the only survivors." Julie spoke to the dock workers. "Can we get them a cab to take them to the Hard Rock Hotel & Casino Punta Cana?"

"The poor people must be devastated and in shock."

We didn't say a word to debate with her lies.

A taxi arrived and we all got inside.

The drive to the hotel was silent.

I looked at my father; he was making eye contact with Uncle Jared and Lieutenant Roberts.

I knew they were plotting something, and I knew by the faces they were making, that something big was about to happen.

19

-Richard

The taxi arrived at the hotel and we walked inside. The hotel was similar to the previous one, except more security guards were standing around.

"Looks like we won't be making a quick escape from this hotel," I spoke to Jared.

"I wonder how many of these cats work for Julie," he responded.

"It's stupid of me to ask," I started to speak, "but, how many cell phones survived the swim?"

I pulled out my phone. My pockets were soaked, but the phone was protected in the Otter Box casing.

"I'm good," I answered.

Everyone reached in their pockets.

"All good," Jared mentioned.

"It's dead, Unc," Jacob mentioned.

"Mine is showing the screen and is responsive," Miracle began, "*pero,* my case is cracked and my phone is cracked on the side."

Veronica pulled out her phone. "It's gone. I see the LCD lights, but no screen at all."

Abel pulled out his phone.

"Barely living," he answered.

"No luck," Jamie determined.

"So, it seems that only half of us have working phones."

"What does that have to do with anything Rich?" Madison asked.

"Shhh" I held my fingers over my mouth.

Julie walked into the building.

"Follow me," she walked to the elevators and walked inside.

We each followed her.

The ride to the top floor was silent; no one made a sound.

We followed Julie to the hotel room.

"This is going to be where you all will stay," she opened the room door.

The ladies walked in first, followed by the guys.

"If you all need me, you can reach me by using the hotel phone to call my number, since I'm sure your phones were all wrecked in the water," Julie finished speaking.

No one replied; I could tell fear was in the children's bodies, as well as the ladies'.

She left out of the room and closed the door behind her.

"Well, mission 'get the fuck out of here' was a complete failure," Jared stated.

I thought aloud.

"Somehow, Julie had some insight on the flight," I spoke. "Veronica, do you think the pilot could have been working with Julie all along?"

"And put his own life on the line?" Jared asked.

"You're right, who would do that?" I thought aloud.

"I did my background search on the pilot. He was clean. It was his eighth year being a pilot."

"So, I really want to know how the men ended up on the plane and knew we would be leaving," I answered.

Abel sat on the bed and picked up the hotel phone.

"Hello, Isabella?" he spoke over the phone.

"Woah, shit," I spoke as I rushed over to the phone and hung it up. "We can't use these phones for calls like that, Roberts," I told him.

"Richard, we need to get——."

"We can't use these phones. Use our cell-phones for all of that," I replied.

"Why would we...?" he started to ask.

"Julie probably has all of the phone lines tapped. She actually probably just focusing on our phone since she knows what's up."

Jared was now sitting on the opposite bed, holding Madison's hand. He kissed her on the forehead.

"No point in hiding that we're cops now," Jared pulled his badge from his pocket and threw it on the bed.

After minutes of silence, Miracle spoke.

"I'm going to take a shower," she walked towards the bathroom and closed the door.

"So, we can't escape via air or boat," Abel spoke.

"And we can't drive over the ocean," Jacob chuckled.

"We're going to have to call in back-up," I thought.

"But the Dominican Republic is meticulous about who sets foot in their water or air," Melanie added.

"Yeah, well we have to find some way to get out of here," Jamie argued.

"We do whatever we have to do, to get out of here alive," I replied. "Veronica, what do you think the status of the cars and our bags are?"

"Once I check my email, I will let you know, but they'd already shipped. The boat was leaving the docks as we boarded the plane," Veronica answered.

"Can't Julie shut down the boat, like she did the plane?" Jared asked.

"She can halt a boat's engine; however, she cannot keep the engine stalled. It can be repowered by the back-up power generators within the boat, so potential passengers would never even know anything was wrong."

"So, why didn't we take a boat out of here?" Jamie asked.

"If we had taken a boat, we would get about halfway, and once we have to pass-over from the D.R. to Puerto Rico, we would be tracked," Veronica explained. "The boat the cars are on is a cargo boat; no passengers are present except the captain of the ship. People have to show passports to go from country to country, but cargo just has a tag and can be delivered worldwide."

"So, we're pretty much fucked, then," Jared spoke.

"Not quite," Everyone looked at me as I spoke.

Miracle

As the steaming water flowed from the showerhead to my body, I couldn't get my mind off everything that happened during the day: Quincy tried to rape me, I was shot at, we jumped from a plane, and we were recaptured by Julie.

I took the towel and scrubbed my entire body, and I couldn't help but let the tears fall from my eyes.

I wanted to scrub the day away from my body.

I got out of the shower about thirty minutes later and dried my hair. My cellphone rang, and I answered it without looking at it.

"Hello?"

"Miracle," Quincy stated in a sing-song voice. "You lookin' good, getting out of that shower. I don't know why you didn't let me see that ass before," he chuckled menacingly.

My heart dropped but I held my phone up to my ear.

"Yeah, why don't you drop that towel for me?"

I put my phone down and ran out of the bathroom.

"Papi!" I shouted.

He quickly jumped up and walked towards me.

"*Quincy puede verme*," I mentioned quickly.

"*¿Mande?*" my mother asked.

My father pulled out his gun and he entered the washroom. He put the phone on speaker.

"Hello?" my father asked.

"Richard! Bro, what's going on?" Quincy stated.

"Where is it, Quincy?"

"Why, what ever do you mean?" he asked sarcastically.

"Look here, you little shit," my uncle spoke as he entered behind us.

"I'm sorry, am I being threatened right now? After you damn near broke the rules and got killed over it?" Quincy cleared his throat. "You may not want to mess with me right now," he added.

"Where's the camera, Quincy?" my mother asked.

"Why do you think there's a camera?" he spoke.

"Let me remind you that having a camera in a private place is illegal," my father spoke.

"Oh, shit, you are a cop," Quincy stated sarcastically. "Let me remind *you*, you're not in the U.S. anymore. Things are played a different way, here."

"You want us to come beat your ass again?" my uncle asked.

"Please… I'd have you all killed before you even left the hotel building," Quincy replied. "Julie's calling me, so I have to go," he quickly hung up the phone.

We were all silent for a moment.

"Go get dressed, baby," my father told me. "Go into the adjoining room with your mother."

"What are we going to do about Quincy?" I asked.

"Uncle Jared, Lieutenant Roberts, and I have a plan to get out of here. We're going to try to make it happen over the next two days, so we need to make sure we have everything up to par."

I lowered my head and walked out of the washroom. I walked into the adjoining room with my mother.

-Richard

"Let's get to calling 'em," I stated.

Abel picked up my phone, put it on speaker, and dialed the police department.

"Chicago Police Department," Isabella answered.

"Isabella, it's Roberts."

"Hey, Roberts. How are you?" she asked.

"Terrible, we—" he began, and I spoke.

"Isabella, we are trapped here in the D.R."

"Oh my, God. What's going on?" she was concerned.

"We need the team to fly here and get us out of here. Julie has this place on lockdown; she controls the boats, planes, everything. We can't leave."

"She got the drop on us being police officers," Jared spoke. "And now, she's holding us hostage."

"Tell me what you need," she spoke; I could hear her typing.

"Blackhawks, as many officers and units that can come, hella ammo," I spoke.

"Heavy weapons; nothing light. We're talking about a dead-on war."

"When's the soonest you think you can have it here?" Abel asked.

"How does tomorrow evening sound?" Isabella stated.

"Tomorrow is perfect. One more thing, Isabella," I stated. "Our personal vehicles are being shipped to Puerto Rico. I need someone to pick them up. I don't have much time to call Puerto Rico, so I need you to do it for me."

"I will do that," she replied. "You all need to stay safe," she mentioned with concern in her voice.

"We're fine for now, but this is why I need for you all to come and get us out of here," I answered.

"You know our motto: 'we make shit happen'," Isabella spoke. "It will happen," she hung up.

"Jacob, Melanie, come over here," Jared called.

Jamie and Miracle walked out of the room, and Madison sat on the bed next to them.

"We've called in reinforcements," Jared spoke.

"Look, we have to get out of here. They'll be here by tomorrow evening, so we need to be on top of our game."

"Why are they coming? Like, what's the point?" Melanie asked. I was wondering why she asked and she was in the room during the conversation.

"They're getting us out of here," Jared stated. "They're bringing heavy weapons and artillery in case it's needed, but we need to find a way to get the hell out of here."

"Are you forgetting, we don't have any weapons, except for the few you all possess. Surely, those wouldn't stand against Julie and her army of people." Madison spoke. "And we can't wait for the C-P-D to arrive before taking on Julie."

"You know Xino?" I asked. "Those are our weapons right there."

"You think he's going to give us weapons to fight against Julie?" Madison asked.

"We can always ask," I stated. "We don't have to give him a reason."

"And," Jared started, "if he says no, we can always use this" he cocked the gun.

"As a last resort, of course," I replied. Jared shrugged his shoulders and I continued, "since half of us have working cell phones, we split into two teams."

"As soon as Isabella calls us and gives the signal that they're on their way, we go live," Abel stated.

Jamie walked to the window of the hotel room; I followed behind her.

"Baby, what's wrong?" I asked her.

"It's just all of this." She began. "We're basically putting our lives in danger because of this fiend. We've almost lost our lives numerous times since we've been here in the D.R. Not to mention we've done countless crimes? And for what?"

"Baby, look," I tried to speak.

"This woman has crossed the line now, and I'm just sick and tired of her. She may be my cousin, but I'll be damned if I let her control and kill us. She's the reason you were in a coma for months, let's not forget that!"

I held her shoulders.

"Baby, I promise this to you, I will keep us all safe. We will get out of here and we will get out alive." I kissed her on the cheek. "I promise."

She hugged me and I returned the hug.

"I love you," I stated while hugging her.

"I love you, too."

***

The next morning came, and Julie came to our room. She opened the door with her keycard and walked inside.

"Wake up, sleepy-heads," she clapped her hands and looked at the beds. She saw lumps under the covers.

"Aww, are we playing hide-and-seek this morning?" she jerked the covers back, only to find pillows.

Julie got nervous and looked in the bathroom; no sign of us. She pulled out her handgun.

"Come on guys, I just want to play," she held her gun in two hands as she opened the closet with her foot. She found Melanie, who appeared to be tied up.

Julie squatted down and lowered her gun. She took the tape from Melanie's mouth.

"What happened?" she asked in concern.

"These guys came and took everyone, but tied me up and left me in this closet." Melanie let a few tears pass her cheeks.

"What'd they look like?" Julie asked.

Jamie tapped Julie on the shoulder.

Julie turned around and Jamie punched her in the face. Madison grabbed Julie's arms, and Miracle helped sit Julie on the bed. Jared entered the room and jogged over to the bed; he grabbed Julie's arms and held them behind her.

"Get your fuckin' hands off me," she growled.

"They'll be coming," I stated out loud as I emerged from the adjoining room.

I was dressed in all black with a Bluetooth earpiece and tactical clothing on. Jared wore similar clothing, as did Abel.

Abel tossed Jared his handcuffs and Jared put the handcuffs on Julie.

"Synchronize watches," Abel spoke.

He tossed me a pistol.

Jamie, Madison, and Miracle walked towards the door and stood Melanie up.

They untied her hands and opened the door.

Jared and I picked Julie up by the arms. Abel directed us out of the room.

"Son of a bitch," Julie tried to break free from our grip and we held her arms tightly.

I hid the gun but held it to her back.

Jared spoke.

"This is what's going to happen, right? We're going outside, and you're going to behave. If not, you'll be bleeding throughout the streets of the D.R. Got it?"

"You can't make me do shit. I wonder how you're going to get me anywhere without getting past Joey and his men."

"We got a little care package for them," Abel stated.

"Isabella, we are about to exit the hotel," I stated over the phone.

"Time until arrival is about five hours and thirty minutes. We still have to break the air." Isabella stated.

"Good luck breaking the air. I'm not letting up on my security," Julie mentioned as we all got on the elevator.

"I didn't think we gave you a fucking choice," I stated.

The elevator opened and we all walked out. Julie was resisting more than ever, attempting to draw attention from someone.

We walked out of the door and saw two vehicles: a white Lamborghini Gallardo, and a black Ferrari. Veronica was standing outside of them with Jacob.

"These are the vehicles we won this morning," she mentioned.

"Alright, Jared, we're in the Ferrari. Ladies, you all travel with Abel and Jacob, and go to the place," I stated. "We meet at the quad at 1700 hours."

"You bitches got a lot of balls," Julie chuckled.

"Shut the fuck up," Jared stated before shoving her into the Ferrari.

I got in the driver's seat and sped off.

"End of the road, Julie," Jared spoke.

"Joey's on his way for me, and Quincy's on his way to Miracle."

I ignored the comment and continued to speed.

Miracle

Hours passed, but due to heavy traffic, we were finally arriving at Xino's gun shop.

Lieutenant Roberts held his gun in his hands and Jacob held the gun that Julie once possessed.

"You ready?" he asked.

Lieutenant Roberts nodded 'yes' and they put their guns in their pants. We all walked inside.

"What's up, my man?" Xino stated as he put the magazine down.

"We're here for a few weapons," Jacob replied.

"Who's the new guy?" Xino asked about Lieutenant Roberts.

"Abel Roberts," he answered stated as he extended his hand for a shake.

"Rule number one: don't try to touch me," Xino walked back towards the counter.

"Is he clean?" Xino stated as he pulled out a few weapons and placed them on the table.

"Cleaner and fresher than a newborn," Jacob stated.

My mother and Aunt Madison walked in, followed by Melanie.

"I knew you'd come back to me," Xino stated as he saw my mother.

"Save it," my aunt stated.

"Something big is about to go down," Jacob stated as Xino put two AK-47s, several .9-millimeter handguns, two Uzis, and some bullet-proof vests on the counter.

"You know what it is," Xino started to speak.

The radio announcer interrupted the music and came on the air.

"Sorry to interrupt your music, but this is a special bulletin. 3 Blackhawks that have just entered the Dominican Republic's airspace. These are military-grade helicopters that arrive when the President flies in and out when a high-powered official enters the area, or there's a war that's either happening or is going to start. These helicopters have a VIN that is registered in Chicago, Illinois, in the United States. Everyone be advised and stay alert. This is not a common thing. Stay indoors and keep cover, as we do not know the seriousness of this matter. We will keep you updated with information as it comes in. *Perdonen por interrumpir la música, pero este es un anuncio especial. 3 helicópteros Blackhawk acaban de entrar a la Republica Dominicana. Estos son helicópteros militares que entran cuando el Presidente viene y sale, cuando un oficial de alto rango entra en el área, o cuando una Guerra va a empezar o está sucediendo. Estos helicopteros tienen un número VIN que está registrado en Chicago Illinois, en los Estados Unidos. Todos tengan cuidado y estén alerta, esta no es una cosa común. Manténganse adentro y manténganse cubiertos ya que no sabemos la seriedad de la situación. Nosotros los mantendremos informados mientras se vaya sabiendo más información sobre el hecho."*

Xino got a text on his cell-phone after the announcer went off the air.

"Yo, I never got your name, bro?" he stated.

I knew he had to have been tipped off about what was going on.

"Jacob," Jacob replied.

"Oh shit, I've just been warned not to give you guys anything," Xino reached his hand under the counter.

Lieutenant Roberts pulled out his weapon and shot Xino in the chest; the suppressor on the gun silenced the shot.

Xino fell to the ground.

We each put on a vest and grabbed a gun from the counter.

"We got it," he spoke over his phone.

"Julie said Quincy was heading for you all. Please keep my baby girl safe and protected," my father spoke.

I cringed at Quincy's name.

"Will do," Lieutenant Roberts stated before putting his phone in his pocket.

We all ran to the car and got inside.

Jacob got in the driver's seat and Lieutenant got in the passenger side. A helicopter flew above us with the flashlight shining.

"Jacob, I need for you to get us to the quad as quickly as you can," Lieutenant Roberts stated.

Jacob sped off, and the helicopter flew above our heads. It was so low, I could hear the propellers spin.

■■■

-Richard

"Approaching the quad now," I mentioned over my phone.

"Will you all let me know what the fuck you plan on doing?" Julie stated as she sat in the backseat.

"Would you just shut up?" Jared shouted.

"You realize that you all have fucked up, right?" Julie questioned as she sat up. "Officers are already covering the quad and are currently following your wives, daughter, and son."

We didn't say a word. I just continued to drive.

Seconds later, we arrived at the quad and officers began shooting at my vehicle.

Pedestrians began screaming and running for cover.

Julie turned slightly and opened the door, with the handcuffs still on, and left the vehicle.

"Julie," Jared stated as she got out of the vehicle.

"Fuck," I spoke softly.

I couldn't potentially grab her without risking getting shot.

All the officers seemed to stop shooting. She walked towards the officers and they unlocked the handcuffs.

"You see, this is why we can't accomplish anything as a people. We're too busy wasting time, on dumb shit."

"None of this would be going down if you would just let us out of here," Jared shouted as he crouched behind the car door.

"You can't and won't leave here until I say so!" Julie demanded as one of the Blackhawks levitated higher into the clouds.

Madeline spoke over the loudspeaker; I was surprised to hear her voice.

"Julie Wilson, give it up. Release the Young party over to the Chicago police department."

"You want 'em?" Julie asked as the officers aimed their guns at me.

As Julie finished her sentence, one of the Blackhawks shot the machine gun at the police officers. Many fell to the ground and instantly died.

"Hubbard, Young, we got you," an officer stated over the speaker.

We continued to use the door as a shelter against the bullets.

The officers shot at the helicopter.

The helicopter gunner viewed the suspect on the monitor and set the missile. They fired the missile, and it caused an explosion.

"Easy with the missiles, Madeline," I shouted.

I kept my head low behind the Ferrari; Jacob sped up beside me and drifted to park the car.

Abel got out of the vehicle and tossed me an AK-47. He, then, tossed Jared an Uzi.

"Stay sharp," Abel got behind his car and held an Uzi.

He and Jacob started to shoot at the officers.

I fired the gun at the officers, and more police officers arrived on the scene.

"What are the chances that these cops work for Julie?" Jared shouted over the gunfire.

"85% chance that every cop works for Julie," I shouted.
"Madeline, lower the helicopter for the ladies," I spoke into my phone.

"Roger that," she stated.

I eased over to the adjacent car.

"Watch out for the police helicopter," I shouted on my phone.

The police helicopter, which was armed with missiles and a machine gun, fired shots at the Blackhawks.

The Blackhawk fired a missile at the police helicopter, and it hit. The helicopter came spiraling towards the ground.

"Incoming!" I shouted, and we hurdled next to whatever was beside us.

The helicopter was in a downward spiral and crashed into the ground a few hundred steps away from where we were. The helicopter exploded upon collision with the ground.

"One down," I thought out aloud.

"Madeline, let's get the ladies on a helicopter," Jared spoke into his phone.

"Lowering the aircraft," she spoke.

The Blackhawk lowered and let down a rope ladder.

Miracle

"Alright, ladies, climb this ladder as quickly as you can and get onto the helicopter."

Melanie was the first on the ladder and began to climb. My aunt was behind Melanie, followed by Veronica, then my mother, and I was last. The Blackhawk continued to fire bullets at many officers, and the ladder started to shake.

"Hold it steady!" Lieutenant Roberts shouted.

We quickly climbed to the top of the ladder, and each got inside of the helicopter.

I saw my father and uncle shoot at the officers.

I hugged my mother tightly as we sat inside of the helicopter.

Several Chicago police officers stood beside us.

"Are you all okay?" one of them asked.

"Shaken up, but we're fine," my mother stated.

"Jamie," a voice stated.

My mother turned slightly.

"Madeline," my mother stood and embraced the woman.

"I'm so glad you all are safe," Madeline hugged my mother tightly. "It's almost over."

"Well, it's not over yet, Madeline," my mother began as they released the hug.

"Our husbands and your boss are still down there," my aunt added.

"Madison, Jamie, we are going to get all of you out of here. We just need for you both to remain calm."

The helicopter's alarm began to ring.

"Evasive maneuvers," the pilot shouted as she made a sharp cut with the helicopter and we all fell over to the left.

A missile flew past us and hit a Blackhawk that was behind us.

It spiraled downwards towards the ground.

■■■

-*Richard*

***

Officers laid on the ground next to us, as well as the destroyed Blackhawk and police helicopter; they were a few hundred feet away. Two Blackhawks were still in the air and Julie crouched behind a car holding an AK-47 with an extended clip; as well as extra ammo in a utility belt strapped across her chest. Only four of us remained.

"Give it up, Julie," I shouted as I held a .9mm and crouched behind a car on the opposite end of the street.

Jared held his shoulder; he'd been shot and was holding the wound.

Jacob put his jacket over his father's wound.

"Julie, we can make a deal. You let us walk, and we won't press charges," Jared shouted.

I could tell he wanted to get out of there to say that.

"You must be fuckin' crazy," Julie shouted back. "The force of the D.R. will be on your asses even if I let you walk away. They'll be on *my* ass if I let you all go."

"What do you want, Julie?" I tried to bargain with her.

"You," she stated after a moment of silence.

"What?" I asked.

"You need to feel the emotion I've experienced in losing my mother. I need for you to feel how my life has been since that tragic day, 18 years ago. I had to fuckin' bury her while I was just a teenager. Closed casket and all," I could hear Julie begin to cry.

We were silent.

"I'm coming out," I spoke.

"What are you doing?" Jared mouthed out.

I stood up and walked from behind the car.

"I'm dropping my gun, Julie," I spoke to her.

She peeked from behind the car.

"And, I promise, Abel and Jared will not open fire on you if you come out," I stated. "Lower your weapons."

"Think I'm stupid?" Julie sniffled. "There are two Blackhawks above just waiting to kill me."

"Airborne units, stand down," I motioned.

The helicopters started to lower.

"They won't open fire, either," I answered in a subtle tone.

Julie slowly rose from behind the car. She approached me with her gun aimed.

I looked to my right and saw Jamie hugging Miracle.

Jared walked up beside me. Julie stopped in her tracks and aimed her gun.

"We're going to get you out of this," Jared whispered with his back to Julie. "Thanks for everything, bro," I mentioned aloud.

He shook my hand and hugged me, before boarding the helicopter. Jacob embraced me without saying any words, and followed his father.

Abel still stood behind the car holding his gun.

"End of the line," Julie stated as she motioned for me to come towards her.

The Blackhawks' engines restarted, and Abel came from behind the car and aimed his weapon at Julie.

"I can't do this," he spoke.

Julie aimed her gun at him.

"Call off your cop, Richard," she told me.

"Roberts, it's fine," I mentioned.

"Young, we are not leaving you here," Abel cocked his gun. "Blackhawks, prepare for a 757," he stated aloud.

At that moment, I knew things were about to get critical. He called for a rare procedure that we would work on in case of emergencies, but never once thought we would ever have to use.

The Blackhawk that wasn't carrying Jamie and the gang levitated into the sky.

"Richard," Julie became impatient.

"Papi," Miracle shouted from the helicopter as she cried.

Jamie continued to hold her.

Abel aimed his gun and prepared to fire the weapon.

He shot a bullet at Julie, but it missed. At the same time Abel fired his weapon, Julie shot hers; her bullet hit him in the chest.

"Young, come to the aircraft," an officer stated.

The Blackhawk fired bullets at Julie, but she ran and took cover behind the car she was previously behind.

The Blackhawk that was in the sky fired bullets at the car that Julie was behind.

I lifted Abel and put one of his arms around my shoulder. I held him up as I walked him over to the aircraft.

I passed him to Madeline, and she pulled his body aboard.

I climbed in next, and the aircraft levitated.

■■

-Miracle

We heard Julie screaming as the helicopters flew away.

Veronica began to cry as she saw her brother.

"Abel," my father stated as Madeline applied pressure to his wound.

He slowly spoke.

"I couldn't have you left in the D.R. by yourself," he stated. "Young, when I scouted you out, I knew there was something special about you. I found you when you were just a young boy," he chuckled.

"And I appreciate every single opportunity you've given me," my father stated. "But I need for you to hang in there."

"I knew there was something special about you. You've taken this force and have made us the number 7 police district in the nation."

"Roberts, don't you leave; hang in there," Uncle Jared spoke.

"And you: When Young picked you to be on his team, I thought you were absolutely insane," Lieutenant Roberts chuckled.

"However, I see how well you all work as a team, instead of separate. You and Young have both gone above and beyond for the force, and now, the force lies in your hands." Lieutenant Roberts coughed.

"Now is not the time for good-bye," my uncle stated.

Jacob held my hand tightly, and I held my mother's.

Lieutenant Roberts chuckled.

"You know, when I joined this force, I was told that you had one chance to make a difference. I hope I've made a difference in each of your lives."

"Roberts, do not do this," my father's voice began to crack.

"Veronica, I love you. You're my sister and my blood, and nothing will ever change that. Jamie, Madison, Madeline, Miracle, Jacob, you have all gained a special place in my heart."

He coughed once again and I started to tear up.

"Young, Hubbard, I thank you all for all that you have done... and I don't normally say this to employees; in fact, I try not to get too attached, but I love you both. The time and commitment you've both dedicated have been nothing short of amazing."

My mother closed her eyes and cried silently, as did my aunt. My uncle began to tear up and my father did the same.

"And another hardest thing about this job is that you're what stands between the choice of someone living, and someone dying. Young, Hubbard, it's yours now," Lieutenant Roberts closed his eyes.

"Abel," Veronica mentioned as she cried harder.

The sun was beginning to set as the aircraft flew through the air.

We were finally leaving the Dominican Republic and heading home.

20

Miracle

The flight was completely silent. The helicopter started to land on the beach next to our home.

Everyone was in tears, and my father took off the chains he was wearing. One chain had the date he joined the force engraved on the back, while one chain was a dog tag with a picture of him and Lieutenant Roberts.

He placed the one with the date around Lieutenant Roberts' neck and gave one to Veronica.

"Oh, no Richard, I couldn't," she spoke softly and broke the silence.

"You've earned it, as well as my friendship and trust," my father spoke.

The Blackhawk landed completely and we all unloaded. The surrounding officers covered Lieutenant Roberts with a dark sheet.

"Richard," Veronica began to speak, but her voice quickly cracked.

"Veronica," my father mentioned. "If you would like, you can stay with Jamie, Miracle, and me.

"Our homes have more than enough room, and we can always use the extra company," my mother added.

Veronica cried again, and I let go of Jacob's hand.

I walked over to Veronica and embraced her, tightly.

"Thank you, Veronica," I spoke.

"Miracle, it is I who should be thanking you—all of you," she looked around. "You've stowed your trust and friendship in me, and I couldn't be more grateful or ask for more than that."

Veronica let out a few tears and embraced me tightly.

"Would you like to stay with us, Veronica?" my mother asked.

"I don't want to be a burden to you all," she answered.

"It wouldn't be a burden," my father spoke. "Honestly, it would be my pleasure to extend my home to you."

"And we have plenty of space as well," my uncle began, "in case Richard gets tired of you," my father and uncle chuckled.

"And, I will not take 'no' for an answer," my father assured her. "Stay with us, at least until you're on your feet."

"Thank you," she whispered.

The officer flying the Blackhawk approached us.

"We will have to take Abel back to Chicago. You will receive full benefits and the force will cover the funeral costs," the officer could hardly finish her statement.

"This is a tragedy that we all wish, could have been avoided," another officer spoke as he walked towards the aircraft.

"I'm flying back to Chicago with my brother," Veronica spoke.

"We'll be up there soon," my aunt spoke. "We just have to make sure that we have everything finished here."

Veronica walked towards the aircraft.

"I'll see you all, later," she added.

"This is unit 3506, we are heading back for Chicago. In need of protection during entry. Entering from south-wing in Blackhawk, VIN Jessica-2-5-6-4-Iris-Larry-2-0-October-Peter-8-6-3-1-4-Zebra," the officer spoke over the radio.

"10-4, units will be advised of your entry and will have full coverage."

"Arrival time is in 240 minutes. Preparing for takeoff."

The aircraft levitated and flew away.

"This has got to be one of the more emotional moments of the job," my uncle stated as we walked towards his home.

"You know that Roberts was the backbone of this force. Now that he's gone, what's going to happen?" my father asked, still in disbelief that Lieutenant Roberts was dead.

"Well, Richard," my mother stated, "the force is yours… Between yourself and Jared, you have to call the shots."

I held Jacob's hand as we walked towards his house.

"Are you all coming inside right now?" my mother asked.

"No Mami, we're going to just sit out here for a moment," I spoke.

She looked at me and walked closer to me. She gave me a hug and a kiss on the cheek.

"*Te amo, mucho, Milagro*," She spoke as a tear fell from her eye.

"*Te amo, tambien*," I spoke. "We're just sitting outside," I told her. "Plus, I have Jacob here to protect us," I blushed.

"My baby girl's growing up," my father spoke.

The adults disappeared in the house and we walked over to the beach. We looked back and noticed the cars sitting in the driveway.

"Looks like Veronica came through in getting our cars back safely," Jacob mentioned. "It's fucked up about her brother."

"The whole situation was insane, but he did come through for us," Melanie stated.

We all sat down on the sand.

"But, I have a question for you two," she added.

I looked at Jacob, and he looked at me.

"I thought you never wanted to speak to me again," Jacob spoke.

"You are an ex, I can admit that, but it doesn't mean I will stop all ties with you or Miracle because we broke up."

Jacob nodded in agreement.

"But, when did you two become one?"

I knew the question was coming.

"It had to be between Quincy trying to harm Miracle, to us heading towards the airport."

"Well, I'm happy for you both. I mean, I could be mad, but staying mad requires too much work. Our friendships aren't worth it."

Melanie reached over to hug me.

"Just remember to hold on to him. Once school starts back and everyone hears the shit he's been through, *¿sabes qué?*, the girls are going to be all over him."

"Well, I'm not worried about all of that," I stated as a flipped my hair and laughed.

"So, what did you all do to Quincy?" Melanie asked Jacob. "I heard it was vicious."

"I wanted to kill him," he replied. "But, we whooped his cocky ass."

"The *puta* tried to rape me," I stated as anger filled my body.

My eyes became watery as I reflected on what occurred.

Melanie covered her mouth.

"I am so sorry, *nena*."

"You don't need to apologize," I spoke, seconds later. "He got his, and I'm not worried about him.

"What about school?" Melanie had a look of shock on her face.

"I forgot I went to school with this fool," I stated as I moved my hair from my face.

"Don't worry about him," Jacob answered as he put his arm around me.

We sat and watched the sunset on the beach.

"Who said we would have a boring childhood?" Jacob chuckled.

"This trip has definitely made me think about life and appreciate those around me, more," I added.

"What would you all say the most 'thrilling' part was?" Melanie was curious.

"Now that I look back at it, whooping Quincy's ass was interesting," Jacob began. "I mean, yeah, I was mad... but, you have to realize, I've never liked Quincy and he's been trying me for the longest," Jacob stated. "But, one of the scarier moments, even worse than the gang shootouts or the robbery, was when we boarded the plane to leave and Julie had men on the plane. And when she shut down the engine, I was sure we were going to die and that was the end."

"That was a fast-paced moment. I think everyone may say that was one of the most thrilling moments," I spoke. "But I have a question for you, J."

"Shoot," he spoke.

"*¿Cómo sabías que estaba en problemas?* Like, how did you know that Quincy was trying to rape me?"

Jacob thought for a moment.

"Well, originally, it wasn't in my intentions to do any fighting. But we were at the house and walked up to the garage, and were about to knock, but then I heard the music volume increase and I heard you scream. That's when I decided to drive the car through the garage."

"It's a good thing you can scream loudly," Melanie chuckled.

Remembering the incident caused me to shudder a bit.

"Yeah, it's fortunate," I spoke with attitude

"But, fuck him," Jacob mentioned as he stood up. "I still have the A-K."

"Don't let Richard or Jared hear you say that," Melanie laughed.

"No, no more killing," I responded. "I just want peace," I looked at the full moon.

"Still hearing from Jessie?" Melanie asked a few moments later.

"She's been pretty quiet; probably because we're done dealing with Quincy."

"Maybe he did have something to do with her death, and since we aren't associated or close to him, she's going to rest. After seeing what he's done, it's not hard to believe he harmed her," Jacob said.

"Well, we should have answers soon enough," I added. "I'm sure my father and uncle will figure out what went down with her."

"Quincy's a little bitch," Melanie stated. "The primary reason Jacob and I respected him in the D.R., is because of you."

"How could I have been so stupid?" I asked aloud, to no one in particular.

"You know we always got your back," Melanie spoke. She looked at Jacob sternly. "Even if we aren't together."

"I'm glad that you both are in my life," I stated, contentedly.
***
About an hour passed and we drove Melanie home.

"Think you still got what it takes, to beat the champ," Jacob joked.

"The champ of what?" I asked with a chuckle.

"The champ of everything," he stated.

He revved his car's engine.

"¿A dónde?" I asked.

"First one back to the house," Jacob stated.

"That's going to be easy," I stated.

"But let's make it a little more interesting," Jacob smirked.

"What were you thinking?" I asked him.

"If you beat me back to the house, I will do whatever it is that you request of me. If you want me to run down the beach naked, I will do that. If you want me to say I'm sexually attracted to men, I will say that. Whatever it is, I will do," Jacob spoke over the sounds of the engines.

"Sounds good," I spoke quickly.

"But if I win, you have to tell me exactly how you feel about me."

I blushed a little and spoke.

"I will do that," I answered.

"It's a bet." Jacob secured both of his hands on the steering wheel. "We go at the light," he shouted.

As the light turned green, we both sped off.

It was a straight shot home; no turns, no crossovers, nothing but street and sand.

Jacob and I remained side-by-side until we got closer to the house. I accelerated more and pulled in front of his vehicle.

I crossed the property line to our homes, a split second before Jacob.

We both got out of our vehicles and closed the door.

"I think the bet was you do whatever I wanted," I chuckled.

"Yeah, that was the bet," Jacob spoke, and I walked towards him.

He embraced me.

"Don't worry, it won't be anything too embarrassing," I joked.

He laughed and kissed me on the forehead.

"I'm not worried," he spoke as we walked towards the house.

21

Miracle

A few months later, once the funeral passed and we were back in Puerto Rico, I received a phone call.

I stood in the kitchen and looked at the caller ID.
"Hello, can I speak to Miracle Young?" the voice asked.
"This is she," I responded. "May I ask who's calling?"
"Hi, Miracle, this is Marquita Monet, I'm calling from Banco Popular de Puerto Rico."
I looked at the number and noticed it was a 773-area code.
"The reason for my call is because we've noticed some unusual spending on your account, and we need to be sure that your account hasn't been compromised. For verification, can you please provide your social security number?"

"Why do I need to verify anything? You called me," I replied.

"I'm just doing my job and what my managers told me to do. Tell you what, please come down to the bank and speak with one of our bankers about your account."

Jacob walked up and hugged me from behind. He kissed me on the cheek.

"Who will I be asking for when I arrive?" I asked.

"You can ask for Marquita, that would be fine," the lady replied.

"Who is that, baby?" Jacob asked.

"Someone from the bank," I stated as I put the phone on mute. "They say there's unusual spending on my account. But any transaction alerts come to my phone"

"Ask for the address on the account," Jacob whispered. I took the phone off mute.

"Ms. Monet, can you provide me with the address on the account?" I asked.

"To protect customer privacy and security, we do not provide information upon request. We ask you to verify the information to be sure that we are speaking with the correct individual and looking at the correct account."

"I'll be there shortly. The thing is, I'm in Puerto Rico now so I'll be visiting a bank here."

"That's fine, I am located in Puerto Rico as well. I will see you soon. Please keep in mind that we close at 8," the woman hung up.

I turned and looked at Jacob.

"Think we should get your father?" he asked.

"*¿Se te olvidó? Nuestros padres están en el trabajo.* Since Roberts died, they've been working like crazy," I spoke.

"Well, I guess it's just me and you, then," he spoke. "I'm not letting you go there by yourself." Jacob looked at me. "Especially after all that has happened."

"Quincy's been MIA. God knows what he's scheming," I replied.

"Don't worry about him. I keep a pistol in the glove compartment," Jacob spoke. He put his hand under my chin, lifted it, and kissed me on the lips. "I promise, I will not let him hurt you," Jacob assured me.

As he moved his hands away from my face, I spoke to him.

"J, you remember that race we had when we first got back?" I asked him.

"The one where I let you win?" he chuckled.

I laughed. "*Eres tonto*, but I'm referring to the bet."

"Yes, Miracle, I remember," he spoke.

"I know what I want you to do," I told him as I blushed a little.

"Tell me what you want. You won the bet fair and square, so I have to do it."

I didn't speak for a moment. Seconds later, I formed my mouth to speak what I wanted.

"I want you to make love to me," I blushed.

His face displayed a concerned look.

"Is this really what you want?" he asked.

"I mean, it will be my first time, and it will be your first time… and I want it to be special, so why not with my boyfriend-slash-best friend?"

Jacob looked at me and moved the hair out of my face with his fingers. He stroked my cheek. He leaned in and kissed my lips.

"I love you," I spoke after the kiss.

"I love you, too," he answered as he put his hands on my back.

He picked me up, and I wrapped my legs around his waist. He held me tightly as he kissed me and walked towards the bedroom.

I slowly rubbed on his muscles as he carried me.

I closed the door behind us as we entered the room.

The kisses became more erotic and passionate as the moment progressed. Jacob sat me on the bed, and took off his tank top, revealing his tightly-packed abs and muscular body.

"I didn't know you had a body like this," I joked as he pulled off his belt.

I grabbed a remote from the table and pressed play. 'Read Your Mind' by Avant began to play from my iPod's dock.

"Shhh," he stated as he pushed me back on the bed, forcing me to lay down.
He continued to kiss me. I put my hands on his back and put my nails in his skin.

He lifted my shirt over my head and pulled down my pants, revealing only my bra and panties.

He kissed down my body and I squirmed a little as he got closer to my thighs with his lips. He held my thighs firmly to stop me from moving, as he continued to kiss my body. I moaned as he marked his territory.

I dug deeper into his back as he pulled down my panties with his teeth.

The sensation was driving me wild as I started to say his name; he hadn't really started yet.

He came up to my face and kissed me some more, passionately sliding his tongue into my mouth.

I looked into his eyes and could see the fire in his eyes. He wanted me as badly as I wanted him.

"J, *te quiero*," I whispered to him.

"I want you, too," he replied as he put his hands on my arms, and slowly lowered my bra straps.

"Make love to me," I whispered. "*Suavemente*," I spoke.

"I promise," he whispered. "Say the word," he looked into my eyes.

The look was intensifying and passionate; it made my body tremble.

"Go, Papi," I responded.

He slowly started to work on my body.

"*Es tuyo,* Papi," I moaned softly.

Chills ran down my body as I realized what was going on.

I was making love to the guy that has been there for me from the beginning. He'd protected me and kept me safe. He was always my confidant and best friend, and now he was my lover.

I looked in his eyes again; no longer did I only see my protector, but I saw a certain passion in his eyes. He was my lover, and he was displaying a side of himself that I'd never seen before... but I liked it — no, I *loved* it.

It was like a fairytale. I held his body tighter and he kissed my lips again.

"I love you," he spoke.

"I love you, too," I responded.

I gasped for breath in between strokes, as it was a new experience and hurt; yet, I was enjoying the moment.

"Do you want me to stop?" he asked as I moaned.

"No," I told him. "*Dame más,* Papi,"

I was living in the moment, for the moment. Jacob was my focus, and everything else in the world: my problems, fears, and worries seemed to fade away.

I put my hands on his head and held it closer to my body. I kissed him on the cheek as I continued to moan in his ear.

"*Damelo,* Papi,*"* I whispered slowly as we continued.

***

22

Miracle

Jacob and I left out of the house and got in my car; I was smiling from ear-to-ear.

"I love you," I stated to him.

"I love you, Miracle," Jacob stated.

He put the car in drive and drove towards the bank. I put my hand on top of his and we listened to the radio.

"Stop smiling so much, girl," Jacob chuckled. "You want our parents to find out and kill us?"

"Shush," I joked with him. "At least we cleaned up," I stated with a smile.

"Yeah. Hopefully, that shower washed away enough evidence," Jacob chuckled.

"*Estupido*," I joked.

I looked at him in amazement. We'd known each other since forever, and have always had each other's backs. I asked him a question.

"Jacob, was it special to you?" I asked.

"Miracle," he began, "it was the most special thing in the world to me; with the woman who means more than anything to me. I don't know why it took over 16 years for me to figure this out, but you're the one I want to be in my life."

As he spoke, I got goose-bumps on my body.

I leaned forward.

"Promise me, now, that I've given you my heart, mind, body, and soul, that you will not do anything to hurt me," I told him.

He pulled the car over and faced me.

"We've known each other all of our lives… You should know, by now, that I will not do anything to harm you."

"*Prométemelo, Jacob*," I told him.

"I promise," he spoke and kissed me on the lips.

As we retreated from the kiss, he looked back at the road.

He put the car in drive and continued to drive to the bank.

As we pulled up to the parking lot, we noticed there were a lot of cars present. Jacob found a parking spot and we walked inside.

Three tellers were working, yet there was a long line of customers. Jacob and I stood in line.

"Long line for the bank," Jacob whispered as he stood behind me and held my waist.

"*Yo se*," I replied as I looked at my watch. "Are you sure it's a Sunday?"

"Last time I checked," Jacob chuckled.

"Miracle Young?" A lady called as she walked out of the back.

I looked back at Jacob. He nodded for me to proceed forward.

I approached the woman.

"So nice to meet you," she began. "I'm Marquita Monet, we spoke over the phone earlier."

"Hi, I'm Miracle. And this is my boyfriend, Jacob." I introduced Jacob.

He extended his hand for a handshake, and Marquita accepted.

"If you would like to step to the back for a moment to discuss your account with me," she began as she walked towards the back of the bank.

We left the line of people and followed her. We didn't enter an office; instead, the door she led us to, led us outside behind the bank.

"Wait, this doesn't feel right. How are we discussing the account on the outside?" Jacob asked as he held my hand; we both knew something was wrong.

"It's all good," she stated. "Don't worry about it," she finished.

Julie came from the side of the bank. I held Jacob's hand tighter.

"Miracle, Jacob, nice to see you both," she spoke.

We were silent.

"I'm sorry, but I believe I just spoke to you." Julie pulled out an Uzi.

"What do you want, Julie?" Jacob asked as he stood in front of me.

"We all 'want' things in life, right, Jacob?" she asked as she chuckled.

She walked up to Jacob and ran the tip of the gun under his chin.

He put his hand over the muzzle of the gun and pushed it away from him.

"Nope, the question is, 'what do I deserve?'" Julie spoke as she walked away.

"You deserve an ass whooping," I spoke.

"Miracle, do we have to resort to using such language?" Julie asked. "Come on now, cousin Julie means you no harm," she paced the floor in front of us and stopped.

"Says the woman with a machine gun," I shook my head.

She looked up and chuckled.

"Marquita, I appreciate the work you've done," Julie replied.

"You're welcome," Marquita replied.

"Yeah," Julie spoke to us, "you know since Veronica went and flaked on me, I had to find someone else with the connections and ability to do things, with accuracy and precision."

She held the gun with one hand and reached into her sports-coat with the other. She pulled out a Cuban cigar and put it in her mouth. Marquita walked over to Julie and lit the cigar.

"So, Miracle, you're glowing," Julie stated as she exhaled the smoke. "You must have done something new," she chuckled.

"Julie—" Jacob spoke.

"Julie, what?!" She put the cigar between her index and middle finger on her right hand. "You all fucking played me, and I will no longer be played like a fool."

Jacob glared at Julie.

"How'd you find us?" I asked.

"It wasn't that hard. I found you once, so I just did it again. I thought you all would have been smarter than to stay in the same place." Julie puffed on her cigar.

"And we thought you'd have been smarter than to come back after us. You're asking for a death wish, huh?" I asked.

Julie ignored the question and Jacob continued.

"What ever happened to Joey?" Jacob mentioned. "You got a woman working for you."

Julie glared at Jacob.

"Joey's in jail," she spoke. "I thought you already knew that."

"No, I didn't know," he spoke.

I realized what Jacob was doing.

"But your slick ass shouldn't have gotten anybody caught."

"Look here, little nigga," Julie spoke as she took her cigar out of her mouth. "You are at my mercy right now. I will pull this trigger and shut all of this shit down right now."

"Pull the trigger," Jacob stated. "Bet you, and your little bitch over there, go to jail. You, for 1st-degree murder, and her, as an accessory to murder, that is, if I die." He stepped closer to Julie. "But you know better than that, right?" He showed no fear and presented the protector I was accustomed to seeing.

I walked closer to Julie, who was less than ten inches away from Jacob.

"The fact that you bitches set me up to fail, is what gets me more than anything. And then you have the balls to talk tough to me?" she laughed. "So, if we must die today, I'm ready. I've written out my will a long time ago and constantly update it," Julie took the remaining cigar out of her mouth, and flicked it on the ground next to us.

"Cameras, Julie, they are watching everything that goes on around this bank," I pointed out.

"Don't you worry your pretty little Puerto Rican ass about that," she retaliated.

■■■

-*Richard*

"All units be advised, we have a situation at Banco Popular de Puerto Rico. Suspects are described as an African-American male, around 21 or 22 years of age; a Hispanic female, about 18 years of age; and a Caucasian female in her mid-to-late 40s. Caucasian female is armed, please take precaution in apprehending the suspects. *Todas las unidades sean advertidas, tenemos un problema en el Banco Popular de Puerto Rico. Los sospechosos son descritos como un hombre afroamericano, de alrededor de 21 o 22 años; una mujer hispana de unos 18 años de edad; y una mujer de raza caucásica a mediados ó finales de sus 40 años. La mujer de raza caucásica está armada, por favor tomen precauciones en la detención de los sospechosos."*

Jared heard the announcement over the radio and spoke.

"Those 'suspects' sound vaguely familiar," Jared pulled a gun from the glove compartment.

"Don't even say that," I told him as I drove in the direction of the bank.

"What if it is them?" Jared answered.

"Why would Jacob and Miracle be behind a bank with a 40-year-old Caucasian," I paused for a moment. "Julie," I spoke as I sped towards the bank.

"How the hell did she find us?" Jared asked as he rushed and loaded the weapon. "She never actually knew our address."

"You know Julie is a genius," I told him as I sped and swerved from lane-to-lane.

"You know other officers will also be reporting to the scene," Jared mentioned as he put on his vest.

I picked up the radio and spoke.

"This is unit 4352, approaching the bank. Have units in the vicinity, but do not have them enter the bank." I stated.

"10-4" the dispatcher spoke. "Unit 4352 in route to Banco Popular de Puerto Rico. Additional units are requested to avoid entering the bank, but remain in the vicinity. *Unidad 4352 en camino al Banco Popular de Puerto Rico. Las unidades de refuerzo se solicitan evitar entrar al banco, pero permanezcan en las cercanías."*

As we approached the bank, my heart started to race.

"Suspects have been identified as Miracle Young, Jacob Hubbard, and Julie Wilson. *Los sospechosos han sido identificados como Miracle Young, Jacob Hubbard, y Julie Wilson."*

Miracle

Julie sat on top of the dumpster lid and held the gun.

"So, tell me," she inhaled on another cigar. "How does the justice system work over here?"

Jacob and I were silent and looked at each other.

"It's about the same as it is in the U.S. You commit a crime, you go to jail, you get a trial, and depending on the crime, if you get one, the jury determines whether you're innocent or guilty," Jacob spoke.

"Sounds about right. You smart," she answered as she blew a ring of smoke. "I think I need a drink," she answered.

"Great, I know a great bar you can head to. Why don't you head down there?" Jacob remarked.

"You know what kid, you got a smart-ass mouth." Julie stood. "And that isn't good."

"What do you want from us?" I asked.

"From you, nothing," she answered. "But as soon as daddy finds out that his princess is in trouble, he'll come. He's the one that owes me, so let's just wait for him to get the party started," Julie stated.

"You really are thirsty, huh?" I asked.

Julie looked at me.

"You know what, I am. Come on, kids, let's go get that drink," she motioned us towards the door of the bank with the gun. She threw the cigar on the ground.

We all walked back inside and walked towards the front.

I was desperately looking around, trying to find an answer and a way out.

Julie put the gun to my back and told me to keep moving.

Jacob turned and faced her.

"Don't touch Miracle with no fucking gun," he shouted to her face.

"Who the fuck you think you talking to?" Julie asked.

"I'm talking to you. You're fuckin' 40 years old, but you still can't do any legit work for yourself. Running around here like a little kid, threatening and demanding that others do your dirty work for you."

Everyone in the bank was looking at us and seemed frozen that they saw the gun in the bank.

"Why do you think I'm here?" Julie asked him. "I could have sent a worker out and I could be sleeping in my bed at home, but Veronica showed me that if you want something done right, you have to do it yourself," Julie adjusted her sports-coat with her free hand.

"Julie Wilson!" a voice shouted from the entrance.

We all turned and looked; my father and uncle were in the doorway, aiming their weapons.

Everyone screamed and got down on the ground.

"Richard!" Julie exclaimed. "So good to see you again, buddy," she pulled me close to her and ran the gun down my cheek.

"Julie, let her go," my father spoke.

"Nah, Richard, I don't think so. You played me when we were in the D.R., so don't even try to kiss my ass now," she answered.

"Julie, what popped off in the D.R. was foul from the very beginning, you know this, just like I know this," my uncle spoke.

"Yeah, but this bullet in Miracle's ass won't be foul, will it?" Julie shouted. "You ready to die, aren't you, Miracle?" she was yelling in my ear.

"*¿Estás loco?* The fuck would I wanna do that for?" I shouted back at her. I tried my hardest not to curse in front of my parents, but I was fearful for my life at this point.

"Julie, you need to take your hands off Miracle and drop the weapon," Jacob spoke.

"Jacob, stop talking to me," she replied, as she rolled her eyes.

In an instant, he grabbed Julie by the arms and threw her down to the ground. He took my hand and we ran through the bank.

Julie shot her Uzi at us, but the bullets missed.

My father and uncle both shot at Julie, but those bullets also missed.

People were now screaming and running to the exit of the bank, including the bankers and the tellers.

My father and uncle got up and chased behind Julie, who was now chasing Jacob and me.

"Come on, M," Jacob stated as we ran through the bank, trying to find somewhere to hide or escape.

"Come on kids, Cousin Julie just wants to play," I could hear Julie reload the Uzi.

"Okay, M," Jacob whispered as we entered a room and crouched beneath a desk. "We need to get out of here, but we may need to split up."

"No, Jacob, we are not splitting up. My father's out there, your father's out there. We're gonna stick together, make sure Julie is killed, and go on back with our lives," I panicked.

My heart was now racing.

Julie entered the room and called our names.

"Miracle, Jacob," she called as she violently kicked the chair over.

Jacob and I remained silent as we hid less than 20 feet away.

She pulled out her cellphone and dialed my number; my phone vibrated, and she heard it.

"Don't make this hard," Julie shouted.

Jacob and I looked at each other; we knew we had to stand up because she heard the vibrations.

We both crawled from under the desk and stood up.

"Ah, there you all are," Julie held the gun firmly and aimed it at me.

My father and uncle entered the doorway.

"Well, is this how it's going to be?" I asked her.

"Too late for words," she stated. "You bitches have made a fool out of me for the last time. This one is for my mother."

She pulled out a pistol and returned the Uzi to her sports-coat.

My father and uncle stood in the doorway with their guns aimed.

They both ran in towards Julie.

A single gunshot rang out.

BANG

***

www.ingramcontent.com/pod-product-compliance
Lightning Source LLC
Chambersburg PA
CBHW050423260626
47156CB00003B/1126